"This is the first book _____ around for a long tim_____ me laughing and at t_____ knows how to plot a g_____ the charac-ters."
—MyShelf.com

"This is a thoroughly enjoyable mystery with a plot that keeps the reader engaged and very surprised by the reveal, always a joy for mystery reading veterans. In this debut Comfort Food Mystery, recipes are of course included as are delectable descriptions of decidedly low-fat but down-home cooking. Trixie is a very relatable and likable character deserving of her starring role in this promising and very well-written series."
—Kings River Life Magazine

"Culinary mystery fans have a new series to sample."
—The Poisoned Martini

"A comfort foodie and cozy reader's delight."
—Escape with Dollycas into a Good Book

The Comfort Food Mystery Series

Do or Diner
A Second Helping of Murder

DINERS, DRIVE-INS, AND DEATH

A Comfort Food Mystery

CHRISTINE WENGER

AN OBSIDIAN MYSTERY

OBSIDIAN
Published by the Penguin Group
Penguin Group (USA) LLC, 375 Hudson Street,
New York, New York 10014

USA | Canada | UK | Ireland | Australia | New Zealand | India | South Africa | China
penguin.com
A Penguin Random House Company

First published by Obsidian, an imprint of New American Library,
a division of Penguin Group (USA) LLC

First Printing, January 2015

ISBN 978-0-451-41510-3

Printed in the United States of America
10 9 8 7 6 5 4 3 2 1

To Patty Tomeny Holgado, Janice Egloff DiFant, Mary Ann Gladysz, and Kathy Prell Friedman. All who are alumnae of St. Margaret's School and are my "Sisters of the Heart." I love you guys! SMS rules!

And to Patricia "Trish" Hoey, avid reader and friend, who had limitless strength and courage. Someday we'll meet again at that big Flush Party in the sky. I'll miss your laughter.

Chapter 1

I wondered why Antoinette Chloe Brownelli wanted to speak to me. It couldn't be good. On the phone she whispered and sounded serious, as if we were going to embark on an adventure worthy of 007.

Antoinette Chloe and I stood in a field—a large, overgrown field that she owned—next to my property. The weeds were choking what was left of the wildflowers and the poor little things were gasping for breath. Some butterflies still roamed over what was left of the pickings, and I could hear the buzzing of a bee. I turned to see a big, fat one land on some goldenrod. The insect might as well get what it could before frost chilled the air and turned the goldenrod to mush, but just in case Mr. Bee wasn't friendly, I prepared to get out my EpiPen.

"Trixie. Thanks so much for coming." Antoinette Chloe Brownelli's purple muumuu with huge white gardenias billowed in the September breeze. Her matching purple flip-flops each sported a big sunflower that covered most of her glittery toenails.

"Of course, Antoinette Chloe. What's up?"

I wouldn't ever dare call her just *Antoinette* without adding the *Chloe*. Most of the time, I thought of her as ACB to save time.

I, Trixie Matkowski—*and don't you dare call me Beatrix*—would do anything that ACB wanted. She's a lovely person under all the stage makeup, the clunky pounds of jewelry, and the lime green fascinator that sported a fountain of colorful feathers. A faux peacock rested on the fountain of feathers that fluttered in the breeze and dangled precariously over her right ear.

ACB's fake feathered friends always seemed to be hanging over her right ear, probably in an escape attempt.

"I've bought back the land that my snake of a husband sold to our mayor. I'd like to build a drive-in on it. I hope you don't mind, since my land is next to your land."

Uh-oh.

"What kind of drive-in, Antoinette Chloe? A food drive-in?"

My mind raced. I didn't want the competition for my Silver Bullet Diner, especially not out here on the outskirts of the village. Competition might be good for the economy, but there weren't enough people in Sandy Harbor to sustain two eating establishments right next to each other.

If it weren't for the seasonal visitors like the fishermen, the summer vacationers, and the leaf peepers and snowmobilers, this place would be a ghost town all year long.

Antoinette Chloe already had a restaurant in the village, Brown's Four Corners, shortened from

Brownelli's Four Corners, that she could barely handle. Why would she want another food establishment?

She moved the greenish-blue peacock into place on her hat, but it slid back down again. "A drive-in movie theater, actually."

Whew! I could breathe again.

"But aren't drive-ins closing all over the United States?"

"That's right, Trixie. So why not strike while the bowling ball is hot?"

How could I argue with crazy logic like that? But as her friend, I was going to try.

"Antoinette Chloe," I said, using my practical voice, "it seems to me that nowadays the only kids who go to movies are kids who don't drive yet— so a drive-in movie wouldn't work without a car. Besides, don't you think that they'd rather be lounging in a plush chair in a nice theater?"

"Psh. Where's the fun in that? The younger generation hasn't experienced the fun of watching a movie with a speaker hanging from the window while the mosquitos are biting. And when it rains, it adds another layer of excitement. I'm even thinking of staying open in the winter. What a thrilling experience that'll be if it snows!"

I'm shivering right now just thinking of watching *Iron Man 29* or *Batman Returns Yet Again and Again* in the middle of a snowstorm.

"I don't know if there are speakers that hang off the window anymore. I think the sound comes in on the car radio," I said.

She waved her hands dismissively. "I'm going

to go retro, so there will be speakers hanging. I want customers to experience the old-fashioned drive-in. You know, the kind with the little hills where you position your car to be higher in the front."

"Don't forget about the playground in front of the screen for the kids to enjoy before the movie starts," I added, getting swept away by her enthusiasm.

"And remember when the movie started, how we'd all scream and race to the cars?"

I grinned. "Those were definitely fun times, Antoinette Chloe."

A warm cocoon of memories enveloped me. I remembered my parents letting us wear our pajamas to the drive-in. How my mom would make a brown grocery bag full of popcorn, and how there'd be some sodas on ice in a cooler. Before the movie even started, my brother, John, would curl up on the back window ledge of the car, like it was his own balcony, but soon he'd be fast asleep.

"Maybe you have a good idea, after all."

ACB grinned. She raised a fist in excitement just as her peacock shook loose of his feathery nest and dove into the high grass at our feet. "What fun those drive-in days were! Necking in the car with Sal . . ." Suddenly, tears flooded her eyes. "Sal and I were going to build our retirement home on this land—right on the waterfront. We had the plans drawn up and . . . and . . . everything. It was going to be our dream home. The perfect place to spend the rest of our lives together."

She picked up the peacock, pulled out a red bandanna from her cleavage, and then slipped the peacock in. After she blew her nose, I pulled her into a hug, disturbing the cloud of perfume that surrounded her. I held my breath, trying not to sneeze.

"Sal deserved what he got—I know that, Trixie. But that doesn't mean that I don't miss him."

ACB's husband, Sal, was serving a life term at Auburn Correctional Facility, a maximum-security prison in New York, for the attempted murder of both ACB and yours truly, and for the completed murder of Marvin Cogswell the Third, who was once a restaurant inspector.

I patted her back. "I thought you and Sal's brother, Nick, were an item now. You motorcycled all over North America with him, didn't you?"

That brought a fresh round of tears, and I felt awful. What did I say?

"I haven't seen Nick in ages," she sniffed. "And we had so much fun on his Harley, with Nick burning up the road and me in the sidecar. I was really a hot biker mama."

I smiled to myself as I remembered ACB's hot-biker-mama attire: black makeup, black hair with a white skunk streak in the part, black flip-flops with glitter, and lots and lots of heavy chains draped everywhere. Oh, and a black helmet that ACB embellished with black sequins, black feathers, and a miniature Harley glued to the top.

"Nick hasn't even called you?"

"No."

"Is that like him?"

She moved away from me and blew her nose. "Two weeks ago, he said that he was going to cook at my restaurant, just like before. He's such a skilled cook, Trixie—a real chef. But because he never showed up, I've been forced to do all the cooking myself. Thank goodness you trained me, or I'd be up Salmon River without my fuchsia waders."

"Did you try calling him?"

"Of course. But I keep getting his voice mail. I probably left about two dozen messages."

"Did you go to his house?"

"Yes. His place was the usual perfection. Everything in its place. I was going to dust for him, but then I thought, Hey, why should I? He hasn't even bothered to call me."

The red bandanna disappeared into the muu-muu, and, with a flourish, she then pulled a flow-ered scarf out of her cleavage, shook it out, and draped it around her shoulders. This was better than a magician's act in Vegas. Thank goodness she had a lot of cleavage for storage.

"Nick and I were close, Trixie, if you get my drift. Very, *very* close."

She gazed off in the distance, and I could tell she was remembering something really . . . uh . . . special.

I smiled. "Let's go to the Silver Bullet and have lunch. It's Meat Loaf Monday, and I'm hungry. Are you?"

"I could nosh."

"Good."

I was in the process of buying the Silver Bullet

Diner, the eleven cottages (there were once twelve, but that's another story), and the big Victorian farmhouse from my aunt Stella Matkowski. It all sat on a prime piece of land that jutted out into Lake Ontario, which was called "the point" by the locals.

Aunt Stella had lost interest in everything since Uncle Porky died, and my husband (now my ex), Deputy Doug Burnham, had lost interest in me.

Aunt Stella and I both decided that we needed a change of scenery, and so she sold me her diner and took off for greener pastures. I suggested that she might want to work up an agreement with a lawyer; she said that I was family, like the daughter she never had, and that the back of a Silver Bullet place mat was more than adequate. Then she tore up the place mat, telling me to pay her a little bit at a time with the profits.

And that was that. Shortly after, I moved to Sandy Harbor and Aunt Stella moved to Boca Raton. It had almost been a year now, and neither one of us had looked back.

Since I walked here from the Victorian, we both headed to ACB's white van that had Brown's Four Corners Restaurant and Catering written on the side along with phone numbers, a Web site address, and a salami dancing with a loaf of bread.

ACB was a slow driver. Granted, we didn't have far to go, but I couldn't relax while she was going about twenty miles an hour on the highway in a fifty-five zone. I kept looking in the rearview mirror, expecting an eighteen-wheeler to zip around the bend and push us out of its way.

As ACB finally turned into the parking lot of the Silver Bullet and parked, the tension drained from my shoulders. I slid down from the passenger's seat and waited for her to catch up so we could walk together.

Whenever I looked at the Silver Bullet, I couldn't believe that it was actually mine. Well, that it would be mine after I kept chugging along with a payment schedule that I devised and tried to stick to.

To the left of the diner, in the middle of the point, was my white Victorian farmhouse with the wraparound porch and forest green shutters. I called it the Big House, not because it was a jail, but because it really was a *big* house. Behind it stood the eleven housekeeping cottages—the Sandy Harbor Housekeeping Cottages, to be exact.

In front of the cottages was a sandy swath of beach that stretched on a nice chunk of land on the New York State part of Lake Ontario. The lake was great for swimming, and the grounds were a perfect place for my guests to picnic, to build sand castles, to make mud pies, and to make memories.

That's what my family did every summer when we rented Cottage Four. Growing up, my diary mostly consisted of three countdowns: my birthday in February, summer at the cottage, and Christmas.

"I love the lines of the Silver Bullet and how it's so shiny . . . like a real silver bullet," ACB said, interrupting my trip down memory lane. "I remember when your aunt and uncle had it delivered back in 1952. Everyone gathered along Main

Street, as if a parade was passing by. I was just a little girl at the time, but I can remember what I wore as if it were yesterday: a pink tutu with red tights. And my hair was done up high with ringlets on top of my head."

"Wish I was around to see it." I meant that I wished I could've seen the diner being delivered—not ACB's pink tutu—but I wouldn't have been born for another . . . oh . . . thirty years or so.

I slipped my arm around hers as we walked, because the parking lot was slick with wet leaves and her flip-flops didn't provide much traction.

"Antoinette Chloe, let's go shopping for a pair of boots for you. I hear that the tractor store got in some of those waterproof boots in lots of bright colors and—"

"Boots?" She paused, shaking off a wet leaf that got stuck between her toes. "I wouldn't be caught dead wearing boots. I'd have to be hiking in a blizzard before I'd give up my flips."

"I've seen you in the snow with your flips on, and it's a wonder that you still have all your toes. Really, you should get boots and socks. This isn't Margaritaville, girlfriend. Sandy Harbor is more like the North Pole."

I was starting to sound like Sister Mary Mary, my fourth-grade teacher at St. Maggots . . . oops, I mean St. Margaret's.

"Socks? You can't mean those ugly cotton things you put on your feet." She stopped shuffling through the wet leaves. "That is so not going to happen."

"You know, I have an extra pair of boots that I can give you and some wool-blend socks. They are all brand-new. What size feet do you have?"

"Eleven," she whispered. "I wear an eleven." She looked around furtively to see if anyone might be able to hear her, but the parking lot was empty except for us. "Yes, my feet are as big as canoes."

"I wear a ten, so my boots might not work, but I'd love to go shopping with you," I said.

She gave me a look, and I decided to drop the subject after this, because I felt like I had started to drift into nagging territory. And that wasn't my intent. Besides, it was obvious that my friend didn't welcome my flip-fop bashing. ACB had her own fashion sense, which obviously included various shades of frostbite, and I was content to leave her to her ways, even if I didn't agree with them.

Finally, we made it to the cement ramp, which was leaf-free, thanks to my handy guys, Clyde and Max. I opened the door, and the scent of bacon and fresh coffee permeated the air. As the sign said, BREAKFAST SERVED 24 HOURS A DAY.

And the diner was packed. Yes! As we made our way to the last vacant booth, I waved at my two waitresses on duty, JoAnn and Kathy.

JoAnn started to hand out two menus, but on second thought picked one of them back up and erupted into a low, throaty chuckle. "Trixie, I bet you could recite this menu by heart."

"I totally can." I turned to ACB. "Antoinette Chloe, you know JoAnn, don't you?"

"Of course I do. JoAnn used to work for me at

Brown's right after she graduated from high school."

"It was my first job," JoAnn said, shifting on her feet, looking a tad embarrassed. "I left for Nashville to cut a record, but the closest I got was cleaning rooms at the Opryland hotel." She put her hand on ACB's shoulder. "And Antoinette Chloe sent me plane fare to return home."

Tears pooled in JoAnn's eyes as she hugged ACB, and then she hurriedly left.

"That was nice of you," I told my friend. In my ten or so months in Sandy Harbor, I'd heard of several touching things that ACB had done for other people.

She shrugged and waved off my comment. "I told JoAnn that I'd pay her rent for a couple of months, that she shouldn't give up on her dream, but her mother got sick, and JoAnn felt she should come home and try again some other time." ACB shook her head. "She never went back, but she sings in the church choir and at funerals and weddings, and, well, I think that makes her happy."

ACB picked up her menu and studied it, while I looked at the purple-black sky. We were going to have rain. A lot of rain.

"Antoinette Chloe, this is Meat Loaf Monday, but it's also *Meatless* Monday, which means vegetarian lasagna is on special tonight, too. Juanita made it, and it's fabulous."

"Sounds good to me. I've been thinking of going vegetarian."

Within minutes, JoAnn appeared again with pad and pencil in hand, looking much cheerier.

"Have you ladies decided yet?" she asked.

ACB handed her menu back to JoAnn. "I'll have the vegetarian lasagna with three meatballs on the side, a salad with Thousand Island dressing, and a glass of chocolate milk. And can I get some extra veggies?"

"I can get you mixed veggies," JoAnn said.

"That'll work as long as there's lots of butter on them," Antoinette Chloe said.

"We can do that." JoAnn nodded and scribbled on her order pad.

ACB tapped a long, sparkling nail on the table. "Oh, JoAnn, could you add a couple pieces of sausage to my order, too? After all, what is vegetarian lasagna without meat?"

JoAnn chuckled. "It's vegetarian lasagna."

ACB and I laughed. JoAnn was always quick with a joke and a tease. Everyone, but especially the truckers and the county snowplow guys, just loved to verbally spar with her.

"How about you, Trixie?"

"I'll have the vegetarian lasagna, as well, with meatballs and one sausage, and house dressing on my salad." *As God is my witness, I'll watch my calories tomorrow, at Tara.*

"What would you like to drink, Trixie?"

"Iced tea."

"Got it. I'll be right back with your drinks."

When JoAnn left, Antoinette Chloe took off her peacockless hat and fluffed up her hair. "Trixie, I also called because I wanted to talk to you about the Miss Salmon Contest. We have a lot of work to do for it, since it's our first contest, and I don't want to overlook a single tiny detail. But I did overlook a big detail—a *major* big detail."

I sat back in the coziness of the red-vinyl booth, not wanting to hear what ACB had to say. I had so much on my mind, running the diner and the cottages, that one more thing was going to make my head explode. So I crossed my arms and let the well-worn vinyl take me away to the 1950s, when the diner was shiny and new, when I wasn't the owner, and when ACB didn't have a major problem with the Miss Salmon Contest.

I don't know what it was, other than age, but the stuffing inside the booths adjusted to everyone's body type. I'd been toying with the idea of getting all the booths reupholstered, but I'd decided against it. Why tamper with a good thing?

But ACB was still talking about the major problem, and I was still desperately trying to tune her out. Anyway, any problems with the contest should be presented to the Miss Salmon Committee, not me. I decided I should probably point that out to her before she got carried away.

"Antoinette Chloe," I said. "We have a Miss Salmon Committee meeting today. Remember? It's being held at my house in exactly two hours. Which reminds me—I need to vacuum. Yet again."

Blondie, my sweet golden retriever, sheds so much hair every day that I could make another dog with all of it. I vacuum twice a day. Three times if I'm having company, and I'm not a cleaning fan.

I was dreading the Miss Salmon pageant meeting. As chairperson of the event, ACB wanted to be the mistress of ceremonies. She was panting to be a part of all the glitz, glamour, and costume changes that the Miss Salmon Contest could muster. However, our mayor, Rick Tingsley, who was running for New York State senator, wanted the podium, the microphone, and the photo ops. Rose Starr of the Salmon Committee was going to talk him into being a judge instead and letting ACB be emcee.

The next ten days were going to be an epic battle, the likes of which no one has seen since the British sailed into this area during the War of 1812.

"But I've overlooked a really, really big detail," ACB continued. "I've been getting e-mails from a bunch of contestants, especially from a girl named Aileen Shubert, telling me that there's no room at any of the hotels in the area and that even the campgrounds are all filled up with fishermen. And Aileen wants to come early and settle in so she can take some time to practice before the big day. Oh, Trixie, this is a huge problem!"

I nodded. "Well, all my cottages are full for the next couple of weeks. I have a huge waiting list."

JoAnn returned with our drinks, and we both reached for them at the same time and took a couple of sips.

"And on top of that, I feel like we have a responsibility to keep an eye on the contestants."

"Won't their parents be with them?"

"No, most are too old for chaperones, and a good dozen are coming a week earlier to work with our resident Broadway choreographer for our special dance productions. Aileen is one of them."

Dance productions? Resident Broadway choreographer? Hm. I hadn't missed a meeting, had I? This was all news to me.

"Who are you talking about, Antoinette Chloe? Who's this Broadway person?"

"Margie Grace, of course."

"Margie Grace isn't a day under eighty-eight years old. She hasn't been on Broadway since they named it Broadway."

"But the contestants don't know that," she said with a smile.

"Can you spell *fraud*?"

"Oh, they'll love Margie. And she might be an old bat, but she can still put together a dance number. She did the Tango of the Shepherds for the Episcopal Church's Christmas play last year, remember? It was brilliant."

"How could I have forgotten that? The shepherds had red roses in their teeth and they tangoed with their sheep."

"It was unprecedented. Creative. Just what I want for the dance number in our pageant." She pulled a little notebook from her—wait for it—cleavage closet again, along with a pen, and started scribbling. "Maybe Margie Grace could choreograph a tableau depicting salmon swimming upstream?"

I bit my lip to stop myself from bursting out into laughter. I didn't think that the rest of the committee members would go for dancing, spawning salmon.

"Getting back to our problem of the girls without rooms who are studying with Margie Grace, what can we do?" Antoinette Chloe sat back into the booth as JoAnn returned with our orders.

Both were presented nicely with carrot curls and radish roses to decorate the plate. ACB's meatballs and sausages were served on an oval side dish with spaghetti sauce and fresh parsley. Her lasagna was a generously sized portion, as was mine.

Just how I wanted everything plated. I made a mental note to compliment Juanita Holgado, my day cook, when I saw her next.

"How many girls do you figure will come early?" I asked.

"About twelve or fourteen."

"Hm. Maybe we could rent some trailers for them. I'd say we could have them park on my land, but they would require water hookups and pump-outs and all that, which I don't have handy." I shook my head. "That's just too much. It just won't work."

ACB buttered a slice of Italian bread. "What about your house?"

Oh no. No way. No way am I going to entertain a houseful of young beauty contestants. "Whoa. My house? Antoinette Chloe, what are you sniffing?"

"Yeah. Your house. The Victorian you call the Big House."

I waved her statement away. "Oh, it's not that big. I should really call it the Little Cottage."

"You have—*what?*—like, four full bathrooms and a couple of half baths?"

My late, and dearly loved, uncle Porky believed in porcelain and lots of flushing, and expected a lot of visiting relatives when he built the house.

"That seems like a high estimate," I protested.

"It's way low. You have more like eight or nine bedrooms."

"Perhaps. I never counted them."

"Trixie, please! Help me out. It'll only be for a couple of weeks. And when the pageant ends, they'll be all gone and everything will go back to normal."

How could I say no to my friend when she was in such a jam?

But there would be endless chatter, lots of toxic hairspray and perfume, and hair in the drains. Not to mention giggling and sneaking out at night to meet up with boys, snacking in the beds, smuggling booze inside, smoking . . .

Oh, wait! I was thinking of my college-dorm days.

"Okay, Antoinette Chloe. Okay. On one condition: You have to move in and chaperone them and get them to clean up after themselves. They can take their dinner at the Silver Bullet. And you can make breakfast and lunch for them at the Victorian."

She sniffed and blinked tears back. If she let them fall, there'd be two rivers of makeup dripping down her cheeks and onto her muumuu.

I couldn't let that happen. ACB's muumuus were like living things, plus mascara stains were a beast to get rid of. Reaching into my purse, I pulled out a little packet of tissues and handed it to her.

She pulled out a few, closed her eyes, and blotted them. "You're a lifesaver, Trixie, and a good friend." She sniffed and blotted again.

But no turquoise or purple eye shadow appeared on the tissues that she set down on the table. No black eyeliner, no black mascara, no orange blush, and no Pan-Cake makeup.

"And *you* are quite clever, Antoinette Chloe. I smell a setup. And the fake tears were a nice touch, by the way."

She laughed. "Well, I was in show business, after all."

ACB always astonished me. "You were?"

"Most definitely. I was a ticket taker at the Sandy Harbor Bijou when I was in high school." Her eyes twinkled and she grinned. "I considered that show business."

She'd set me up again, and I walked right into it.

"Sheesh. I didn't see that coming."

Suddenly, the smile left her face and she became quite serious. "I agree to your terms, Trixie. Matter of fact, I welcome them. I've been so . . . lonely lately. I'm sure chaperoning the girls will cheer me right up."

Oh my. My friend was displaying a full menu of emotions tonight. She was ecstatic over her drive-in idea, mad at Nick for disappearing without saying anything to her, worried that the pageant contestants wouldn't have a place to stay, sad that Sal was in jail and that her dreams of a retirement home on the water were dashed, and then joking about being in show business.

I was exhausted by it all and worried that Antoinette Chloe was headed toward a nervous breakdown.

"Trixie, it's just awful being so lonely," she continued. "Sal tried to kill me, and now his brother is ignoring me. I mean, is it me? What's wrong with me?"

This time her tears were real, and they did drip down her cheeks. But, thankfully, she caught them before they hit her muumuu.

My heart was breaking for her. But I didn't know what I could do other than to help her get some answers from Nick. Maybe if she had that, it would help her move on.

"There's nothing wrong with you, Antoinette Chloe. Maybe it's the Brownelli brothers, but together we'll find out where Nick went off to." I patted her hand and vowed to give Nick Brownelli a piece of my mind. "And when we do, you can hear what he has to say for himself; then you can take him or leave him."

"Yes!" She pounded her fist on the table, and it made me jump. The customers around us were also airborne. I swear our meals shot two inches into the air, then landed back on their plates.

I slid her ice water closer to her, thinking that a cold drink might refresh her, but she ignored the water and picked up the steak knife at her place setting and held it upright on the table.

Oh, this didn't look good! For everyone's safety, I got ready to spring into action.

She rapped the handle of the knife on the table. "As soon as I find Nick, I'm going to make sure that he never lies to me again!"

Could she be any louder?

Everyone turned to look at Antoinette Chloe as

if this was a dinner show. And, boy, she didn't disappoint the spectators.

Very dramatically, she gripped the knife with both hands and lifted it over her head, and before I could blink, she plunged it into a plump sausage on her plate.

"Take that, Nick Brownelli!"

Chapter 2

*T*he Miss Salmon pageant meeting at the Big House was a disaster. The committee members got loud to make their points over each other, and Blondie started barking like a mad dog.

I phoned Sandy Harbor deputy sheriff Ty Brisco, one of my first friends when I moved here. Ty's a transplant from Houston, Texas, and he can really work a pair of jeans and a white cowboy hat. If he adds his snakeskin boots and his brown suede bomber jacket, women of all ages melt like butter on toast.

But not me. I'm not interested. I'm still shell-shocked from my divorce from Deputy Doug of Philadelphia.

"Ty, can you come over and take Blondie? I have a real heated meeting going on here, and she's barking her head off."

"Sure, Trixie. I'll be right over to get her. We'll go for a long walk."

"Thanks, Ty." I just loved his drawl. I could listen to him read the phone book.

It wouldn't take Ty long to walk to the Big House. He lives above the Sandy Harbor Bait

Shop on the other side of the Silver Bullet in a fabulous apartment that Uncle Porky and Mr. Farnsworth, the bait shop's owner, built. It also has a huge corner window that overlooks the lake and the Big House. Sometimes I can see Ty in that window, looking at the lake.

"Trixie! We need you in here!"

The melodious voice of ACB bounced off the walls of my house. Blondie howled. I wanted to howl along with her.

"I'm coming." I guess I couldn't stall any longer.

I didn't see Ty yet, so I got Blondie's leash and headed into the kitchen until he arrived.

"What did I miss?"

Pam Grassley, the third-grade teacher at Sandy Harbor Grammar School, raised her eyes to my vintage tin ceiling. "Someone needs to take charge of this meeting. I haven't got all day."

I looked at Blondie's pink leash loaded with fake rhinestones. Some were missing. When I looked up, the committee members were staring at me.

"It's your kitchen, Trixie. You should run the meeting," Jean Harrington, the co-owner of the Gas and Grab on Route 3, said.

Thankfully, there was a knock on the door, and I hooked Blondie's leash on her collar. She knew it meant a walk, and she just about jumped out of her fur.

"That's Ty Brisco. He's going to take Blondie," I explained. "Come in, Ty."

The committee members quickly fluffed their

hair, applied lipstick, and waited in anticipation for Ty to walk into the kitchen.

Sheesh.

"Well, hello, ladies." Ty tweaked his white cowboy hat with his thumb and finger.

Yes, his jeans were perfect, his snakeskin boots were polished, and he was wearing the hell out of a brown suede bomber jacket that probably was as soft as it looked. And his eyes were as blue as Lake Ontario on a clear summer day.

Not that I noticed.

I handed him Blondie's leash, and he leaned over and whispered, "Bad meeting?"

"The worst."

He winked. "I'll keep Blondie for the rest of the day. I think I'll go for a jog."

"Good-bye, Deputy," said Kathy Prellman, the owner of an auto-repair shop. Kathy could take apart a motor and put it back together again, and she looked like a swimsuit model. Actually, she still modeled for the Ford Models agency in New York City from time to time. She was going to be the head Salmon judge.

"See you, Kathy. Ladies." He tweaked his hat again, and we all watched him walk away.

"Nice butt," ACB said, expressing what we were all thinking.

"Let's get down to business," I said. "I'm sure that we all have things to do, so let's rock."

I decided that I'd lead the meeting after all, because I had to cook at the diner in about ten hours, and I needed to get some sleep.

"We need to discuss accommodations for the

out-of-town contestants. I understand from Antoinette Chloe that there are twelve contestants who need a place to stay for a week or so before the Miss Salmon pageant to practice routines with Margie Grace. I've volunteered to house them all here. This house. They'll have to double or triple up. Antoinette Chloe will move in to help me and to chaperone. She will prepare breakfast and lunch for them. They can walk over to the Silver Bullet for dinner."

"What will be the charge for dinner?" Kathy asked.

"I didn't think of that," I said honestly.

"I'll cover the cost," ACB said. "I should have thought about the lack of accommodations in town when we decided to go forward with this idea."

There were protests around the table, and it was finally decided that we'd charge the contestants a minimal amount and ACB could cover the rest.

More items were raised, and Margie Grace agreed to put together a dance that would signify the importance of salmon to Sandy Harbor. Again, that was ACB's idea, and when I glanced at Margie's notes, I saw a doodling of two rows of fish heads complete with legs and arms.

I could just imagine the contestants wearing salmon heads and tap-dancing or doing a kick line.

We accomplished a lot more, including accommodating the five contestants from the Sandy Harbor Golden Age Apartments. All five were in wheelchairs and they called themselves the Wheeling Grannies. We were proud of the fact that the Miss Salmon pageant was open to all ages eighteen and up, and Margie Grace assured us that she'd be able to work them into her program.

I brought up a few more items—an emcee for the event was one of them. Several names were hashed around, including Antoinette Chloe, Ty Brisco, Reverend Clem Reynolds of St. Luke's of the Lake, and Chef Nick Brownelli.

The mention of Nick's name sent ACB into a fit of hysterics, then rage.

The alarmed committee members voted for ACB to be emcee, probably just to shut her up—which worked, I might add. She turned into a ray of sunshine, giddy with being selected. As she talked about designing a formal muumuu for the event and decorating new flip-flops, one by one the committee members put their dishes into the sink and backed out of the kitchen to the front door.

As I walked them out, all of them expressed concern for Antoinette Chloe and her mental health. Kathy, Pam, and Margie were at the Silver Bullet when ACB shouted Nick's name and violently stabbed her side order of sausage. It had left them quite shaken and worried.

After everyone else left, I sat down across from Antoinette Chloe at the table and took a deep breath. I might as well jump in with what I had to say.

"Antoinette Chloe, do you think you might need someone to talk to? How about seeing a counselor or Reverend Clem or someone?"

She raised a penciled eyebrow. "What for?"

I put my hand over hers. "Maybe you can talk about Sal and how you feel about his incarceration."

"He tried to kill me. How do you think I feel?"

"I know, sweetie." And, trust me, I did. Sal tried to kill me, too. However, I pressed on. "But maybe you could talk about Nick? You said that you were lonely without both of them. And then you stabbed the sausage when you thought about Nick. You seemed pretty mad."

"I'm definitely mad, Trixie. And I'm feeling sad and lonely and betrayed, and all because of the Brownelli brothers. But why should I go to a counselor? I have you to talk to." She studied a huge purple ring. "And I have to keep busy: the Miss Salmon pageant, for one, and I have to get Brown's remodeled—yep, I'm going to do that—and then there's the drive-in. I want to break ground on that soon. Hopefully next Thursday."

"You are definitely going to be busy." That was good for a person like ACB.

"Absolutely."

"Can you fit a counselor in?" I patted her hand.

"Like I said, I have you!" She squeezed my fingers and then stood and stretched. "How about going to Nick's house with me? Maybe there's something I missed. Something that would give me a clue as to where he went."

"So, you're not going to a *real* counselor and you are still going to search for Nick?"

"Yes to both. So, will you come with me to Nick's house?"

"Now?"

She nodded.

I looked at the clock on my wall. I guess I didn't need all that much sleep. "Let's go, Antoinette Chloe."

"I'll drive," she said.

"Let's both drive. I don't want you to have to come back here to drop me off."

"Good thinking. I'll meet you at Nick's. He's at 1302 Third Street, and I have the key."

I gave her the thumbs-up sign, but I had a queasy feeling in my stomach. She was a friend, though, so I grabbed my purse, slipped into my yellow raincoat and headed for my boring gray car to spy on ACB's boyfriend, the brother of her incarcerated husband.

Nick's house on Main Street was a cute Craftsman bungalow. It reminded me of a cartoon house with windows that looked like two eyes; the roof seemed like it was wearing a beret, and the front porch could be its teeth.

I stared at the house, willing it to talk like a cartoon and give up its secrets.

ACB was already there, as the front screen door was open and banging on the side of the house in the wind.

Walking up the stairs, I cautiously stepped over the threshold as my eyes adjusted to the darkness. No wonder ACB left the door open.

"Antoinette Chloe? I'm here."

"I'm in the bedroom."

I half expected to see Nick's body on the floor at

my feet. I don't know why. Maybe it was due to Deputy Doug and all his cop stories. Or maybe it was because I was addicted to all the cop shows with or without initials.

Hearing a sob, my heart pounded louder. "Hello? Antoinette Chloe?"

I followed the sobbing down the hall and came to what had to be Nick's bedroom. It was a mixture of cooking-related items and motorcycle paraphernalia. There were paintings and framed photos of plates of meat right next to various blueprints of motorcycles. There was a display of chef hats in various shades of yellowing, along with a rack of motorcycle bandannas and caps.

His bedspread and curtains went with the motorcycle theme. His rugs had the name CHEF NICK'S—BOSTON, MASSACHUSETTS.

I wanted to ask ACB when Nick had his own restaurant. But now was not the time to ask her anything. She was sitting on the bed, hugging a black T- shirt to her chest.

"This is Nick's," she said. "I remember when he wore it. We were riding with the Rubbers."

"The what? The who?"

She turned the shirt around for me to see. "Roving Rubbers, 2013 Ride-a-lot Against Cancer," I read aloud.

"I remember this day." ACB looked up at the Harley-Davidson ceiling fan. Her pale blue eyes pooled with unshed tears. "I was riding in Nick's sidecar, and he kept smiling down at me. We had these helmets that were connected by wire, so we could talk. But we didn't need to talk. His big brown eyes told me everything. They told me that he loved me. Why would he leave me without a word, Trixie?"

"I don't know, Antoinette Chloe. That's why we're here. To find out what's going on. If Nick loved you like you think he did, then maybe he left you a note or something."

She raised her hands in frustration. "I looked for a note the last time I was here."

"Maybe it slipped behind something. Maybe it slipped under the fridge or an end table. Come on. Dry your eyes, and let's look around."

The red bandanna appeared in a flash, and ACB dried her eyes and blew her nose. In another flash of red, the bandanna disappeared again.

"Let's rock and roll, Trixie."

Finally, ACB was back from the land of the love-lorn and ready for action. "Let's search the kitchen first," I suggested. "That's where I'd leave a note."

For a man who always looked unshaven and grubby whenever I'd seen him, Nick was an immaculate housekeeper. Not a fork was out of place. Not a fragment of uncooked spaghetti was on the floor. Not a piece of eggshell was left on the stove. His stainless-steel fridge didn't have one magnet on it or one fingerprint.

And there wasn't a note to be found anywhere.

"Trixie, let's try the living room."

The living room was sloppier. There was a Harley blanket draped over the couch, which was a little crooked. Oh, and the lines of his vacuum cleaner were not all going in the same direction. What a slob!

No note. No tablet. No laptop. No cell phone. There was nothing electronic that we could check for a clue. A Harley calendar had nothing written on it except an entry for two days ago that said *Doc Stanley. Noon.*

"Who's Doc Stanley?" I asked.

"Dentist. He's on Seventh North Street in that ugly building that our not so beloved Mayor Tingsley owns."

"How about calling Doc Stanley? Find out if Nick went to his appointment."

"I'm way ahead of you." ACB was already punching in numbers on her cell phone. I heard her ask if Nick Brown or Nick Brownelli had seen Dr. Stanley on Tuesday.

It didn't take long before she shook her head and mouthed the word *no*. She clicked off her phone and it disappeared into her muumuu. No wonder she never carried a purse.

I shrugged. "It was worth a try."

"Nick would never miss a dental appointment. He took great pride in the fact that all his teeth were his—no bridges, no caps, no root canals. He's had just a handful of cavities."

ACB walked over to the couch and slid off the Harley blanket. She put it around her and flopped down on a brown recliner next to the couch. This must have been her spot when they were watching TV. She started drifting off into her memories again, and I quickly realized I was losing her.

"And my Nick had a great smile. It was like Sal's, but when Nick smiled, little dimples appeared. I loved to watch for those dimples. And his teeth were such a brilliant white. You know, Trixie, they reminded me of Ty Brisco's teeth."

That was more than enough dental discussion, but it did remind me that I was long overdue at the dentist myself.

Time to corral ACB and get her to focus. I needed to get back and get some sleep before my shift, or I'd fall asleep in the dough for the dinner rolls that I planned on making.

"Let's search Nick's garage," I blurted, startling Antoinette Chloe out of her daydreams.

She blinked then turned to me. "Excellent. Let's go."

After she locked the front door, we went to his two-car garage. As clean as Nick's house was, his garage was even cleaner.

Tools hung on Peg-Board in order of smallest to largest. Little plastic boxes with drawers were labeled: #4 NAILS, HEX BOLTS, WASHERS, FLATHEAD SCREWS, and on it went, cabinet after cabinet. Then the big red metal cabinets began and stood guard all around the circumference of the garage.

"Antoinette Chloe. Is that Nick's car?" It was a white Sebring convertible with a black rag top.

"Yes. And that's his motorcycle." She ran her hand lovingly over the black leather seat, then the sidecar.

"Does he have any other vehicles?"

"No." Her eyes grew as wide as my platters at the diner. She knew where I was going with my question.

"So, if Nick left town, it had to be by some other way. Like what?"

"Bus," she said. "But he'd have to get to Watertown or Syracuse to catch a bus. Both are about an hour's drive away. If he took a plane, he'd have to do the same thing."

She continued. "Nick would never take a bus. He hated them. The same with a plane. He said they're both too confining. So is a car, but he always rolled down the windows and the top, rain or shine or blizzard."

"And did you notice that he didn't . . . uh . . . disconnect the sidecar? I think he was still planning on riding with you."

"Oh, Trixie! Oh! I think you're right!"

I looked into the sidecar, not really expecting to see a note from Nick, but stranger things have happened. The metal floor looked like Nick had even shined it up, and there wasn't a blade of grass, a leaf, or a grain of sand to disturb the mirror finish.

"Sorry, Antoinette Chloe. No note."

She shook her head. "I just don't know where he went. I think he would have told me."

"We can always search more at another time. Maybe you'll think of something that he told you that you've forgotten about."

"Maybe . . . but I've racked my brain already."

We walked to the door, and I waited until she locked it. "I have to get some sleep before I drop in my tracks."

"I have to see how my new chef is doing, and make some phone calls," she said. "Thanks for coming here with me, Trix. You're a real pal."

"Anytime. You know that."

"Thanks. I don't have too many friends, but you are at the top of my list."

She gathered me up into a great bear hug, and I tried not to gasp for breath from either my lungs being squished or the fog of scents.

After I could breathe again, I hugged her back with equal enthusiasm.

"See you later, Antoinette Chloe."

"Later."

"If you remember anything about Nick that will help us locate him, give me a shout."

"You got it."

"Do we have any pickled eyeballs?" Barb Hern was subbing tonight as a waitress on the graveyard shift. That was my usual shift.

"We do. How many would you like?"

"A dozen. We have some fisherman out front who said that they've heard that your pickled eyeballs are the best."

I pulled out a gallon jug of my hard-boiled, pickled eggs from the fridge. They were a perfect dark pink color because they had been soaked in beet juice.

Putting them all in a pretty bowl lined with endive, I rang the bell for pickup. Barb returned with more orders. I checked the wheel. Most of them were for the haddock special, but several were breakfast orders: omelets, pancakes, various toasts, eggs, muffins, and quiches.

I got to work doing the Silver Bullet Shuffle, a type of dance that reminded me of being in the chorus line of Sister Mary Mary's fourth-grade play.

I leaped to the fridge, twirled to the Ferris wheel toaster, and spun to the steam table.

The fried fish were floating in the oil, which meant they were done. I plated them and added a generous scoop of mashed potatoes, unless they had asked for fries. I had the fries bubbling in another fryer, out of the way of the fish.

Soon the last order was completed, and I rang the brass ship's bell that signaled Barb that her orders were done.

Barb pushed through the double doors and picked up her order that I'd put on big oval tray for her.

Several hours of twirling and leaping later, I heard the back door squeak open, and my morning chef, Juanita Holgado, entered the kitchen.

"*Hola*, Trixie. Good morning. Sorry I'm a little late."

"I didn't notice, but *hola* and adios, Juanita. The kitchen is all yours. You'll see that I made pea soup for the soup of the day and that dinner rolls are on the racks."

"I could smell the fresh bread from the parking lot. Delicious."

"The daily special is—"

"Spaghetti and meatballs. Go. I can take over."

As I took off my apron, I ticked off a bunch of things I needed to do today. First, I wanted to pick up Blondie from Ty and head home. If I was going to house a dozen or so beauty-queen wannabes—and, yes, that included ACB—I'd better do some serious cleaning.

I saw Ty and Blondie jogging around the grounds. She looked so beautiful with her tail wagging and her blond hair shining in the morning sun.

Ty didn't look so bad himself. It was cool this morning—about sixty degrees—and he was in navy blue sweats. His long strides looked effortless.

I, however, was breathing hard with my short, choppy steps. I vowed that when the New Year began in four short months, I'd exercise more, and not just kid myself that the Silver Bullet Shuffle was my aerobic workout.

And I had to cool it with the carbs. For every dinner roll that came out of the oven, all hot and begging to be smeared with a couple gobs of butter, I must have eaten fifty.

I waved to Ty, and he jogged over. "I suppose you want our dog back."

Blondie wiggled and looked like she was about to jump out of her skin. Squatting down, I hugged her and got a load of puppy kisses in return.

"If you have more exciting things to do with her, please keep her. I'm only going to clean for a horde of Miss Salmon pageant contestants."

"What?"

"There's no room in the inns or the trailer parks in the vicinity, so the Big House is going to be sorority central for a while."

He laughed. "Yikes!" Then he snapped his fingers and raised a perfect black eyebrow. "Beauty contestants, huh? Need any help?"

"Sure, Ty. The ladies who entered from the

Sandy Harbor Golden Age Apartments need wheel-chair transportation. How sweet you are to volunteer! I'll write you in."

"Oh . . . um . . . okay. Anyway, I was going to take Blondie to the dog park. She can run around and play with the other dogs, and I can read on a nearby bench."

"Blondie will love it." Then I thought about Nick and our quest to find him.

I should probably tell Ty about Nick being missing. "I want to tell you that Antoinette Chloe and I went to Nick's place to see if there were any clues as to where he might be—you know he's missing, right?"

"Of course. ACB called yesterday."

Ty shared my abbreviation for Antoinette Chloe Brown's name.

He shook his head. "She also filed a missing-persons report."

I nodded. "She must've called it in right after we left his place. We couldn't find anything. No notes. Nothing. And the place was so clean and sterile that every worker in the Health Department and Housing Codes Enforcement would cry in happiness."

"I hit the computers, but no luck," he said. "He hasn't used a credit card; he hasn't used his cell phone. He hasn't reserved a plane or a bus seat. We are all keeping an eye out for him."

By *all*, I knew that he meant all three deputies of the Sandy Harbor Sheriff's Department. Yeah, that's right: three.

"His car and his motorcycle with the sidecar still attached are in the garage."

"I know. I checked."

"How? ACB has the key."

"It was as simple as looking in the window, Trixie. After all, I am a detective." He said it sarcastically, but there was a twinkle in his eye.

Okay, I deserved that. "I didn't mean to insult your cop-ness, Ty, but he's been missing for a long time."

"What do you mean?"

"Nick's been missing two weeks, not two days. ACB is beside herself with worry."

"Then she should have called us earlier. I can imagine she's upset, but I've already kicked up the investigation a notch," he said.

"How so?"

"I put Nick's information in on the New York State Police system. The troopers are looking for him, too."

"Oh, good!"

"What? Do you think that all I do is jog and hang out with Blondie all day?"

"Of course not. You eat three meals at the Silver Bullet, too."

He patted his flat stomach. "You need a diet menu."

I laughed. "I've been meaning to get around to that."

Looking over at the lake, I thought about how I wanted to bring something up, but I didn't want to accuse Ty of not doing enough.

"What's on your mind, Trixie? Spill."

"What do you mean?"

"Well, you're petting Blondie so much, she's losing fur."

"Okay. I didn't want to get ACB alarmed, because she thinks that Nick's coming back for her, and I kind of encouraged that kind of thinking, but—"

"But?"

"But I have this feeling in my gut that Nick just didn't up and run away. I think something happened to him."

"I do, too, Trixie. I do, too."

Chapter 3

*M*y cell phone rang just as Ty jogged away with Blondie. I checked the number. It was ACB.

"Hello, Antoinette Chloe."

"Trixie, do you remember that you were supposed to meet me at my land? We are about to break ground for my drive-in."

"Already? Antoinette Chloe, you told me next Thursday." When that woman had a bee in her bonnet, or various flora, fauna, poultry, and birds, she worked fast.

"Well, Excavating Ed Berger had a job fall through, so he and his backhoe and other equipment are available. So we're rocking and rolling today."

"You don't need me." What was I supposed to do? Watch Ed the Excavator and his crew move dirt and cut trees?

"Joan Paris of the *Sandy Harbor Lure* is going to be there, so it's a photo op for our mayor. Besides, it'll be good publicity for us, too. And as my best friend, I'd like you to cut the ribbon with me."

Aww . . .

"Hurry, Trixie! Oh, this is so exciting!"

I walked to my car and drove to ACB's land. There were four other cars parked in a line along the highway, and I pulled in behind them.

ACB was there, holding a long yellow ribbon that looked like crime-scene tape at first glance. At second glance, it definitely was crime-scene tape.

ACB handed an end to the mayor and the other end to Ed Berger, whose loud, obnoxious backhoe was running.

"I'm so glad you're here, Trixie," ACB shouted over the noise. She handed me a pair of scissors, and as Joan Paris began taking pictures for the *Lure*, ACB and I posed like we were cutting the crime-scene tape.

ACB had on a subdued muumuu—yellow and blue bird-of-paradise flowers on a fuchsia background. I wished I had the time to change from my tomato-print chef's pants and red chef's coat. Sandy Harbor mayor Rick Tingsley was all suited up with a red-striped tie. His light blue shirt was stretched across his belly, with a couple of buttons straining to keep the shirt closed. The buttons were fighting a losing battle.

Joan Paris was dressed in a black fitted skirt, aqua sweater, and tall black boots. She always looked fashionable, even when she was taking pictures in the mud.

When ACB brought out the champagne and glasses, Mayor Tingsley was the first to hold his glass out. Ed Berger shook his head at the champagne and made a motion that he was going to get to work. It was useless to talk over the roar of the motor, so we smiled at each other, drank champagne, and watched Ed dig. Joan took more pictures.

At about the third scoop of dirt, I spit out my champagne and dropped the glass into the grass.

"Stop! Ed! Stop!" I ran in front of the backhoe, waving my hands and screaming. "Stop! Stop!" I ran my hand across my throat in a gesture for him to cut the motor.

"Oh my goodness!" Annette Chloe flip-flopped across the field to where Ed had started digging. "Oh no! It's Nick! Those are his tattoos. That's his Harley shirt!"

I tried to keep her away from the dirt-covered body of Nick Brownelli. He was on his back, and his face and eyes were covered in mud. There was a dark spot on the left side of his neck, and I thought it must be blood from either a knife or a gunshot wound. Dirt clung to it.

"Mayor Tingsley! Call the sheriff's department!" I shouted. I couldn't do it. I had a two-handed grip on ACB's bird-of-paradise.

But Mayor Tingsley was puking in the weeds.

"Joan! Call the cops!" I yelled.

"I'm on it!" she said.

Excavating Ed appeared and, with hands on hips, said the brilliant words "I hope this isn't a Native American burial ground."

Good grief. "Ed, get a grip. This is Nick Brownelli! He's Italian!"

"My Nick!" ACB twisted out of my grip and knelt next to Nick in a clump of sod. "My beloved."

She reached for his hand and held it. "Who did this to you?" She was sobbing and her tears were dropping on his hand.

I gently pulled her hand away. "Antoinette Chloe, don't touch anything. The cops will want to preserve the crime scene."

ACB's future drive-in was now a crime scene with a dead body in its dirt.

Who would have thought that the crime-scene tape would be an omen?

We waited for an eternity with ACB's head on my shoulder and my arm around her. The seat of my cute tomato pants was feeling damp.

Finally, Ty arrived. I could see Blondie in the back of his cop car.

He rushed down to where we were and looked at me. "Is it Nick?"

I nodded.

"Did any of you touch anything?" he asked.

"I held Nick's hand." Antoinette Chloe hiccuped.

Ty shrugged. "I guess that didn't hurt the crime scene too much."

He took charge. "Joan, would you take pictures, please? All angles."

She nodded and walked gingerly around the overturned ground.

Ty walked back to his car and returned with a full tote bag. He took pictures, too. He asked us all to move back so he could take wider angles. Then he talked to Ed Berger, our puking Mayor Tingsley, and Joan Paris. He must have realized that

ACB was too distraught to make any sense, so he didn't speak with her—at least, not yet anyway.

Just after he asked me to follow him away from the scene so he could ask me questions, the crime-scene investigation van of the state police rolled in and a team of six exited and walked toward us. They all huddled with Ty like a football team, then broke and spread out around Nick's body.

ACB and I sat on the sidelines of the field. I put my arm around her, and she rested her head on my shoulder. She cried and cried, and out of the blue, she looked at me and said, "At least he didn't just take off and leave me, right, Trixie?"

How was I supposed to answer that?

"Uh-huh." That was my usual default response.

"I want to leave here, Trixie," ACB said.

"I agree. Come over to my Big House and I'll make us a cup of tea."

"Not right now, Trixie." We got to our feet with a minimum of grunting. "If you don't mind, I'm going to go home and change and take a shower and take a nap. And tomorrow I think I should drive to Auburn prison and tell Sal about his brother. I know Nick and Sal were on nonspeaking terms ever since Sal tried to kill me . . . but I think he deserves to know that his brother is dead. And I'll need to know what arrangements he wants me to make for Nick."

"Wait until you're ready, Antoinette Chloe. You just had a big shock. Besides, Hal Manning will be examining Nick for a while."

Hal Manning was the owner of the Happy Repose Funeral Home and Sandy Harbor's coroner. I didn't want to go into details with ACB, but based on my faux training with my ex, I was fairly sure that Nick's body wouldn't be released for a while.

How did I know this? Deputy Doug, my ex-husband, always brought his work home, and over dinner he'd tell me every detail of every crime scene he ever presided over. Eventually he stopped coming home for dinner—due to his affair with a very fertile twentysomething—and our big Colonial in Philly became silent—other than when I talked to myself.

But I digress.

"Antoinette Chloe, I'll drive you home. You can take a shower or whatever you want, but I don't want you to be alone. Pack up and move into the Big House. You've moving in to chaperone the Miss Salmon contestants anyway, so just do it sooner."

"That's nice of you, Trixie."

"What are friends for? Let's go."

ACB gave a last look at Nick's body, and my stomach sank. She loved Nick so much, and it was a real shame that her last memory of him had to be of his body covered in a royal blue . . . uh . . . tarp? I'd prefer to think of it as a blanket.

I motioned to Ty, and he came over. I told him what our plans were, and where we'd be in case he wanted to question us.

"I want to take your statements as soon as possible." He looked over at the state police investigators, who were sifting through the dirt. They always called in the troopers for assistance when something big hit Sandy Harbor. Little towns just didn't have the wealth of technology that the troopers had. "I'll be over after we finish up everything here."

Hal Manning had arrived and was peeking under the tarp covering Nick. He nodded at Joan Paris, and she waved back a greeting in return. Everyone knew that they were living together above the Happy Repose, and that Hal was known to spill some particularly juicy bits of information about the cases he was working on to Joan.

After a little pillow talk with Hal, Joan might spill to me. In our book club, we discussed much more than books.

Boy, I sure wanted to find out what happened to Nick. And I was certain that Antoinette Chloe wanted to know even more than I did. She was going to jump out of her flip-flops if she didn't find out soon.

Obviously, someone killed Nick, dug a hole, and placed his body there. I had already ruled out suicide, because even if he had dug the hole and killed himself, someone would have had to bury him. *Duh.*

I opened the door of my car for Antoinette Chloe and she got in. Without a word, which was unusual for her, we drove to her house.

ACB's Victorian house in the middle of the town was a plethora of paint. Every piece of gingerbread trim had a different color. It stood out on her street like a flashy Vegas showgirl next to a congregation of Amish.

We went into her house, and though I had been in her home before, every time I visited it was a fresh experience. To say that it was overdosing with boas, hats, fascinators, and tchotchkes is an understatement. Swags of silk flowers were draped everywhere: cabbage roses that somewhat matched her living-room couches; rows of artificial ivy, hibiscus, hydrangea, and other silk flowers that I couldn't tell the genus or species of the real flower that it was supposed to represent.

Antoinette Chloe was in a decorating category by herself.

"Make yourself comfortable, Trixie. I'll be right back."

I went into the kitchen, where at least I could escape some of the kitsch. But even the kitchen was still crammed with several hundred salt and pepper shakers in every shape and size ever made in this country and beyond.

My head swiveled in awe.

Then I closed my eyes and thought. The Miss Salmon contestants were arriving in no less than five days. Five!

About a dozen were moving into my house, and I needed to start getting things ready. I figured I would rally ACB to help me, as it would force her to take her mind off Nick. Besides, in the committee meeting, she said she would chaperone and cook. But first I needed her to be a maid . . . er . . . a room attendant and help me to get the rooms ready.

And she needed to move in to her room. Our two rooms were off-limits to everyone but us two.

Speaking of which, I wondered how ACB's new chef was working out at her restaurant. I'd have to remind her to check, or we could swing by.

I heard a thump, then another. The noise was coming from upstairs. Hurrying to the stairway, I had to dodge black plastic garbage bags being tossed over the railing.

When ACB came into view with two other bags, I shouted up to her. "What's all this?"

"My muumuus and flip-flops. I won't toss my suitcases. I'll put my makeup and nail polish and accessories in those. Speaking of my nails, I'm missing my pinkie nail from my Salute to Glitter gel nail kit."

I couldn't care less about her glitter gel nails. There were twelve bags and they were still coming.

"I'll start loading these in my car," I yelled.

"Thanks, Trixie."

I wondered how everything would fit in my small, alleged gas-saving car. We should have taken her van.

After everything was finally loaded, we made our way to Brown's Four Corners restaurant to check on the new chef and how things were coming along without ACB.

We both were pleasantly surprised and impressed. The dining room had a good crowd, and as I glanced around, the plates looked nicely prepared. The waitresses looked happy and efficient, and the place looked much cleaner than in the past.

ACB flip-flopped her way into the kitchen and

gasped. "Wow! Everything is so clean since I've been in here last. What did you do, Fingers?"

Fingers?

"I hired a crew. Had it steam cleaned and power washed from top to bottom with an antigreaser. Remember, Antoinette Chloe? You approved it."

"Yes. Yes, I did. Fabulous, Fingers. Great idea." With hands on hips, she looked around and grinned.

"Fingers, I'd like you to meet a friend of mine, Chef Trixie Matkowski. Trixie, this is Chef Phil Gallman."

"Nice to meet you." He had a tough-looking face, like he was a boxer or a wrestler, but when he smiled he looked young and sweet.

He held up his hand in a wave to me, and I discovered why his nickname was Fingers. He was missing two of them.

"One big meat hatchet," Fingers said in response to the question I was dying to ask. "At the Culinary Institute of Brooklyn." He laughed and put three plates of fried haddock and french fries with coleslaw under the heat lamps. He rang a bell, and a waitress came into the kitchen immediately.

"What took you so long, Debby?"

She giggled. "What took you so long to make it?"

Swaying her hips, she sashayed away, knowing Fingers was watching. He gave a low wolf whistle.

"Do you need anything?" ACB asked.

"Not a thing, Antoinette Chloe. We're making

money, and I have everything running like a well-oiled Harley."

Another biker? How does Antoinette Chloe find these guys?

"Okay, Fingers. Keep up the great work. Call me if you need me. I don't feel like cooking these days, but I will come if you need the help."

He nodded as he took a handful of orders from Debby.

It seemed like Fingers was taking over ACB's job as owner. Obviously, she trusted him to take care of the money, too.

Wow.

She'd known him for less than two weeks. I felt like saying something to her, but I thought now wasn't the best time.

Finally, we walked out the door and crammed into my sardine can of a car.

"If I can forget about Nick, the next several days will be fun," she said. "I can look forward to the contestants arriving and the pageant itself."

I turned down Main Street and headed to the Big House. Right now I was wishing it was bigger.

"Just a few more days before we welcome the contestants, Antoinette Chloe. I have to get the Big House ready and get some groceries. I could use your help."

"You got it, Trix."

But I didn't get any. She couldn't stop thinking about Nick and spent her time constantly phoning Hal Manning, trying to pry something out of him about the circumstances of Nick's death. She hung around the Silver Bullet, hoping to corner Ty Brisco for the same thing. She made numerous calls to everyone and their relatives. Any man or woman in uniform who came into the diner, she asked if they were working on Nick's case.

In between all that, she spent her time on the phone with the contestants and giving them directions, and meeting with Margie Grace about the performance part of the program.

Oh yes. A tableau of salmon swimming upstream. Now, that had to be Broadway bound!

At some point, we gave our statements to Ty. And then gave the same statements to the state police investigators. Ditto to every resident of Sandy Harbor who wanted to hear the story from the horse's mouth.

Just call me Seabiscuit.

Somehow I managed to get everything ready by myself, in between cooking at the Silver Bullet and taking care of my eleven cottages when Clyde and Max needed me.

On Saturday morning, three out of the twelve contestants arrived. One of them was Aileen Shubert, who was finally happy to find a place to stay.

I prepared a sandwich-and-salad buffet for the girls and added another table in the kitchen, along with folding chairs so they could all sit together for meals. Besides, I wanted to get to know them.

But there was no time for a lot of talk. As soon as they finished, ACB whisked them all away in her van to Margie Grace's Dance Studio (aka Margie's back deck) to introduce them to their new instructor and choreographer.

And I got stuck cleaning everything up.

I was just about to plop my butt into an Adirondack chair to relax on my covered porch, the one facing the lake, when Clyde and Max appeared.

"Hi, guys. What's up?"

"The fishermen wanted me to ask you if they can have another cleaning station set up. Apparently they have to wait in line to use the two we have."

"Hmm. Where would we find another stainless-steel table at this time of the season?" I thought aloud. "We could supply another couple of trash cans and hook up a hose for running water. It could drain out into buckets or a drum. I could make up a sign to use that station last if the other two are being used." But all that planning was for nothing if I couldn't find a table of some sort.

Clyde snapped his fingers. "I have a table behind my house you can have, Trixie. It's in good shape and I don't really use it anymore. I'll use the one here or the one over at the bait shop, if I need to."

"Thanks. I'll pay you for it."

"No need." He shook his head. "No need at all."

Both Clyde and Max had been in the Army with Uncle Porky. They came to visit and never left, so Uncle Porky gave them jobs as handymen.

"I'll bring it over in my truck," Clyde said. "Max'll help me load it. Right, Maxie?"

"Yup." Max was a man of few words.

Just as soon as they left, I noticed Ty walking up the path toward me with a white bakery bag. I really hoped that he was going to share whatever was in that bag with me, and maybe tell me some news about the investigation into Nick's murder.

Usually, Ty's lips were tightly sealed when it came to pending investigations, but every now and then he'd let me in on something that was going to be public knowledge sooner or later.

"Good evening, Trix," he drawled.

"Hi."

"No company?"

"Blissful silence, for now. The girls that arrived today, including ACB, are all practicing their Miss Salmon number over on Margie Grace's deck."

He laughed. "I know." He made like he was holding a clipboard and pretended to read off it: " 'Earlier, I dispatched Sandy Harbor deputy sheriff Vern McCoy to the residence of Mr. Joe Jensen at 4578 Shipwreck Drive. Mr. Jensen, our complainant, reported that when he was about to go to the Elk's Lodge to get set up for bingo, he noticed that all of his fishing rods had absconded from the back end of his pickup truck. Well, Deputy McCoy, being the excellent Sandy Harbor deputy that he is, heard laughing and giggling and went to investigate. After the subsequent questioning of an individual known to Deputy McCoy as Antoinette Chloe Brown, she informed said deputy that she noticed said fishing rods doing nothing but reclining in the back of the Jensen truck bed and asked Agnes Jensen, spouse of victim, if she could borrow them for the dance practice currently in progress. However, said Agnes forgot to tell said spouse, Joe. Property recovered. Investigation closed.' "

I couldn't stop laughing. Legalese rolled off his tongue like Dinerese rolled off mine.

"Oh, but wait. You haven't heard the best part."

"Do tell, Deputy Brisco."

" 'Deputy McCoy related that he saw a bit of the aforementioned, quote, Run of the Salmon, rehearsal, complete with the Jensen fishing rods, unquote, and he had to leave because he, quote, peed his uniform pants, he was laughing so hard, unquote.' "

"Oh no! Then what?"

"I told him to go home and change his pants."

I couldn't breathe. I couldn't do anything but laugh hysterically.

Ty leaned against the railing, facing me. As I regained my composure, he reached into the bag and handed me an almond bear claw. Mrs. Sarah Stolfus must have made her baked-goods delivery. I had standing orders with her and she supplied the Silver Bullet, keeping the revolving case stocked full of delicious desserts.

I loved her bear claws, her hand pies, her Danishes, and her . . . well, you get the drift. And I had to get exercising.

Ty looked out over the lake and stared for a while. Based on our yearlong friendship, I knew that he was mulling something over and that he'd talk when he was ready.

In the meantime, I munched on the bear claw, enjoying the sweetness of the glaze and the cinnamon that gave it just the right taste. Then I wondered if Sarah delivered the apricot and cheese Danishes like she usually did. Talk about delicious.

Pilates. That's what I was going to do.

Ty finally turned to me. "We're releasing Nick's body the day after tomorrow. Tomorrow I'm going to go to Auburn prison and break the news to Sal. I don't know if he knows yet. I asked his counselor there to try to keep the news away from him until I got a chance to tell him. But who knows?"

The mention of Sal's name got my attention. I shuddered, remembering the wintery day that he almost killed ACB and me.

"Ty, did you know that Antoinette Chloe wants to tell him herself?"

"No way."

"Way."

"I don't want her doing that."

I sighed. "Why not? She was Sal's brother's girlfriend. Besides, ACB wants to find out if Sal knows what Nick's last wishes were. She feels that she should be the one to take care of the funeral arrangements. She was talking about driving to Auburn, but I told her that she has a lot of time yet, since Nick's body wouldn't be released for a while. Now she'll be itching to go."

"Why can't she call him instead? I can get a call through to him via his in-house counselor. She can talk to him then."

"Ty, really. This isn't the kind of news that you want to tell someone over the phone."

He rubbed his forehead. "Why does she care about being polite? He was planning to run away with his girlfriend! And he tried to kill ACB!"

"What can I say? She still has feelings of what might have been for Sal. They were married for more than twenty happy years before it all turned to crap. And they had so many nice plans for their retirement. Unfortunately, that was the money he took to run away with his girlfriend with."

A reddish-purple-gold sunset was taking place behind him, but he didn't notice. He'd taken his cowboy hat off and was studying the inside of it, for some reason. Then he raked his fingers through his straight black hair with its chestnut sun streaks.

Not that I'd noticed.

"Trixie, can you get anyone to babysit the contestants tomorrow?"

"Antoinette Chloe can if—"

"No. I mean, can anyone take care of things while you and ACB are gone for the day?"

"Well, I can have someone from the Miss Salmon Committee come over."

"Then spring them into action for tomorrow."

"Ty, can you back up a bit? Or can I buy a clue?"

"I want to go to Auburn to talk to Sal before ACB does, and since I probably can't stop ACB from going by herself, I want to bring her along."

"Then why do you need me?"

The eyebrow went up, and the half smile appeared.

"Oh, I see. You need a bodyguard."

He slipped his hat back on and tweaked the brim. So sexy.

As he walked away, I wondered why he wanted to get to Sal before ACB.

Oh, I know! To see Sal's reaction to the news of Nick's death. Would it be sadness, gladness, or satisfaction that he saw gleaming in Nick's eyes?

Ty would definitely be looking for some kind of tell—a twitch of the eye, a movement at the corner of his mouth, or some other nervous tic.

Thinking about it, Sal could easily order a hit from prison. But would he do so on his brother? They had been great buddies in the past up until Sal tried to kill me and ACB. They motorcycled together. They cooked together at Brown's Four Corners.

I just can't imagine why Ty would suspect Sal of something so heinous.

Heinous? Heinous was Sal's middle name! The man was in jail for one count of murder and two counts of attempted murder. And one of those counts was for my attempted murder, for heaven's sake.

Then I thought of something else the brothers had in common: ACB.

Could Sal be jealous enough of Nick to arrange a hit on him from jail?

Chapter 4

*W*e met at the crack of sunrise for breakfast at the Silver Bullet. With it raining like Noah's flood and ACB yakking nonstop, it'd be a long trip to Auburn Correctional Facility, the home of the first electric chair.

She was in the backseat, refreshing her makeup, which meant more coats of everything. When she pulled out a gallon jug of perfume, I asked her to wait until we got outside.

It's not that I objected to perfume; I just needed to breathe a bit. And she'd already sprayed at least three times.

She said that she was wearing the muumuu that Sal had bought her for their twentieth anniversary. It had stems of gladiolas circling it. Their roots started at the hem, and their green stalks ran vertically up the garment until the flowers started blooming at her knees, all the way to her neck. She wore several necklaces—from chunky faux stones to a circle of seashells. Her earrings were six-inch starfish, and matched the starfish on her flip-flops. Her fascinator was a nest of plastic pelicans in a nest of feathers in a nest of white lace.

I couldn't help but smile every time I saw my friend. ACB definitely marched . . . er . . . flip-flopped to beat of her own drummer. She dressed the way that pleased her, and probably the Brownelli brothers, too. If ACB had ever continued with her fashion career in New York City, she would have shaken the place to its very girders.

Ty had warned ACB at breakfast that Auburn probably wouldn't let her in the door with her jewelry and hat, and that she could be sure of a thorough search due to her dress.

"Do they think that I have an Uzi strapped to my thigh with duct tape?"

Ty shrugged. "Stranger things have happened, Antoinette Chloe."

Ty broke free of us and breezed through the prison equivalent of Homeland Security, thanks to his law-enforcement status. After he unloaded his gun in the designated Unload and Store Firearms Here area and stashed it in a special locker, he waved to us as if he was cleared for takeoff. The door and bars, and doors with bars, and bars without doors, clanged open and shut behind him.

Ty was indeed right. ACB received more scrutiny than a twenty-dollar bill at the discount store. A team of female correctional officers took her into a special room, and I could hear ACB using very, very special words.

When she came back into the waiting room, she was wearing a totally boring white jumpsuit with Auburn Correctional Facility stenciled on the back. Her hair was flat and her fascinator was gone, along with every piece of jewelry. Even her long, glittery, fake fingernails were gone. They let her keep her flip-flops, minus the starfish.

Sobbing, she showed me her hands. "No fingernails. They thought I might be smuggling in drugs under them. Can you believe that one?"

I could believe that others might have done so.

She burst into tears. "Look at me! I look like . . . white bread. So colorless and boring."

Yes, compared to her usual dress, but I thought she looked younger and skinnier. I didn't know she even had a waist under all those muumuus!

I took her arm and we headed to the ladies' room. "Antoinette Chloe, you have to wash your face. You have streaks of makeup and mascara running down it."

"I had to lock up my purse. All my makeup is in it."

"Mine's locked up, too, so I can't help you there. I guess you're just going to have to go . . . commando."

That got us both laughing, and after some scrubbing and scraping of her face with industrial paper towels and hand soap from a dispenser on the wall, she looked in the mirror, and a fresh batch of tears started.

I thought she looked just wonderful and told her so. "You have a fabulous complexion and barely have wrinkles. I can't say that about mine and I'm thirty years younger."

"Oh, stop."

It seemed as though we were in the eighth-grade locker room at St. Margaret's Grammar

School instead of a two-stall ladies' room in a New York State correctional facility.

Who would have thought?

"Antoinette Chloe, I'm not particularly thrilled to be seeing Sal. I still have flashbacks about him holding a gun on us, but we are in this together, just like before, so let's go to jail!"

"I'm glad you're here, Trixie. I need you for moral support."

I took a deep breath. "You got it!"

My heart was pounding so hard that I thought it was going to pop out of my chest. It had better not. This was one of my best blouses. However, I needed to know if Sal ordered a hit on his brother because he'd been dating ACB. It seemed like something he was capable of, and when ACB was still married to Sal, she had told me how he was maniacally jealous of anyone who even looked at her. She'd told me about a couple of incidents where Sal actually threw punches at unsuspecting guys who just looked at ACB. She's so flashy, she attracts swivel necks wherever she goes, so I'm sure that it was just Sal's imagination.

ACB gripped my hand as we were escorted through the doors and bars, and then through more bars and doors. Finally, the metallic banging stopped, and we waited as two different correctional officers met us. They snickered as they noticed our hands clutched together in fear.

"Grow up," I said. "This is America." Let them think whatever their tiny minds could fit.

"Is there a problem here?"

I'd know that drawl anywhere. I turned to see

Ty behind us, looking every bit the six-foot-four-inch cop that he was. The two correctional officers were almost entirely dwarfed by his shadow.

Ty put a hand on my shoulder and the other on ACB's. Suddenly, I felt better about being here. ACB must have, too, because she let go of the death grip on my hand.

"I'll escort my friends to the private meeting room, if you two don't mind. Has the prisoner been moved?" Ty was authoritative and commanding.

"Yes, sir."

"Good. Thank you. I know the way."

Ty led us to a fairly large room with a gray steel table and several gray steel chairs.

Sal stood as we walked into the room, and it was then I realized why we were given the Homeland Security treatment. There were no walls between Sal and us.

Sal had the good sense to look uncomfortable when he saw me. As for ACB, his eyes kept darting back to her, looking puzzled.

"I know you, don't I?" he asked ACB.

"Don't be an idiot, Sal."

"Antoinette Chloe?" he asked incredulously. "You look so, so . . . different. In a good way, of course. You look so beautiful . . . and young! Did you lose weight?"

"Save it, Sal. I look like a ghost. You've just been without a woman too long."

I really had to help my friend work on her self-esteem.

She sighed. "We came here to tell you some bad news."

"Ty already told me about Nick. It breaks my heart. My baby brother! Oh, Nicky . . ."

Sal seemed genuinely sad. His shoulders shook and his eyes pooled with tears. He wiped them on the sleeve of his orange jumpsuit. Then he put his hand over ACB's.

Ty cleared his throat. "I'm sorry, Antoinette Chloe. I know you wanted to tell him first. But the matter came up in the course of my conversation with Sal."

Liar, liar, jeans on fire! I knew he had wanted to beat ACB to Sal all along.

She quickly pulled her hand away from Sal. "I want to know about his final wishes, Sal. Did he ever tell you anything as to what he wanted for his arrangements?"

"Didn't he tell *you*, Antoinette Chloe? I hear that you and my brother were quite the hot biker duo. How could you do that to me? My own brother!"

"You can't tell me what to do anymore, Sal. We're divorced, remember? I didn't cheat on you, like you cheated on me with that bimbo."

"It's the biggest regret of my life, babe."

I jumped out of my chair, outraged. "What about the man you poisoned, pal? The bimbo's boyfriend. And what about the fact that you tried to kill me and ACB? Don't you regret any of that?"

I felt Ty's hand on my sleeve, tugging me back into my seat. "Hey, let's not rehash old crimes. Trixie, you should sit down before the two stooges bust in here."

Antoinette Chloe sighed. "Sal, what would you like me to do with Nick?"

He shrugged. "The cemetery out in the country—what's the name of it?"

"Restful Souls. We have a double plot there. Remember?"

"Can you add on a plot for Nick?"

"I'm not going to be buried next to you, Sal. Not anymore!" She shook her head. "My soul will never be able to rest."

"Okay, then give my plot to Nicky. You and my brother can share a dirt nap together."

Ty must have seen it coming, because he caught ACB's fist just inches before it connected to Sal's unshaven jaw.

"Antoinette Chloe, you sit over there." He pointed to the chair farthest away from Sal. "Trixie, why don't you join her?"

I gave Sal a dirty look and joined ACB.

He leaned over like he was sharing a joke with Ty. "What a woman!"

Ty nodded. "I can't argue with you there, but how about answering Antoinette Chloe's question like the gentleman I know you are?"

Sal hung his head. "It's hard to remember what I was like before."

"You've only been in here five months," Ty pointed out.

Sal pushed up his short sleeves. "Are you kidding me? Just look at this amateur clink ink. I'd never put up with this bad ink on the outside."

"I recognize the crest of the Double R. It's not a bad ink job, Sal," ACB said from across the room. "Of course, I can barely see it from way back here."

To me, it looked like a big rubber tire with two *R*'s inside it. Not a difficult design for even a clink ink artist.

"I don't recognize the insignia," Ty said.

"Me and Nicky belonged to the Roving Rubbers, a rough bunch of upstate New York chefs," Sal said, flexing his biceps. I saw Ty perk up at that.

"'Where the rubber meets the road—'" ACB sang.

"'We will rove!'" Sal and ACB finished together.

"You know, the Rubbers accepted me as one of their own, Sal. After all, I'm a chef now," Antoinette Chloe said.

"The hell you are!"

"I sure am. Who do you think is running *my* restaurant these days?" ACB said.

Uh, probably Fingers, her new cook!

"Uh, let's not start anything," Ty interrupted. "Out of curiosity, just how tough are the Roving Rubbers?"

I knew what Ty was going for. Sal could have used a fellow Rubber to wipe out Nick.

ACB laughed. "I know the RR code. For instance, we swear that we'll always use real butter instead of margarine. Oh, and we don't use cookware or utensils that aren't made in the United States."

"Probably the toughest is our leader, Toxic Waste," Sal said. "He owns Bill's Bavarian Restaurant up in Ogdensburg, but he's anxious to open an additional restaurant. And, yeah, he's tough. He's done some time."

"State time?" Ty asked.

"Community-service time. In one of the parks up there."

"Oh, I'm absolutely terrified," I said under my breath. "Those Rubbers are just wild."

ACB stifled a giggle.

"What did he do?" Ty asked.

"He had a lot of outstanding parking tickets."

I could see that Ty was trying not to laugh, too. "Any of the Rubbers have a grudge against Nick?" he asked Sal.

"Yeah. Me. 'Cuz he was with my woman," Sal snapped, then calmed. "Actually . . . that's not true. Nick is . . . was . . . a good guy. Though now that I think about it, Toxic Waste did have some beef with Nick."

"What kind of beef?"

"Nick made a play for Toxic's position. He wanted to take his place as head of the Rubbers because Toxic lost a Michelin star. Apparently, Nick didn't think he was worthy to run a club of chefs. But Toxic blamed Nick for making him lose that star. It's a long story." Sal shook his head. "Oh. And Nick stole Toxic's girlfriend. That didn't sit well with Toxic. He's very loyal and protective of all his women, you know."

"What a guy," Ty said. "So, Sal, talk to Antoinette Chloe. What about Nick's arrangements?"

"Well, first, Ty, I'd appreciate if you'd find out who stuck a blade into his neck," Nick said.

"I will. And if you can think of anything I should know, tell your counselor, and he'll put you through to me. Personal calls are limited, but legal calls aren't."

Sal looked sadly at ACB. "Sweetheart, why don't you get another double plot? I'll pick up the tab—just call my lawyer and he'll give you money. It was supposed to go for my appeal, but let's face it: I'm never getting out of this hole." He turned to Ty and chuckled. "Ty and the district attorney, along with yours and Trixie's testimonies, did too good of a job putting me in here. So, do that, babe. Get another double for yourself. A beautiful woman like you will find a guy worthy of you. That way, Nicky and I will rest together, and you can rest with your new man. How's that?"

There were tears in Sal's eyes. That little speech was hard for him to say.

"All right, I'll make arrangements through Hal Manning, then. Of course, I'll put a write-up in the *Lure*. I'm sure Joan Paris will help me. I'll have one night of calling hours and a little service at Hal's Happy Repose Funeral parlor and another service at the Restful Souls Cemetery."

"That's nice of you, Antoinette Chloe," Sal said.

"I loved Nick. A lot. He was a good to me after you were sent away, and we had a lot of fun with the Rubbers. I needed that."

Several sharp knocks interrupted the ACB and Sal truce. The Two Stooges. Sal stood immediately.

ACB stood, too, and waited until they entered the room. "Can I hug my ex-husband before you take him away? For old times' sake?"

They were going to deny her request, but Ty held up his hands. "I'll vouch for Antoinette Chloe. She's clean. Besides, you're going to search the prisoner anyway before you take him back to his cell, right?"

The shorter guard nodded. "Yeah. Go ahead and hug, but make it quick."

I had tears in my eyes as the two of them hugged. They were both in prison jumpsuits and both of them were in their own lonely prisons. Sal deserved what he got, don't get me wrong, but ACB's life had fallen apart—twice. Yet both times, she picked herself up, dusted her muumuu off, put on fresh makeup, and made another hat.

I admired her, and I hoped she knew that.

She broke away from Sal, kissed him on the cheek, and turned to Ty. "Let's get out of here. I have a bunch of beauty queens to take care of."

Ty sighed. "It's a tough job, but someone has to do it."

I was glad when the gate opened, then closed as we were outside the walls of Auburn. Thankfully, the medieval-looking prison with its guard towers, turrets, and razor wire were behind us.

The ride back was uneventful. Once again, ACB was mostly silent and just stared out the window. I could hear her sniff every now and then, and I handed her a pack of tissues from my purse.

"Thanks, girlfriend," she said, plastering on a few coats of foundation.

"Need anything else, ladies?" Ty asked. "Coffee? A pit stop?"

"I just want to get back to Sandy Harbor," ACB said. "Prison is too depressing."

No kidding!

I wanted to get back and see how the Miss

Salmon Committee was taking care of things. They said they'd get the rooms ready for the rest of the contestants who were due to arrive shortly.

"We could always have lunch at the Silver Bullet," I said. "The specials today are goulash and Spanish rice. Both come with a couple of sides and fresh Italian bread that Juanita makes from scratch."

"I'll have to take a rain check. There's a couple of things I need to do for the case. One of them will be to search Nick's house. And, Antoinette Chloe, I wish you'd told us sooner that Nick was missing."

"I do, too. But I thought he was just . . . roving. I never thought that he was dead." She sniffed. "I think I'll go to Margie Grace's with the girls," ACB said. "Then I'll stop and see Hal Manning. But thanks for the lunch invitation, Trixie."

"Do you want me to go with you to Hal's?" I asked.

"No. I'll be fine."

Ty dropped us off at the Silver Bullet, where ACB had left her car. She hugged us all and drove away in her van.

"Save me some of that goulash, Trix." Ty put his hand on my shoulder. "I need to stop in at the office and bring everyone up to speed."

"Can you bring *me* up to speed?" I asked.

"As to what?"

"As to what you got out of Sal. You were in there with him for a long time before we all met him together."

"You pretty much know what I know."

"'Pretty much'?"

"Trixie, stay out of it. I'll do my job and you do yours."

"But ACB is my friend. I want to find out what happened. Maybe then she'll be able to put everything to rest and move on."

But from the look he gave me, I knew that he wasn't going to give up anything. So I waved goodbye as he got into his cop car. Then I went into my diner to see if everything was running smoothly.

And to see if Sarah Stolfus had made a delivery of fruit hand pies. *Cherry, please.*

Everything was okay, but Sarah Stolfus hadn't made her delivery yet. So I began the short walk to the Big House.

Hmm . . . after going to Auburn, a real big house, maybe I shouldn't call my Victorian the Big House.

Along the way, my cell phone rang. It was Antoinette Chloe. *What on earth?*

"Hello?"

"Trixie, I lied to Ty. I'm not going to the Miss Salmon practice now. I'm going back to Nick's house. I forgot to pick up a couple of things when we were there last. Come with me, please?"

"Do you really need me?" I asked. "Just get your things and get out of there."

"I can't stand the thought of going into Nick's house now that I know that he's dead."

There were so many things I needed to do, but nothing was more important than helping a friend—even if it meant going with her into her deceased boyfriend's house yet again.

"Okay. I'll be right there."

Fifteen minutes later, we were going through

the front door. ACB ran immediately to the master bedroom. At first glance, it appeared that nothing had been upset, but I knew that Ty and his gang of state police would descend on the place soon.

I followed her.

She opened the bottom drawer of the dresser and pulled out a . . . black leather thong. Her name was tooled on the back strip of leather.

"Where is that camera?" she asked, pulling out dozens of black T-shirts and tossing them on the floor. Finally, she found a small red camera and let out of whoop of excitement.

"A camera?"

She giggled. "I can't even tell you what naughty pictures are on that camera, but I'm so glad that I found it!"

"Let's get out of here."

"In a minute. I want to look at my sidecar and Nick's bike one more time," she said. "I'll take a couple of pictures. You know, for memories."

"Let's hurry."

We went into the garage, and ACB took tons of pictures. Then she froze like a statue and slapped her head.

I was glad that she wasn't wearing a hat, or it would have flown to the next county.

"I'll have to sell everything," she said. "Crap! I never thought of how I'd have to sell Nick's things. His house, his bike, my sidecar. His convertible. Oh, I forgot about the big shed out back! And look at all these tools and tool cabinets! I'm getting overwhelmed. Who should get the money?

Sal can't use it where he is. Oh, I guess I can donate the money."

She was rambling and looked like she was ready to fall apart.

"What about your drive-in, Antoinette Chloe?"

"I don't know. I lost my enthusiasm for that project. I'll have to think about it, but for now, I can't even think about the drive-in. Especially after we found Nick's . . . body on the land I wanted to build it on."

"Are you done here?" I asked, concerned that she was going to burst into tears at any moment. "Why don't you take a break and go back to my house and lie down?"

"I can't. I have to go to Joan's office at the *Lure.* I have to put an obituary for Nick in the paper. And I really have to see Hal Manning."

Hmm . . . maybe Joan had a scoop or two after pillow talk with Hal, although Hal had loose lips even without pillows being involved. A visit to both of them might prove helpful.

"Antoinette Chloe, how about if we work together and find out what happened to Nick?"

"Just what I was thinking. I owe it to Nick to find out who killed him."

"We still have to take care of the pageant girls, shuttle them around, feed them, and put on the pageant. We both have to cook at our restaurants, too. In between, we'll have to follow any leads about Nick. Oh, and you have to take care of funeral arrangements. His house and contents can wait for a while, don't you think?"

What was I doing? I was adding to her anxiety, for heaven's sake.

"Yes. All that can wait, but Hal Manning can't. Let's go, Trixie."

So we went to Hal's Happy Repose Funeral Home. His office was very modern, if we were still in the disco era. Shag rugs in various colors covered everything, even the walls. I'd been to calling hours here before, and the room was tasteful and nice, but I'd never been in his lime green shag office.

I wondered where he did his coroner duties.

"Sit down, ladies. Obviously, I know why you're here."

Reaching into a small fridge, he pulled out two bottles of water and set them down in front of us. I went for one.

"The world has lost a good man and a good cook," Hal said.

"Chef," ACB corrected.

"Chef," Hal repeated. "It was a shame that he had to die that way."

ACB dabbed at her nose with a yellow bandanna. "What way, Hal?"

Hal hesitated just a second, but I pushed.

"I think that Antoinette Chloe has a right to know, Hal. They were very close."

"He died from a knife cut to his jugular vein. He bled out on the dirt not far from where Ed dug him out."

Eew. Picturing that, I took a couple chugs of water. It sloshed around my empty stomach.

"A big knife?" I asked. "Like a big bread knife or a meat cleaver?"

"Nope. He had a small but perfectly placed cut. It had to be a thin, very sharp knife."

I grabbed ACB's hand and squeezed it. She was turning white under all the makeup that she slathered on during our ride back from Auburn.

Twisting open the cap of the other bottle of water, I handed it to her. "Take a couple of deep breaths. And drink some water."

Hal Manning definitely had loose lips today, but nothing else he mumbled about had much to do with Nick.

ACB made the other arrangements and wrote out a check for Hal. Then we told him that we were on our way to see Joan.

"Tell her that I'm in the mood for spaghetti and meatballs," he said.

ACB shook his hand. "Go to my restaurant. Tell Debby that it's on me. Oh, Joan's going to be late getting home because she's going to be working with me on Nick's obit. I want it to be perfect."

We drove over to the *Lure* office. Sisters May Sandler and June Burke, retired schoolteachers, were in the reception area. One was typing on a huge computer, and one was on the phone. They worked at both the library and at the *Lure* parttime and were two of my first friends when I arrived in Sandy Harbor.

When they saw us, they waved. We waved back.

"What do you need?" May shouted.

ACB pulled a green bandanna from her cleavage closet. "I would like to write an obituary for Domenick Brownelli, and was hoping that Joan could help me."

"I'll call her and see if she's available."

But Joan opened the door to her office and walked toward us. Thin walls, I guess.

She hugged us both and escorted us to her office. It was filled with autographed pictures and framed front pages of some of the *Lure*'s hottest stories.

Nick's obituary was painful for Antoinette Chloe, but she pushed on.

Finally, she had a finished product:

Domenick "Nick" Floyd Brownelli, age 55, of Sandy Harbor, New York, rode his Harley into the sunset on Tuesday, September 1, 2014.

Nick is survived by his brother, Salvatore "Sal" V. Brownelli, formerly of Sandy Harbor, now of Auburn, New York, and Nick's girlfriend, Antoinette Chloe Brown, the current owner-operator of Brown's Four Corners restaurant in Sandy Harbor, New York, and who will definitely miss her beloved Nick.

Nick was predeceased by his parents, Mary Columbo Brownelli and Domenick Salvatore Brownelli, formerly of Quechee, Vermont.

Nick was a master chef. He co-owned Chef Nick's, a five-star restaurant in Boston, Massachusetts, until he left to join his brother, Sal, as a chef at Brown's Four Corners.

Nick enjoyed riding his Harley with the Roving Rubbers, a New England motorcycle club. He raised thousands of dollars riding in numerous charity events. Antoinette Chloe could be found riding along with him in his Harley's sidecar.

Calling hours will be at Manning's Happy Repose Funeral Home on Friday from 7:00 p.m. to 9:00 p.m. Burial will be at the Restful Souls Cemetery on Route 491 on Saturday at 9:00 a.m.

Nick will be missed by all whose lives he touched.

"I like it," Antoinette Chloe declared. "Thank you, Joan, Trixie."

I nudged ACB. "Tell me about Nick's restaurant in Boston."

"Oh yes. It was quite fabulous, from what I knew of it. Very classy, very posh, and it was a gold mine."

"Why did he leave it, then?"

"He had a falling-out with his partner. I don't know what it was about, but from what I heard, he walked out one day and threatened to burn it down. Then he smoked his Harley through the dining room and out the back door, never to return again."

Joan leaned forward. "Sounds like one hell of an exit."

"I know—I wish I had been there to watch it! But I know only what Nick told me." ACB's face glowed with excitement.

"Did he ever see his partner again?" I asked.

"Only once that I know of. I was with Nick when he ran into him . . . Chad, that is. Chad Dodson. I wasn't divorced from Sal then, but he was still in jail, awaiting his trail, and Nick thought I should get away from everything, so I hopped into his sidecar. We rode in one of the fund-raisers, and we were at a postevent barbecue when Chad rolled in. He was in a vintage 'fifty-six Thunderbird convertible. It was candy-apple red with a bright white interior. What a ride!"

"And then what?" Joan asked.

"Well, Nick didn't know that Chad was the organizer of this particular event, or he probably wouldn't have entered. During Chad's speech, Nick's blood began to boil. He said to me, 'How dare he talk about bikes when he's never even sat on one? Dodson is just too damn pompous to believe.' And then, after they'd both had way too much to drink—Chad celebrating a successful event and Nick drowning his anger—they crossed paths. They were having some words, and then Chad pulled this switchblade-looking knife out of nowhere and slashed Nick on his arm. They rolled around on the ground, punching and kicking each other, and Nick broke Chad's nose in the scuffle. In the end, Chad bled all over his fancy shirt and khakis, and Nick was livid that Chad ruined his Roving Rubbers tattoo by causing him to need stitches."

"A switchblade-looking knife, huh?" I said to myself.

Joan punched keys on her computer. "Aren't switchblades illegal in New York?"

"I don't think Chad Dodson gave a hoot."

"Chad Dodson? Of the Boston Dodsons? As in the banking family?" Joan's hands flew across the keyboard.

"I guess so. He seemed pretty rich and WASP-ish." ACB stood. Finally we were leaving.

"Sounds like Nick had an enemy," I said.

"I thought it was just a guy thing. You know, macho posturing, but now that I think back, Chad did threaten to ruin Nick like Nick had ruined Chad. Then Chad said that he'd kill Nick."

"Antoinette Chloe!" I hoped that she noticed the urgency in my voice. "This could be important!"

"Do you think so? It was about six months or so ago. I think that it was just something said in the heat of the moment. You know, after a few beers and all that. If Chad Dodson wanted to kill Nick, why didn't he do it before now?"

I shrugged. "I don't know the answer to that yet, but a knife was involved. A thin knife. Like a switchblade. Antoinette Chloe, I think we have Suspect Number One. Now, where can we find Chad Dodson?"

Chapter 5

Joan Paris volunteered to search for Chad Dodson on her newspaper's computer system. She said that it wouldn't be too hard, since it seemed like he was the Paris Hilton of his family.

Antoinette Chloe and I drove back to the Big House—my Victorian, not the correctional facility.

I paused as I pulled into my usual parking spot. "What's going on in my house?"

"The rest of the girls arrived today," ACB said.

"Today? I thought I had two more days!"

Geez. I must be really out of it.

"No. Today. It was always today," ACB said.

"I don't have anything ready."

"Don't worry. Connie DiMarco and Irene Mitchell made up the rooms, greeted the girls, and are going to feed them."

I let out my breath, not realizing that I'd been holding it. Thank goodness ACB had things under control.

All the contestants had indeed arrived and were being fed by Connie and Irene, two of our Miss Salmon Committee volunteers.

Everyone introduced themselves as they sat around the table.

"I'm Aileen with an *A*. Shubert, like the famous theater in New York City."

She had blond hair with white streaks that fell to her shoulders in a shiny mass of loose curls, which she kept tossing.

I've always wanted to toss my hair, but it's too thin and too short. Oh, well.

A redhead with spiked hair said that she was Wanda Pullman, "like the train car."

Betsy Dyson, "like the vacuum," was tiny with a pixie haircut. And then there was Lisa Something, whose name wasn't like anything, so I promptly forgot it, along with the names of the rest of the contestants.

The total count of those residing at the Big House was twelve contestants, Antoinette Chloe, Blondie, and me.

That was a lot of females!

Oh, and there were four cockatiels on the side porch. Apparently, one of the contestants didn't get the word that there wasn't a talent portion of the pageant, just salmon dancing and spawning.

I couldn't imagine what her talent was, but right now, the birds were making a mess—at least according to Connie, who declared emphatically that she wasn't going to clean it up.

Blondie had come alive and was running around the ladies, vying for attention.

"Fabulous goulash, Miz Matkowski. Just like my mom used to make."

Huh? That's when I noticed all the white foam boxes in the trash. They all had takeout from the Silver Bullet. *I thought the committee was going to feed them. . . .*

"I had the Spanish rice. It was divine."

"I had corned beef and cabbage, and brought half of it back for a snack later."

"And the desserts . . . I'm never going to fit into my gown!"

That reminded me. I needed to find a gown to wear. All of the committee members agreed that we'd go formal and fancy. Well, ACB insisted on it—and we agreed, if only to stop her from talking.

That reminded me again. I hoped ACB would get some sleep in the room next to mine. She'd had a tough day.

I'd had a tough day, too. That was why it didn't help that I couldn't get a minute of sleep before I went to cook at the diner.

The contestants were as loud as they could be. Blondie was about to jump out of her fur from excitement. She ran from room to room, seeing where she could get the most attention.

I just wanted quiet—just four hours of peace so I could take a nap.

Hearing flip-flopping in the room next door, I hoped that ACB would do a little chaperoning and quiet the sorority girls.

Instead, it seemed that the party had moved to ACB's room and she was holding court.

I knocked on the door and stuck my head in. "Hey, ladies, I have to go to work in a while, and I haven't slept for a long time. Can you all go to your rooms and read quietly or something? Or go to sleep early? I hear that Margie Grace is going to be ruthless tomorrow."

There were groans, but they filed out of ACB's room.

"Sorry, Trixie. I wasn't thinking," ACB said. "I was just enjoying them so much."

"I know, pal. It's just that I'm exhausted. I'll never make it through my shift if I don't catch some sleep."

She nodded. "There won't be another sound."

But there was. The party moved outside onto the porch that faced the lake, and said porch was right underneath my window.

"I think that our dance routine is really lame," I heard one of the girls say.

"It makes me laugh. I don't know why I entered Miss Salmon anyway. It doesn't exactly shine on a resume."

"The five-hundred-dollar prize is laughable. So is the ride in the funeral guy's Cadillac in the Salmon Parade. Now, that is definitely lame."

"But we're getting fed for a minimal amount, and this house is fabulous. *And* there are a lot of cute fishermen roaming around."

"Only if you like your men in rubber waders."

That brought peals of laughter. I supposed it was funny, but I wished they'd quit bashing the pageant.

"And what about Antoinette Chloe? What's with those muumuus?" I heard Aileen Shubert pipe up. "And that makeup! With all those silly hats and flip-flops and jewelry!"

More laughter. Okay, they could bash the pageant all they wanted, but bashing Antoinette Chloe went too far. I didn't want her to hear them and have hurt feelings.

So I threw on a bathrobe and shot down the stairs through the living room and kitchen, and flung open the screen door.

"Do not talk about Antoinette Chloe like that," I said through gritted teeth, looking pointedly at Aileen. "She's my friend, and she's done a boatload of things to make you all feel very comfortable. And she's doing everything she can to make the pageant a success. And the salmon dance might be lame, but it's . . . uh . . . artistic and . . . um . . . interpretive. Yes! It's an interpretive artistic dance, the latest thing on Broadway."

"Oh, I didn't know that!" said Aileen Shubert. "That puts a new slant on our dance."

Aileen was leaning against the bannister, and her legs were so long that they started at her boobs.

"And I'm sorry for talking badly about your friend. She's just a little . . . overwhelming," said a girl with empty orange-juice cans in her hair for rollers.

I tried the cans for a while when I was her age, but after one night trying to sleep on those things, I tossed them into the trash, where they belonged.

"Trixie, we are really sorry," said . . . um . . . her name had something to do with a train. *Something Pullman. Oh, Wanda!* "We should have been more considerate, especially since her boyfriend was murdered. She told us about it tonight. She said that calling hours are tomorrow. I'd really like to go."

There was a chorus of *Me too*s.

"Do you know if the police have any clues as to what happened to her boyfriend?" Aileen asked.

"I think they have a couple of leads," I said.

She fluffed her hair, and magically it fell into place and looked even better.

Why couldn't mine fluff like that?

"We want to support Antoinette Chloe," said . . . her name was right on the tip of my tongue.

Donna? Melanie? Bonnie? Oh, I give up. My brain is fried.

"That's nice of you, but please go to bed," I said. "It's almost midnight, and you have a full day of swimming upstream tomorrow, and I need some quiet for a while."

They all got up and walked past me in single file. I was just about to close and lock the kitchen door when Ty scared the snot out of me.

"What on earth do you want?" I snapped.

"Are you cranky, or what?"

"Yeah, I'm cranky. I haven't slept a wink and I'm exhausted. I wish I had someone to call to replace me tonight."

"Still nothing from Bob?" he asked.

Oh, sure. The missing Bob. He was supposed to be cooking the night shift with me, but it didn't matter because I hadn't laid eyes on Bob since I took over the Silver Bullet almost a year ago.

"Juanita said she got a postcard from him from Biloxi, Mississippi."

"Aren't there a lot of casinos there?" Ty grinned.

"I believe so."

"I'll bet Bob is having a great time."

"Ty, what's up?" I asked. "You didn't walk over here to chitchat at this hour."

"Actually, I'm keeping an eye on your house. There are a lot of fishermen here and out-of-towners, and there are quite a few good-looking ladies here."

Good-looking? Without looking down, I ticked off what I was wearing: a pair of oversized navy sweats, my purple T-shirt that said CHEFS DO IT IN THE KITCHEN, and a yellow bathrobe that was really a terry-cloth beach cover-up.

Ty never seemed to catch me at my best, but that was going to change when I got all sequined up for the pageant.

Not that I wanted to impress him. No way.

"Have a seat, Ty." I pointed to a forest green Adirondack chair. I took the one next to it. "I have a bit of time before I have to get dressed and cook."

We sat in silence, looking at the brilliant stars in the sky. They were so close, I could reach out and touch them.

"Anything on your mind?" I asked.

"Just the Brownelli investigation," he said.

"Will you tell me why you had to see Sal first? Why you didn't let ACB tell him about Nick?"

"I wanted to see his reaction."

"I figured that. What else did you find out from your talk with him?"

"Nothing all that exciting. I was just feeling him out."

"Like if he arranged for his brother to be killed from prison?" I asked.

Ty looked like his mouth was going to drop wide-open.

"Fess up. I know that you suspect Sal of ordering a hit on Nick. And I think I know why."

"Why?"

I had his undivided attention now. "Judging by how he's still in love with ACB, I think you believe he might have been extremely mad at Nick for dating Antoinette Chloe. Am I right?"

"You might be."

He wasn't going to give anything up. Sheesh. I know that there are cop rules about not telling civilians anything, but I wanted to help ACB.

"But what I don't know is who would have told him about ACB and Nick being an item."

"You can get visitors in jail, you know. And mail," Ty said.

"Nick would've had to be the one who visited Sal. ACB had never visited Auburn before this morning, with us. Maybe Nick felt guilty about dating Sal's ex-wife, so he confessed all to Sal."

"I wanted to check out Nick's visitors while we were visiting, but their computers were down."

I hoped that Nick didn't tell Sal about the leather thong tooled with her name, or the dirty pictures that ACB had to get out of the house today.

"I'll bet you found out his visitors the second Auburn's computers came online. Was Nick a visitor?" I asked.

More silence from Wyatt Earp.

"C'mon, Ty. Did Nick visit Sal?"

"I'm not being coy, Trixie. You know I can't share any information about an ongoing investigation, but let me just say that you have a couple of interesting theories."

I understood that he couldn't spill certain things from an intellectual perspective, but he definitely could tell *me*. We'd been friends for almost a year and even exchanged a polka or two. And, above all, I wasn't going to tell anyone.

Even though Ty couldn't tell me officially, I'd bet the Silver Bullet that Nick had visited Sal. They were brothers and they were close at one time.

"Cowboy, you think I have interesting theories? Wait until you talk to ACB and find out what she has to tell you about an incident that occurred a couple of months ago."

He leaned over in his chair.

"It's going to knock you right out of those crocodile boots."

"Tell me," Ty said.

"Antoinette Chloe should probably tell you."

"Oh, she will. Where is she?"

"She was up for a while, then she went to bed. She's had a horrible day: Auburn, a strip search and a half, going makeupless, and making arrangements for Nick and composing his obit. By the way, calling hours are tomorrow night."

He nodded. "I can't have her holding back information. I want her to meet me at my office the first thing in the morning."

"I'll tell her, but you'd better define *first thing*. From what I've seen, Antoinette Chloe is not an early riser."

"Eight in the morning."

"Yikes. Up early two days in a row?"

"Okay." He rolled his eyes. "Eight-fifteen and not a second later. I'll make it nine o'clock if you want to give me a sneak preview."

"I'm sure that ACB can fill in the details, but long story short, Nick got into a pretty nasty fight with his former restaurant partner after a motorcycle fund-raising event. They'd split up their partnership earlier after some kind of disagreement. But at the event, Nick gave the guy a broken nose, and in return the guy slashed Nick's beloved Roving Rubbers tattoo with a—*are you sitting?*—switchblade."

"How long ago was the fight?"

"About six months ago."

"No contact between the two since then?"

"Not that ACB knows of." I stood up. "Excuse me, Ty. I have to get ready for work."

"You have to work tonight? Pardon me, but you look like you need some sleep."

"I do, but the pageant girls decided to have a pajama party."

He raised a perfect black eyebrow. "Sorry I missed it."

"Oh, for heaven's sake. You could be their father."

"Nah, maybe an older brother."

I smiled. "I'll give your message to ACB. Nine o'clock?"

"Yes, ma'am."

"It's a great lead, isn't it?"

"Definitely. Do you remember the name of the guy who cut Nick? His partner in the restaurant."

"Chad. Chad Dodson."

"The name sounds familiar. Should I know him?" he asked.

"He's from a big banking family in Massachusetts."

"Massachusetts National Colonial Bank and Trust? They've led the United States in foreclosures for the past few years."

Ty never ceased to amaze me. "I'll take Banking for one thousand dollars, Alex."

"I wonder how Nick met Chad. Nick didn't seem to be the kind of guy who'd run in Chad's circles."

"Maybe ACB can help fill in the blanks."

"I think I'll get a head start." Ty tweaked his hat and went down the stairs two at a time. "See you in the morning for an early breakfast."

I jumped into the shower, a cold shower. Maybe it would help me stay awake. I smiled as I slipped into my tomato-print pants and red chef's coat with my name embroidered on it. Underneath that was CHEF, SILVER BULLET DINER.

I put my wet hair into a ponytail. It'd dry eventually, maybe on the walk over. Then I tried to do something about my puffy eyes with the dark circles underneath. I didn't have time for cold tea bags, so I pulled out all the concealer I could find and blotted it under my eyes.

I was tempted to wake up ACB and ask her for makeup help, but since she was going to have another difficult day with Nick's calling hours at night and her nine o'clock interrogation in Ty's office, I decided to let her sleep.

I got to the diner about fifteen minutes early, so I made myself a cup of coffee behind the counter. I was glad to see that the place was mostly full, and I hoped it'd stay that way. The time would go by faster if it was busy, and I wouldn't be able to think about how I hadn't slept in a day or two.

"How's everything, Nancy?"

"Fine. Judy and I have been hopping all night. The customers just love the goulash and the Spanish rice, but they can't stop talking about Antoinette Chloe stabbing the sausage and calling out Nick's name when she did it."

"That wasn't her best moment," I said. "Are they saying anything else about her?"

"Some are speculating whether she was the reason Nick Brownelli found himself in a ditch. Most people are imitating her. There isn't a sausage that's safe in this diner," Nancy quipped.

I sighed. Small-town gossip can be overwhelming, but there wasn't much I could do to stop it. Besides, I should be concentrating on my diner right now.

"I hope there's enough goulash and Spanish rice to last until the morning. I don't want to run out."

Nothing bothers me more than when customers come in for the daily special and it's gone. However, from a business standpoint, I suppose it's a good thing.

I walked through the double doors and saw that Cindy Sherwood, who usually cooked from four to midnight, was mighty happy to see me.

"Trixie, I gotta fly. I have a date."

"Anyone I know?"

"I don't think so, but I'll bring him by for dinner sometime. I'd love for you to meet him."

"Can't wait, Cindy. I'm sure he's wonderful."

Cindy worked very hard both here at the Silver Bullet and at home watching her brothers and sisters while her single mother worked at the box factory in Oswego. I knew that their family struggled to keep afloat.

"Cindy, before you go, take home some bread and luncheon meat. And I ordered way too much tuna fish. Take some of both."

"No. I couldn't, Trixie."

"Yes, you can. Go freshen up for your date, and I'll get it ready for you."

She wrapped me in a big hug. "I know what you're doing, Trixie," she whispered. "And thanks."

I turned her around and gave her a tiny push toward the ladies' room by the walk-in freezer. "Go. Get ready. And come back here before you hurry out."

I found a cardboard box and loaded it with everything I thought would be good for the kids' lunches and dinners. I decided that they needed breakfast items, too, so I put in cereal, yogurt, and some cans of orange juice.

After I waved Cindy off, one of my third-shift waitresses, Chelsea Young, whom I enjoyed immensely, arrived. Chels was a free spirit, a flower child who should have grown up in the sixties. She was tall and slender with a lot of energy, and her platinum hair was streaked with all the different colors of the rainbow. I hoped some of her energy would rub off on me.

Josephine Pirro, the other graveyard-shift waitress, was a very pretty twentysomething with big black eyes and long lashes. Her hair was thick and black with a little wave in it. She was short and could stand to lose a few pounds—*like me*—and she was a chronic giggler. Everyone loved to make Jo laugh—it didn't take much. The truckers teased her often, but they never stepped over the line. If they did, Jo would point her finger at them and give them a stern warning, all punctuated by giggles.

It was going to be a fun night with Jo and Chelsea, and I needed some fun to put some pep back into my step.

I decided that I'd bake something fun as well. I was going to make some dog biscuits for Blondie. I even had a cookie cutter in the shape of a dog bone.

Very cool!

I got out all the ingredients, but before I could start, Jo came in with a large order, mostly for the daily specials, with a couple of orders from the breakfast menu.

I glanced through the pass-through window to see who was in the diner. Vern McCoy was with Lou Rutledge. They were the other two members of the Sandy Harbor Sheriff's Department. They saw me peeking at them and waved. They were sitting with John Nunnamaker, the commander of the American Legion, and Mr. Farnsworth, the owner of the bait shop next door.

I didn't see Ty—not that I was looking for him. He was probably investigating Chad Dodson. By the time ACB moseyed over to the sheriff's department office on Main Street in the morning, Ty would probably know more about the brawl at the Boston barbecue than Antoinette Chloe did.

I went back to making Blondie's dog biscuits. As I was kneading the dough, I had a scathingly brilliant idea: I'd put six treats each in a bunch of plastic bags, tie them with a pretty ribbon, sell them at the counter, and donate the money to the ASPCA.

Feeling like a woman with a mission, I made a triple batch.

In between orders, banter with Chelsea and Jo, and making the dog biscuits, the time flew. Before I knew it, it was seven o'clock and Juanita Holgado was arriving for her morning shift.

Juanita picked up a bag of biscuits. I didn't have ribbon or a cute basket here in the kitchen, so I'd have to go back to the Big House and get both.

"These are terrific, Trixie." She held up the plastic bag to take a better look.

"Thanks. I'm going to class up the packaging and add ribbon, maybe a label. All proceeds will go to the ASPCA."

"Brilliant, *chica*. My Pancho will love them."

I untied my apron. "I am dead on my feet, Juanita. I'll talk to you later."

"Adios."

My feet were throbbing, but surprisingly I felt really good for being a zombie with no sleep. I had energy spurting up from I don't know where.

When I got back to the Big House, the noise level was breaking the sound barrier. The girls were dressed and getting ready for dance practice, but they were having a grand buffet of cookies, Danishes, donuts and other sweets.

I took Antoinette Chloe aside. "Where are the committee ladies? Aren't they supposed to help you cook breakfast and lunch?"

She looked quite satisfied with herself. "Yes, but I gave them the morning off and had all this delivered from Gas and Grab. Jean Harrington gave me a discount."

"But why didn't you let the committee cook?" I asked.

"I didn't want them to try talking to me about Nick. The obit is in the *Lure* this morning, and my cell phone hasn't stopped ringing."

"Oh," I said, and changed the subject. "I'm guessing you're going to Margie Grace's today."

It wasn't hard to guess. ACB was dressed for a morning on Margie's deck. It was one of those rare occasions when ACB was muumuu-less. She had a sweatband wrapped around her head, and it wasn't just any sweatband. She'd embellished it with sequins and feathers.

She wore bright orange and red sweatpants and a sweatshirt. And, of course, both were embellished with sequins and glitter glue.

Her earrings had a metal pair of white-and-black sneakers hanging from them, but instead of the real thing on her feet, she had on—*you guessed it*—orange flip-flops.

"Antoinette Chloe, your flip-flops are so . . . plain."

"Well, of course, dear. These are the flip-flops I dance in. However, the ones I wear as emcee will just dazzle you."

"I'm sure they will!" And that reminded me that I needed a dress.

When no one was looking, I grabbed her arm and steered her to the front room, well out of the hearing of the girls, who seemed to be enjoying their sugary breakfast.

"Antoinette Chloe, Ty Brisco wants to talk to you at nine a.m. in his office downtown."

"Why so early?"

"It would have been eight o'clock, but I got you an hour's reprieve because I told him a little about the incident in Boston between Chad and Nick. However, he wants to hear it all from you. And beware. He types with two fingers and a thumb, so it'll take forever."

"Oh, dear. I can't be there all day, Trix. I have to get to Margie's for the rehearsal!"

"Then you'd better get going, and talk slowly to the nice deputy about the Boston barbecue brawl while he types. Or you could always type it for him. Actually, you're probably a better typist."

"I feel funny about naming names. I don't want to point the finger at someone based on an old incident."

"It's not that old. Besides, Ty will eliminate

Chad Dodson as a suspect if things don't point in that direction. Don't worry."

"Well, okay, but I'm still worried about another thing."

"Talk to me, friend."

She hesitated, looking at her fake fingernails. They were too long and clawlike for my taste, and the one on the little finger of her left hand was unlike the others. All the rest were a sparkly leopard print, but her pinkie finger was bright pink with white daisies.

She sighed. "After I put these all on, I remembered that one of them was missing, and I had only nine. And I wasn't going to take them all off, so I added one from another box. I like it! Maybe the next time I'll do all ten in a different design."

Her tone was clipped and her voice warbled. I could tell something was up.

"You never answered me, Antoinette Chloe. What else has made you nervous?"

"I think I might have found Suspect Number Two."

Chapter 6

Antoinette Chloe played with her necklace of blue scallop shells and red sea horses, and I waited until she was ready to tell me what was on her mind.

"Toxic Waste, the guy that Sal mentioned when we were visiting, called me earlier this morning. He said that he'd heard about Nick's passing from Mad Dog Morgan, his second in command. Anyway, Toxic said that he would like to speak at Nick's wake or at the cemetery and wanted my permission to do so."

"So far, so good," I said, waiting for the rest of the story.

"I asked him if he was going to speak on behalf of the Rubbers, and he said yes, but that he also had a lot of personal things to say about Nick to send him off on his final ride."

"Like what?"

"Like how Nick welched on a deal. Apparently he was supposed to sell Toxic a vintage Panhead Harley, but Nick sold it to someone else. And then there was even more bad blood when Nick tried to start a coup to overthrow Toxic as leader of the

Rubbers because Toxic had lost his three-star Michelin rating. It was knocked down to two stars. When the Michelin evaluator was at the restaurant, Nick brought him curled-up slices of pizza instead of the sauerbraten that he ordered. According to Nick, it was just a joke. He swore he thought the guy was a friend of Toxic Waste's."

I must have looked confused, because she explained.

"The highest rating that Michelin awards is three stars. And only chefs with three-star ratings can be the leader, according to the Roving Rubbers operating manual."

"That doesn't sound so awful to me. It's certainly not worth killing over, and I definitely hope he doesn't bring this up during a eulogy that's supposed to be nice," I said.

ACB took a breath. There was more. "The third strike against Nick was when Toxic's longtime girlfriend, Leslie, left him for Nick. Toxic Waste was a basket case—a total wastebasket!"

She chuckled, pretty proud of that joke.

She continued. "Nick didn't ask Leslie to leave Toxic, but when she did, the two of them struck up a romance, and it got pretty serious—I mean, Nick asked her to marry him. The plans were made, the announcement was in the paper—the whole enchilada."

"This is a biggie," I said. "I can totally understand Toxic being mad, and then some. What happened?"

"Nick left Leslie at the altar."

"Well, I can see her being furious and hurt and

embarrassed," I said, shaking my head. "And that was pretty cowardly of Nick."

ACB was quick to defend him. "Nick said he felt trapped. Once he'd asked her to marry him, the relationship stopped being fun, and she became overbearing and obnoxious. He tried to call it off a couple of times, but Leslie would always guilt him into staying. She kept telling him that he was just getting cold feet and he'd get over it."

"And then?"

"This was about the same time as his motorcycle ride through the dining room and kitchen of his restaurant. Between all the drama with his partner, Chad, and his fiancée, he split, moved to Sandy Harbor, and started cooking at the restaurant with Sal. Then when Sal got into trouble, Nick saw me through it all, and we started dating. You know the rest."

"Getting left at the altar is a horrible thing. I'd be furious," I said.

ACB sighed. "I guess I'd better tell Ty about everything, starting with Chad Dodson. I might be a while."

"Oh, I don't know. Ty can type at least eight words a minute," I said jokingly, but then turned serious. I wanted to ask my friend a very personal question—a question that was burning a hole in my brain. "Antoinette Chloe, was Nick that great of a catch?"

"He was a dream, Trixie. A real good bad boy. Know what I mean?"

"Uh . . . no."

"He was tall, dark, and handsome. He kind of

looked like Elvis. He looked hot in black. And those lips and tongue of his . . . well . . . you know."

Well, actually I didn't know. It had been a long time, and Deputy Doug . . . nah, I wasn't going to go there.

"*And* the man loved to cook—breakfast in bed, lunch in bed, dinner in bed." She sighed, remembering, and then tears welled in her eyes. "He was something real special, Trixie."

I put my arm around her and led her to the door.

"It's eight forty-five. You'd better get to Ty's office before he comes to fetch you in his sheriff's car."

She sighed. "Do I look okay?"

"You look fine. Is that a new muumuu?"

"I ordered it from Hawaii—Muumuus 'R' Us. I love hibiscus."

"It looks great," I said. "Go. See you later."

She turned to wave good-bye, and just as I went to walk into the kitchen, a movement caught my eye. Was someone listening to our conversation? I mostly just caught a shadow. Then Blondie came bounding into the room. It must have been her coming down the stairs.

Blondie needed some attention, so we snuggled together on the couch as I thought about all the people who had a grudge against Nick Brownelli.

First, there was Sal Brownelli. With nothing to do in Auburn Correctional Facility except get tattooed, he might have become obsessed enough about ACB and his brother's relationship that he could have arranged for a hit on Nick. Sal still loved ACB dearly, and he had nothing to lose. It wasn't as if he was going to ever get out of jail in his lifetime, so what would another life sentence tacked onto the one he was already serving be to him?

Second, there was Chad Dodson, millionaire from a rich family and former partner of Nick's in a five-star restaurant that bore Nick's name. Something had happened to their partnership and friendship, and they disliked each other enough to draw blood at a barbecue.

Third, we had Toxic Waste, the leader of the Roving Rubbers. Nick had reneged on a Panhead deal, he tried to unseat Toxic, and Toxic's girlfriend, Leslie, ran to Nick Brownelli—he of the full lips and bedroom meal delivery.

As I sat there petting Blondie's soft fur, I wondered if there were any other people that Nick had ticked off. If so, Nick's calling hours this evening might prove to be an interesting experience if someone decided to bring out some hard feelings.

But I didn't want ACB upset by any derogatory remarks about Nick. She had enough to deal with. And besides, she had loved him and probably still did.

ACB loved Nick. Nick had loved ACB. Sal loved ACB. ACB still had some retro feelings for Sal. ACB still loved Nick. What a mess!

That was enough of that! I got up from the couch and let Blondie spread out. She could be such a lazy pup sometimes. Stopping in the kitchen, I greeted the pageant contestants.

"Hi, ladies! Is everything okay? Do you need anything?" I asked, turning to a contestant who had her hand raised. I stifled a smile. "Hello. You don't have to raise your hand to speak to me."

"Uh . . . Miz Matkowski, we didn't know you were a judge at the pageant until Antoinette Chloe told us." The speaker was a beautiful olive-skinned woman with almond-shaped eyes and long, shiny black hair.

"Call me Trixie. And you are?"

"Cher. Cher LaMontagne. I'm from Poughkeepsie."

"That's a long way from here. How did you hear about Miss Salmon?"

"My father's a fisherman. He was up here not too long ago, and brought a copy of the *Lure* back with him. I saw an article about the pageant in there, so I decided to try it."

"Well, Cher, I am a judge, but don't hold that against me. Though now that I think about it, I do have an unfair advantage over the other judges, since I get to know all of you ahead of time. I should probably talk to the committee members about it and sequester myself as much as possible."

"No, don't do that, Trixie!" said Aileen Shubert. "We love your company. And we are so sorry we talked about Antoinette Chloe behind her back. We feel absolutely awful. She really is a lovely person."

"Yes. Yes, she is."

"And we are all carpooling tonight to go to her boyfriend's wake," added a redhead with streaks of gold in her hair. She wore a black athletic bra and black spandex capris with a fuchsia stripe down the sides.

A person who looked that fabulous in exercise clothes didn't have to exercise. That's my theory and I'm sticking to it.

"I hate to interrupt your sugar high, but shouldn't you all be getting to Margie's?" I asked.

There were groans all around and a couple of *lame*s. Then someone whispered "Judge," and their tone completely changed.

They had started to rush out of the kitchen when I called them back.

"Hey, ladies! Please put your dishes in the dishwasher! And put what's left of the pastries away. The empty boxes go into the recycling bin. And wipe off the table."

There was a litany of "Sorry, Trixie," and I left them to clean up. Going upstairs with my sweetie of a dog following me, I thought of my big, comfy brass bed with each step.

I was just about to collapse onto it when I remembered that I needed an evening gown. I made a U-turn toward the attic stairs and Aunt Stella's cedar-lined closet. She'd told me to help myself to whatever I wanted and to donate the rest, but I hadn't had a chance yet.

Aunt Stella and I weren't really close to being the same size. For one, she was about a foot shorter than I. She had bigger boobs than I, and I have hips with their own zip code. But I figured it couldn't hurt to try—you never know!

Walking past the bedrooms, I couldn't resist looking wherever the doors were open. Most of the rooms were cluttered but clean. Most of the beds were made. I had to smile as I walked by

ACB's room. It was a complete disaster. I wondered how she could ever find anything in that mishmash. It crossed my mind that maybe someone had been in ACB's stuff, but ACB would probably be the only one who could tell. And even she would have trouble. I shook my head as I climbed the narrow stairs to the attic.

The closet with Aunt Stella's clothes was just to the left of the entryway. It was a huge thing, and I remembered playing with dolls in it with my sister, Susie, when we were kids.

I opened the doors and caught the scent of cedar—the same scent I remembered from all those years ago.

I slid the hangers one at a time to take a good look. There were a couple of classic gowns—the kind that never go out of style. Of them, there was one that I really liked. It had a glittery copperish bodice and the rest was a creamy crepe. It'd never be long enough, but maybe I could pass it off as tea length.

Closing the closet, I took the gown back to my room and hung it on a hanger on the back of the bathroom door to let it air out.

I'd try it on later, but first I needed to sleep for a good twenty-four hours.

I don't know how long I slept, but the sound of a phone ringing annoyed me like the buzzing of a grass trimmer.

Would someone please answer that?

Then I realized that the buzzing was my cell phone and it wasn't going to stop.

I slid the green arrow thing. "Huh?"

"Trixie! Thank goodness!"

"What's wrong, Antoinette Chloe?" She must have had me on speed dial.

"Chad Dodson is in town! He's riding around in that classic red Thunderbird of his. I saw him pull up to the Crossroads and go in."

"Hmm . . . he's probably in town for Nick's calling hours. Maybe we could talk to him tonight and find out what the bad blood was between him and Nick."

"Should I tell Ty that I saw him?"

"You should. Yes."

"But, Trixie, I'm just so tired. It was a long day with Ty, and although he's positively a piece of eye candy and I just adore the way he speaks— you know, like a Houston cowboy—I am simply tired of thinking. I think I'll just point Chad out to Ty tonight."

"That'll probably be okay." I yawned. "Antoinette Chloe, what time is it?"

"Five o'clock."

"No way!" Where had the time gone? I had a million things to do. Plus I had to get ready for the calling hours. "I'll see you in a bit. Are you coming back here?"

"Yes. I have to get ready for tonight."

"Just what I was thinking. See you in a while."

I jumped in the shower. Every now and then, I scored on the perfect water temperature. Today was that day, and I didn't want to get out. Finally I forced myself to turn off the water, and I blow-dried my hair with lots of product in it so I could have some version of a hairdo for a while, until it drooped.

I slipped on my only black dress, bought purposely for wakes and funerals. Then I went down to the kitchen to get something to eat and to let Blondie out.

After emptying the dishwasher, I put everything away, made a tuna-fish sandwich on rye, poured myself an iced tea, and went out to the porch.

The fishermen were gathered around the cleaning stations and filleting their catches. Large white coolers were scattered around the lawn, and the gulls were squawking overhead.

It looked like they had had a successful catch.

A group of men were eating at the picnic table next to Cottage Two. A family was playing badminton. Cottage Nine's residents were grilling something and it smelled divine, like burgers or steak. A couple was going out in a canoe.

I loved the fact that my cottages were full and that people were enjoying themselves.

Looking to the right, I saw Ty walking my way. He looked like he had on a pair of black khakis and a black blazer. As he got closer, I noticed that his hat was black, his shirt was white, his alligator boots were polished, and he didn't wear a tie.

He looked marvelous, actually, not that I was looking or anything.

"Howdy, Trixie." He tipped his black cowboy hat. "You're looking mighty fine."

"Thanks." His compliment made me feel warm and fuzzy inside, and it'd been a long time since I'd felt warm and fuzzy. "Have a seat, Ty."

He sat down in his usual chair. "I thought I'd find you sitting here, enjoying the nice day."

"It's a beautiful one for fall, isn't it? It's really warm. Would you like a tuna-fish sandwich or something to drink?"

"I'm good. I had an open steak at the Silver Bullet. Dee-licious."

"Was it crowded?"

"Packed."

"Good.

Ty ate most of his meals there. I really should give him a meal plan or a flat fee for the month.

"Ty, why don't you figure out how much you spend per month on meals at the Silver Bullet? Then I'll work out a flat fee for you."

"That's not necessary."

"Just do it," I said.

"Yes, ma'am."

"How did your day go with ACB?"

He groaned. "I think ACB has ADD. Attention deficit disorder. It's very hard to get her to focus."

"She has a lot on her mind, Ty, and she was probably nervous."

"She spews whatever's on her mind—that's for sure—and it's hard to corral her when she's loose like that."

I laughed. "I think she's upstairs, getting ready."

"She's right here. Sorry I'm late. I was looking for my motorcycle earring and I couldn't find it," Antoinette Chloe said. "And I do have a slight case of . . . oh, look, a bunny!" She pointed at the lawn and laughed. Nothing was there.

Ty got a kick out of that and he laughed loudly,

but his laughter was drowned out by the roar of engines. Motorcycle engines. A lot of them.

We went to the side porch to look. A procession of motorcycles, two by two, roared down Route 3 and turned into the parking lot of the diner. There had to be thirty of them.

The noise was deafening, and I couldn't hear myself think. The two at the head of the line took off their helmets and looked up at us on the porch.

"That's Toxic Waste, Trixie," Antoinette Chloe whispered in my ear. "The other guy is Mad Dog Morgan."

Toxic Waste shouted over the noise of the engines. "Antoinette Chloe, we're all sad to hear that Nick took his final ride."

"Thanks, Mr. Waste."

"Please accept our final tribute to him. We'll go into your parking lot so we don't tear up the lawn."

"I'd appreciate that," I said, thinking that Toxic Waste looked a little like Billy Joel in his younger days.

Because Toxic was considerate of my lawn, I was prone to like him. But my internal juror was still pondering whether he was a murderer.

They revved up their engines and headed for the parking lot, where they did a series of maneuvers that would have earned them a spot at some type of marching-band competition.

From corners they zigzagged, did a promenade from a circle, and zoomed in and out of from between one other. When they were done, we clapped, and Toxic and Mad Dog returned to where we were standing.

"That was amazing!" ACB said, clapping.

"Thank you. We practiced a long time so we wouldn't crash into one other." He grinned. "Antoinette Chloe, we'd love to provide you with an escort to Manning's Happy Repose."

Any suspicions she had about him were soon forgotten as ACB just about vaulted over the railing. "I'd need my sidecar, though."

ACB's mode of travel was to attach her sidecar to the side of Nick's motorcycle like a barnacle.

"Um . . . no sidecar. You'll be in your automobile, and the Rubbers will escort you to Manning's."

"Sweet!" ACB said.

"Can you give us five minutes, guys? I have to get a couple of things," I said.

"Of course," said Mad Dog. He reminded me of James Earl Jones, only taller and bigger.

I turned to Ty. "You're coming with us, too. Right?"

"I wouldn't miss being escorted by the Rubbers," he said. "Go ahead and get ready to go, Trixie. I'll tell these gentlemen the appropriate route to take. We wouldn't want the homes of Sandy Harbor vibrating right off their foundations, would we?"

Toxic laughed. As I walked away, I heard Ty introduce himself as one of three deputies in Sandy Harbor.

I was hoping that Ty wouldn't start interrogating Toxic right then and there. However, there would be only a brief period of time when Toxic and now Chad Dodson would be in town.

That's probably what Ty was thinking.

Grabbing my pocketbook, I yelled up the stairs to ACB. "Are you almost ready?"

"Almost! I decided to change my muumuu."

ACB came down the stairs wearing a black muumuu with white outlines of flowers—gardenias, maybe. A black fascinator was positioned on the right side of her head. There was a small blackbird, which looked more like a vulture than anything else, in a feathery nest on the hat. As for jewelry, she wore a gold chain with black balls on it and a set of matching earrings and a matching cocktail ring. Black flip-flops rounded out the outfit, which was definitely subdued for her.

We got into Ty's black SUV. I insisted on sitting in the back, so ACB could enjoy the Rubbers' escort in the front.

"Did you notice they are riding with a position vacant?" she asked. "That's for Nick."

"That's really nice," I said. Even though Nick had stolen Mr. Waste's girlfriend, he came to pay his respects. Maybe he wasn't going to say anything negative at the services like he insinuated to ACB. I really hoped not.

Just in case, I should take him aside and suggest he shouldn't say anything stupid, or I'd rope his motorcycle to the cleats of the first boat out of the marina.

I was looking forward to meeting Chad Dodson, and wondered if Joan Paris found anything through her sources. I'd look for Joan at the funeral home and get an update.

We pulled into Hal Manning's parking lot and parked by the front door. The Roving Rubbers parked on the side of the road. Smart. They filed up the steps of the funeral home one at a time, across from one another, helmets in their hands like a military honor guard. They waited there until we all passed between them.

Nice.

Ty offered an arm to both ACB and me. We both took them, and he escorted us inside.

The funeral home smelled sweet with the scent of flowers. We were the first ones there, which was our plan. When ACB saw Nick lying in the front of the Crystal Room, she burst into tears.

Ty held her up, and Hal Manning and Joan Paris arrived at her side, armed with bottled water and tissues.

After an appropriate amount of time, I motioned to Joan with my eyes and a slight movement of my head for her to follow me to a corner of the room.

"Did you find out anything about Chad Dodson?" I asked.

"I printed out a boatload of stuff. It was easy. He's all over the news, but mostly he appears in the society pages of the Massachusetts papers and the *New York Times*. I'll give you all my material before you leave. In summation, I just want to say that Chad is one hot guy—oh, and he's a philanthropist. He likes to spread his parents' money around."

She pulled out an envelope from her purse, and I slipped it into mine. "Does Chad have a real job?" I asked. "Like at one of his family's banks?"

"Not my definition of a job," Joan said. "He invests in different ventures—like Chef Nick's. One of his restaurant investments went into a chain and sold nationally. It did well until the owners sued him for fraud. They settled out of court for an undisclosed sum, and Chad was forced to relinquish his investment in the restaurant. It looks like he was trying to get back in the game again by partnering up with Nick. Though the two of them must have clashed over something, and Nick walked away from their venture. And I'm sure that Chad couldn't afford another lawsuit, so he had to let the restaurant flop. Rumor has it that he lost a lot of money because Nick backed out."

"So, Chad's not in the family business?"

"Not anymore—rumors are still rampant that they kicked him out of day-to-day operations or anything important—but it appears that they consider him their public-relations guy. He keeps their name in the paper and he does charity work, but only for the big charities. You won't see him dishing out meals at his local soup kitchen, even though I doubt there is a need for one on Beacon Hill. Instead you'll see him at some black-tie event for Soup Kitchens Around the World and Beyond for five thousand dollars a plate."

I chuckled. "I know the type."

Joan nodded. "Chad has some other investments, but they're not exactly bringing in big returns, especially in this market."

"So if he invested in Nick Brownelli and Nick quit on him, could he afford to lose the investment?" I asked.

"It doesn't seem like he could. Nick's place was on prime real estate in downtown Boston. I don't know if Nick had any money to invest in the place or not, or if it all was funded by Chad and Nick was recruited as the master chef. You know, he lent his name to it."

"Nick was that great of a chef?"

Joan shrugged. "From what I found, he sure was!"

And I thought that Nick was simply a short-order cook at Brown's Four Corners. I remembered him as unshaven, with a filthy apron and a greasy baseball hat.

Don't judge a meal by its picture on the menu, Uncle Porky always used to say. I should remember that.

"Joan, I'd better see if Antoinette Chloe needs any support."

"Go ahead. I'm going to say good-bye to her, head back to the *Lure*."

I glanced over at ACB, and she looked like she was doing fine. She was smiling and shaking hands with everyone in line. Then I watched as her smile melted from her face.

Chad Dodson.

He shook her hand and gave her a hug. Joan Paris was right: He was hot if you liked the rich surfer-guy look. He had sun-bleached hair—more likely salon bleached. He had a perfect tan. It was so perfect I thought it had to have been sprayed on. And his teeth were dazzling white. If his investments sank, he could always try out for a toothpaste commercial. He was tall and slender, dressed in tan pants and a turquoise golf shirt. Chad must be going golfing after Nick's wake.

I should heed Uncle Porky's saying about the not judging a meal by its picture and give Chad a chance, but I didn't have any patience for smarmy, spoiled, rich kids with shady tendencies.

I listened in. He was totally charming the pants off Antoinette Chloe, telling her how lovely she looked and how Nick just adored her. He said all the right things. Then he lowered the boom.

"Miz Brown, I'd like to talk to you about Nick's estate. I realize that now is not the time, but I'll be in town for a day or two."

"Where are you staying?"

"In my motor home. This town is crowded, and I haven't found a place to park it yet, but—"

Antoinette Chloe looked at me.

"What?" I asked, hoping that she wasn't going to ask me what I thought she was.

"Trixie, why doesn't Chad park in the back of your lot? There's room over there, by the woods."

"Oh, I couldn't impose—"

"Yes, you can!" ACB said, nudging me with her shoulder.

What on earth was I supposed to say?

"Of course you can park your motor home in the back of my parking lot. It's to the left side of the Silver Bullet Diner, off Route 3. You can't miss it."

"I'm also towing my car."

The red Thunderbird.

"There's room for your car, too."

He put his hand in my right hand, and . . . oh, no! He was going to kiss it.

I winced as his lips touched the back of my hand, and I forced myself to smile and stay put when I wanted to run to the ladies' room and scrub my hand.

Who does that anymore? Maybe scores of other women would swoon over that, but Trixie Matkowski wasn't one of them.

Feeling someone watching me, I looked up. Ty Brisco. He had a grin the size of Texas. He knew just what I was thinking about Chad Dodson: *This is one smarmy man.*

Chad left for parts unknown, and Ty walked over to me.

"Interesting guy," he said. "What do you think?"

"He makes my skin crawl, and I don't know why. At least not yet anyway."

Ty raised his chin in the direction of the front door. "Well, you think that was interesting, wait until you see what's going to happen next."

Chapter 7

As if by command, four armed officers—complete with ugly-looking rifles—escorted a shackled Sal Brownelli into Hal Manning's Happy Repose Funeral Parlor.

ACB fluttered over to him like a butterfly. But the armed guards sprang to attention, not letting her come closer than three feet from Sal.

I watched as Chad Dodson and Sal exchanged a slight nod. It crossed my mind that Sal and Chad had to have met before. Maybe they knew each other well.

"Hello again, sweetie," Sal said, turning his attention back to Antoinette Chloe. "You look great."

"I didn't know you were coming."

"Last-minute decision by the correctional officials. Sorry about my clothes."

"Orange is the new black," ACB joked. After an awkward silence, she added, "Come over and say good-bye to Nick."

Sal's shoulders slumped as he looked at the casket. "Nicky . . . Nicky . . . my brother. My only brother."

Even the guards looked sad.

"Who did this to you, Nicky?" Sal cried, then shouted louder, "Sheriff Brisco! Where are you?"

Ty walked over to them. "I'm right here, Sal."

"You find out who did this to Nicky. Ya hear?"

"I'm doing my best."

Sal nodded. "Thank you." One of the guards pointed to the door. "Looks like I gotta go now. Bye, Antoinette Chloe, my love. I forgive you for taking up with my brother."

ACB put her hands on her hips. "Salvatore Brownelli, you have absolutely no say in who I go out with. We are divorced. And, dammit, you tried to kill me."

"A slight mistake on my part."

Antoinette Chloe's lips moved, but nothing came out. She turned and flip-flopped over to me. "Ugh! The nerve of some men."

"Yes, I know." Then I decided to change the subject. "Antoinette Chloe, why don't you invite everyone over to the Silver Bullet for some refreshments and sandwiches when this over? I'll give Juanita a call and tell her to get a few platters ready."

"Oh, thank you, Trixie! I closed my restaurant today. I should have had everyone over there, but I just didn't think!"

"Don't worry. Juanita will do a great job. A little buffet will do."

She gave me a kiss on the cheek. Then I noticed that the Miss Salmon contestants had started filing in.

Chad Dodson's eyes sparkled with interest. His

teeth glowed like a beacon. And instead of looking at Nick, I noticed that they all gravitated toward Chad Dodson, with the exception of Aileen Shubert. She greeted ACB but ignored both Nick and Chad and went to sit in a dark corner.

The Roving Rubbers were next in line to pay their respects. Hal Manning held open the door as they walked in. Most of the gang wore black leather chaps, black leather vests, black or blue jeans, and lots of chains and spikes.

Toxic Waste pulled out something white from his vest pocket, and I held my breath, hoping he wouldn't make a scene. But instead he said, "Nick, you were a five-star chef and a five-star biker. Even though your Rubber days are over, you always will hold a place in our hearts. And even though you stole my woman and did her wrong, the best man won in the end."

What did he mean by *the best man won*? Won what? And who was he referring to as the best man—himself or Nick? *Hmmm.* Maybe how Toxic Waste won this contest was the more appropriate question for me to ask myself. Did Toxic murder Nick to win and be the "best man"?

He unfurled the white cloth—a chef's hat—and placed it next to Nick.

Mad Dog stepped forward next, and I noticed that he had a black item in his hands. "Nick, we called you Saint Nicholas for a reason. You were a saint. I hope that whoever did this to you rots in hell."

He shook out the black object and showed the

crowd. It was a T-shirt with SAINT NICHOLAS on the top and the Roving Rubbers logo in the middle. Underneath the logo it said, LAST RIDE.

Mad Dog put the shirt next to the chef's hat.

Finally, nine o'clock rolled around, and Hal Manning stepped forward and announced that there was going to be a brief prayer service. The place cleared out quickly. In the end, only ACB, Ty, and I were left.

By the time we got to the Silver Bullet, the place was packed to the rafters. Four waitresses were working and pouring coffee, tea, and soft drinks for everyone. Juanita and Cindy were busy in the kitchen, making sandwiches and salads.

The trays had come out lovely, even though they'd had very little time to prepare. They'd made wraps of cold cuts and chicken salad on Italian rolls. Small sub sandwiches were on another tray with a mound of potato chips in the middle. A big pan of chef's salad was sitting on the butcher-block table, along with three varieties of dressing.

"It's all ready to go, Trixie," Juanita said. "But I'm sure we'll have to make more right away. This is quite a crowd."

I tied on an apron and started helping with the sandwiches. Pretty soon we ran out of chicken salad, so I made tuna. "Let's bring out the first round and keep making more. By the time the first wave of people goes through the buffet, we'll have more sandwiches ready."

"Great idea," Cindy said. "And luckily, I made brownies and a white sheet cake today. We can put those out later."

"Perfect," I said, grateful for my wonderful staff. In between getting the buffet ready, Cindy filled orders for customers who wanted meals off the menu.

ACB knocked on the door. "Thanks for everything, ladies. I truly appreciate it. And Nick would have, too."

My chefs all hugged her.

"I'll be at the cemetery tomorrow," Juanita said.

The others chimed in.

"Thank you so much." ACB looked like she was on the brink of tears. She turned abruptly and went back into the diner.

Juanita took me aside. "I asked Linda Blessler if she'd cook tomorrow. She said that she'd be happy to cover. I hope you don't mind."

"Mind? Not at all! Thank you for thinking of Linda. She's a wonderful cook and a terrific person. I should have thought of her myself."

"Trixie, Toxic Waste and Mad Dog want to talk to you," said Nancy, one of my waitresses, bringing in an empty tray. "And we need more sandwiches."

"Okay on both counts." I carried out a platter of subs and set it on the buffet table. I found both Mr. Waste and Mr. Dog at the counter.

"Hi, gentlemen. What can I do for you?" I asked.

"We were hoping you could help us out. We don't have anywhere to stay. The Wishing Well Campgrounds won't let us stay, even though we had reservations. Seems like the owner doesn't like motorcycle gangs. Mad Dog called him on that, and they argued. After that, I called every other campground in the area, and nothing is available."

Oh no! Not the Rubbers, too!

"Guys, I don't have anything but land. I don't have shower facilities for all thirtyish of you. And I don't have ... uh ... sanitary facilities."

"No problem, Miz Matkowski," said Toxic. "I have a pal in the portable-crapper business. And he has showers, too. I took the liberty and called him. He's dropping off six of each tonight."

"Oh."

"And we're all thinking of staying a couple of days. Antoinette Chloe said that she has Nick's stuff that she's going to sell. His bike and car, too. She's waiting for the sheriff's department to release his house, I believe she said."

"Well, I guess it's all settled, then," I said, resigned. "You can camp on the land on the other side of the Big House. That's my Victorian. It'd be to the right of Chad Dodson's big rig in the parking lot."

"Thanks so much, Miz Matkowski," said Toxic.

"Call me Trixie."

"And the Roving Rubbers would love to get a couple of recipes from you—your chicken salad is the best I've ever had. You know we're all chefs, right?" said Dog.

"I do know you'll all chefs, and I'm flattered that you want some of my recipes, but I don't cook anything fancy. I am strictly in the diner-food business. I make simple comfort-food meals—the kind Mom and Grandma used to make—and a lot of it," I said.

"Works for me!" said Toxic.

"Well, then, I'd be glad to give you any recipes that you'd like."

They both shook my hand and headed back to the buffet.

Well, how do you like that? Wasn't it just convenient that the two suspects I had in mind for Nick's murder, Chad Dodson and Toxic Waste, were going to be camping right on my property?

As soon as I could, I was going to have a chat with them both. I know Ty had warned me not to get involved, but he didn't understand. Antoinette Chloe is my friend, and she'd asked me to help her figure out what happened to her beloved Nick.

And that was just what I was going to do.

The group at the cemetery the next day was quite an eclectic bunch—a collection of Rubbers, Miss Salmon candidates, Chad the bon vivant, and friends of ACB and Sal Brownelli. Thankfully, they were all respectful and no one spoke ill of Nick.

Pastor Trish O'Brien of the Sandy Harbor Community Church said a nice, solemn prayer that guaranteed Nick would motor right into the gates of heaven.

I just hoped that said gates would be open for him.

As soon as the service was over, Antoinette Chloe stepped forward. "I'd like to invite you all to my restaurant, Brown's Four Corners, for breakfast. It's in the middle of town at the intersection of Main and Flower streets. You can't miss it."

Chad Dodson looked exceedingly respectful, but as soon as we were walking to our cars, he asked if ACB could find the time to talk to him about Nick's estate.

She told him that she'd chat with him over breakfast.

Ty drove us both to Antoinette Chloe's restaurant. The parking lot was full of motorcycles. The Miss Salmon contestants weren't present, due to their practice at Margie Grace's all day today. This was going to be their last practice on Margie's back deck, because Margie had to babysit her granddaughter for the next couple of days in Alexandria Bay.

The next time they practiced their routine, it would probably be in my yard. *Good grief.*

While ACB went into her kitchen to check on things, Ty and I sat at a table for four.

"Ty, you've been awfully quiet. Is everything okay?"

"Just thinking," he said.

"About what? Can I help?"

"No. You can't help. Not yet anyway," he said, moving to the side as a waitress filled his coffee cup.

Antoinette Chloe joined us and held up her cup to be filled. "Thanks, Debby."

Chad Dodson appeared at her side. "Do you have a moment, Miz Brownelli?"

"Sure. Have a seat."

He nodded to Ty and me. "What I have to discuss is private."

She waved him away. "These are my friends, Chad. You can talk freely in front of them."

"I don't think—"

"Chad, have a seat and tell me what's on your mind."

"Nick owed me almost a million dollars."

Antoinette Chloe jerked her head so fast that the fake blackbird in her fascinator almost dove into her coffee. It missed, hitting the table instead and lying there, stunned.

"It's not possible to get that kind of money from Nick's . . . estate. First of all, there isn't one. I have to sell the contents of his house and then the house itself before there's any estate."

"What about his life insurance policy?" Chad asked.

"Life insurance?" ACB's eyes grew wide. "Honestly, I never thought of that. I haven't gone through Nick's papers yet, since Ty hasn't released Nick's house."

Ty nodded. "Do you know something about Nick's life insurance policy, Mr. Dodson?"

"Oh no. Undoubtedly not!" Chad said as he raked his hand through his hair. Those rows stood up like spikes in an otherwise perfectly feathered hairdo. "How long will it be before you release his property, Deputy?"

"I don't know yet. We're still investigating, but do you have any proof that Nick owed you that money?" Ty asked. He had on his cop poker face. It was impossible to read him, but I just knew something was going on. He was asking leading questions.

"I have our contract, and proof of the fact that he wrecked everything before he drove away, never to return."

"Where've you been for the past several months, Mr. Dodson?" Ty asked.

"Deputy, why do I have a feeling that I should be calling my lawyer?" Chad asked, raking another row of his hair. "I'll answer this one last question: I've been following Nick's whereabouts very closely. My lawyers have filed all the paperwork possible, but, as they told me, I couldn't get blood out of a stone. But now I can. Oh, and I'm sure you know that Nick's house wasn't even in his name."

"Whose name is it in?" I asked.

He raised his chin toward ACB. "Antoinette Chloe Brown."

When she heard her name, she was obviously startled. "Nicky put it in my name? My name? Are you sure?"

"He did, and I'm sure. I had my lawyers check. You know, you can find anything about anyone if you have the resources." Chad tried not to show it, but I could see his lip curling a bit in a self-satisfied smirk.

"Then it's not Nick's. You can't lien it," Ty said.

"I know. I was counting on his life insurance policy," Chad said.

I didn't really know anything about the way insurance works, but it didn't seem like a life-insurance policy could be touched by anyone other than the designated person or persons. And I was banking on the fact that Nick had probably named ACB as his only beneficiary. And that Chad knew it.

Chad flashed a major smile at ACB. "I was hoping that fairness would rule. That Antoinette Chloe, being an honest person and a lovely woman, would give me the funds due me, or some form of recompense, at the very least."

Ty raised an eyebrow. "Pay her former brother-in-law's debts out of the goodness of her heart?"

"I know it sounds like I'm naïve, but I have faith in my fellow man, or, in this case, a delightfully charming woman."

Smarmy. The man was smarmy.

Antoinette Chloe was ever the lady. "Chad, I'll see what I can do. And I'll consult my lawyer. How's that?"

He picked up her hand and kissed it. I winced. But ACB didn't look like she minded at all.

Chad stood. "You'll find me in my motor home in the Silver Bullet's parking lot for a couple of days yet."

"Matter of fact, Mr. Dodson, I'd advise you not to leave town until you hear further from me," Ty said, putting his forearms on the table.

"You can't be serious!"

"I'm very serious," Ty said.

Chad's face flushed. "Do you think I killed Nick?"

"You're a person of interest, and I'd like to talk to you in my office this afternoon. Shall we say two o'clock?"

"I have nothing to hide, Deputy."

"Excellent. See you at two, then."

Chad turned and hurried out of the restaurant as if his expensive chinos were on fire.

I didn't realize that I was holding my breath. This was too much drama on only one cup of coffee.

"Ty, do you really think that he killed Nick?" ACB asked, her eyes wider than the flowers on her muumuu.

"Like I said, he's a person of interest. I also want to talk to Toxic Waste. Call him over, will you, Antoinette Chloe?"

"What do I say to him?"

"Just thank him for coming. I'll do the rest," Ty said. "And, Trixie, you don't have to talk."

Humpf!

"Oh, William! Billy Gerard!" ACB waved him over. "Over here, William!"

Mr. Waste hurried to our table after Antoinette Chloe wouldn't stop calling his name.

"It was a nice service," Toxic Waste said. "Very nice."

"Thank you," ACB smiled. "And your gifts to him—the shirt and the chef's hat—were very thoughtful. I want to thank you and the rest of the Rubbers for coming."

"How long will you and the Rubbers be camping, Toxic?" I just couldn't call him William . . . or even Billy. He was definitely a Toxic Waste.

"I think we'll stay for a couple of days. We're actually all thinking about attending the Miss Salmon Contest."

"I want to advise you not to leave town without a green light from me," Ty said.

"What the hell? You got to be kidding," Toxic said. "The Rubbers have a lot of things to do."

"I don't kid about murder, and I'm not talking about the Rubbers, just you."

Icicles dripped from each of Ty's words.

"How long?" Toxic asked.

"As long as it takes. I'll let you know."

"Is this because my fiancée left me for Nick?" he asked. "Or because of the screaming matches that I had with him? He started it!"

I felt like I was at recess on the grammar-school playground, and Toxic was whining to Sister Mary Mary.

"We'll talk in my office. Four o'clock," Ty said flatly.

Toxic Waste looked like he had swallowed some toxic waste. He was turning purple. "Is that all?"

"We'll talk at four," Ty said.

Toxic Waste left the restaurant as if his black jeans were on fire.

ACB chuckled. "You're really clearing out my breakfast guests, aren't you, Ty? Oh, well. More for me."

The buffet was ready, so ACB led us there first. Other tables followed.

It was a nice buffet with scrambled eggs, eggs Benedict, a beautifully arranged meat-and-cheese tray, a basket full of warm rolls, home fries, sausage, bacon, ham, relishes, and an extensive array of pastries. There were baked beans, macaroni and potato salads, chef's salad, and other items too numerous to mention.

"My new cook is fabulous," she said. "I hope he doesn't quit."

"He's not a local guy, is he, Antoinette Chloe?" I asked.

"He just graduated from Paul Smith's at Lake Placid. I asked the placement office to put an ad

on their bulletin board or on their computer—
whatever they do. Fingers answered my ad, and I
hired him immediately."

"What a great idea," I said.

"I know."

The three of us ate, talked, drank more coffee,
and people-watched. Finally, Antoinette Chloe
stood up and clanked her spoon on her coffee cup.

"Again, I'd like to thank you all for coming, for
your cards, your kind expressions of sympathy,
and for your support. Please don't hesitate to
visit Brown's Four Corners in the future. We have
a fabulous new cook, as you can tell. Thanks
again!"

The crowd started to clear out. Some lingered
over their coffee, but almost everyone shuffled
out. I could hear the Rubbers rev up their motorcycles.

And then there were three.

I stretched. "I'd better get moving and see
what's happening at the point."

I started to stand, but Ty put a hand on my arm.
"Now that we're all alone, I'd like to talk to you
both."

Crap. This sounded like something I wouldn't
want to hear.

ACB was concentrating on reattaching the blackbird to her fascinator and wasn't paying much attention to Ty.

Ty snapped his fingers loudly. "Antoinette Chloe,
please listen."

"Oh, sure. What's up, Ty?"

"We found a fake fingernail in the collar of

Nick's shirt." He pointed to ACB's pinkie finger. "It would fit exactly here. We think that Nick might have been taken by gunpoint or knifepoint from his toolshed to the land where we found him—your land, Antoinette Chloe."

"He must have been scared, poor Nicky."

"Uh-huh. And we found a fake animal—a little yellow rabbit—on your land, too, not far from the body."

"Oh, good! That's probably the bunny that fell off one of my favorite fascinators."

"Antoinette Chloe, don't talk," I said, knowing where this was leading.

Ty sighed. "And we found the murder weapon, a filleting knife, wrapped in a fascinator, just like the kind you wear, not far from Nick's body."

"It has to be my Easter fascinator! The one I've been looking for. That's the one with the robins and bunnies frolicking on the grass. I was going to make it into a fall tableau with autumn leaves and salmon jumping, and wear it to the Miss Salmon pageant, but you found it with a knife wrapped in it? The knife used to kill Nick?"

I wanted to put my hand over her mouth, but it would've ruined her Wild Irish Rose lipstick. "Would you listen to me? Don't talk to Ty without a lawyer."

Ty shrugged. "I'm not the enemy, but that's the hat, Antoinette Chloe—robins and bunnies on pink grass. I knew that it was yours."

"Any prints on the knife?" I asked, holding my breath, praying that ACB's weren't there.

"It was wiped clean. But there was something

else nearby—a silver earring with a little motorcycle hanging from it."

"I was wondering where that went!" she said, completely oblivious. "I wanted to wear them today to the cemetery, but I could only find one."

"Antoinette Chloe. Shut up!" I said tactfully.

"Why?"

"Because everything Ty is mentioning is all your stuff! And it was all found at the scene where Nick was found."

"I know. I'm lucky he found it." She laughed, then sobered. Finally the situation hit her. "Oh! Oh, merciful heavens, no!" She turned to Ty. "Are you going to arrest me?"

"I'm afraid so, Antoinette Chloe." He shook his head. "Please stand and put your hands against the wall. You have the right to remain silent. You have the right—"

"Ty, no!"

"Trixie, please stand back."

"C'mon, Ty. Antoinette Chloe? Really, Ty? *Really*?"

"It's okay, Trixie. It's okay," ACB said. "Ty will figure this all out, and you'll help him. Okay?"

He handcuffed my friend, and it was like nails on a chalkboard when those metal teeth clicked into place. Then he patted her down. Tears ran down my cheeks. She looked so sad, so tired, so unlike Antoinette Chloe.

"Are they comfortable, Antoinette Chloe?" Ty asked.

She sniffed, then nodded. "How could you think that I'd kill my Nicky?"

"The clues lead straight to you," he said. "I'm

really sorry, but there's the Easter hat, the motorcycle earring, the fake nail, the bunny . . . it's all yours."

"Ty Brisco!" My anger was bubbling like molten lava, and finally I blew. "You call those clues? It's a trail that a first-grader could follow. It's like Antoinette Chloe tossed everything out her car window, for heaven's sake."

"Maybe she's a sloppy criminal," he added.

"I'm just sloppy," Antoinette Chloe. "I'm not a criminal."

I remembered walking by her room in my house. The door was open, and I had peeked in. Okay, ACB was a slob when it came to her room. No, maybe she wasn't a slob. With everything going on, she just didn't have time to put anything away. I wondered how she could find anything in that room.

"Trixie, what about the Miss Salmon pageant? I'm the mistress of ceremonies. I bought an evening muumuu."

"Don't worry, Antoinette Chloe. I'll bail you out in time."

She nodded. "Thanks."

"We have to get going now," Ty said.

"One more thing. Trixie, will you tell Fingers to just . . . carry on? Oh, and the payroll is due tomorrow, and . . . Oh, I can't think."

"I'll take care of everything," I said, with more confidence than I actually felt.

"I can always count on you," ACB said.

I followed as he escorted ACB to a sheriff's car. Vern McCoy got out from behind the wheel and opened the back door.

"Sorry, Antoinette Chloe. We had to do it," Vern said.

"I understand, Vern." ACB then yelled back to me. "Trixie, call Janice Malloy for me."

"Who?" I yelled back.

"Janice Malloy. She's a lawyer. I graduated from high school with her."

After Vern drove away, Ty turned to me. "I'll drive you home."

"I'd rather walk!"

"Get in my SUV, please," he said through gritted teeth. He meant business, and I wasn't in the mood to argue anymore or walk to my house.

"Give me ten minutes. I want to talk to her cook."

I didn't need ten minutes. Five was more than enough. Fingers knew where the time cards were, where her payroll books were kept, and even where she hid her blank checks. No computers for ACB.

He gathered up everything and put it in a box for me.

She sure must trust Fingers . . . er . . . Phil Gallman.

I walked slowly to my ride home. Getting into Ty's car, I put the box at my feet and didn't say a word.

"A penny for your thoughts," he said unoriginally.

"They aren't worth that much," I shot back.

Ty sighed. "Nick had an insurance policy, just like Chad Dodson claimed. In fact, the policy was taken out through Chad's bank or some kind of insurance holdings his family has. Anyway, Nick's policy is worth almost a million bucks."

"How do you know that?"

"We've been searching his house for a while now, remember?" he said. "All his important papers—important to Nick anyway—were in a metal file cabinet on the floor of his bedroom closet."

"And who's the beneficiary?"

"Your friend Antoinette Chloe Brown."

Chapter 8

*T*y cleared his throat. "And I believe that's what we in the business call—you know, the job that you said a first-grader could do—we call that motivation."

"Don't be crazy, Ty. ACB didn't even know that she was the beneficiary or that Nick even had a policy. Chad Dodson was the one who knew that. And he had inside information. He even knew that Nick signed his house over to her, for crying out loud."

"How could Antoinette Chloe not know that little tidbit?"

"It's not as if she had to do anything. Nick paid the premiums. Obviously he wanted to surprise her," I pointed out.

"Oh, I don't know if she was surprised," he said. "I wonder if she was acting."

Ugh. Sometimes, Ty got me so crazy, I wanted to pull his cowboy hat down past his ears. "ACB doesn't know how to act. What you see is what you get with her."

He shrugged. "Yeah, you're probably right."

"And did it ever occur to you that someone was

trying to frame her by littering all her stuff on her land?"

"Of course it did."

"So, where do I find Janice Malloy?"

"Over at Malloy's Hardware Store and Gift Emporium. Her law office is above the store that she runs with her husband, Gary. She's an excellent criminal lawyer."

"Will ACB get her one phone call?" I asked.

"We'll give her as many as she needs."

"Good."

"Trixie, this isn't Auburn or Attica. We have two holding cells—one for men, one for women. The last woman we had there was an out-of-towner who got lost and ended up here in Sandy Harbor during a blizzard. She stayed in the cell because all the hotels were full with other stranded motorists. She thought it was quite the adventure staying overnight in a jail and couldn't wait to go home and tell her pals."

"I'm hoping that ACB will think of this as an adventure, too."

We sat in silence for a few miles; then I asked, "How can I get her out?"

"You can't. Not until after she's arraigned and if bail is set. That'll be tomorrow morning."

"Who will be presiding over her case at court?"

"Judge Martin Butler, the town justice of Sandy Harbor. I'll catch him before he goes out fishing tomorrow."

"Where's his office?" I'd make sure that I was there when ACB was arraigned.

"At the Happy Harbor Bar and Grill. It's in between the bottle-and-can-return place and the Laundromat, Bubbly Clean, on Fifth Street. He owns the bar, and court is held there when the bar is closed on Mondays and before eleven on weekdays."

Does anyone have just one job in Sandy Harbor? The one lawyer in town owns and operates a hardware store and gift shop. The town justice owns and operates the bar and has court right there. It's just like the Wild West!

"What time will ACB be arraigned?"

"Nine o'clock," he said. "Are you going to be there?"

"Of course. My friend needs my support."

"You can visit ACB tonight, you know. That's not a problem," Ty said. "In fact, I'll be there."

"I will see you at the jail, then. And please be nice to ACB."

He raised an eyebrow. "Geez, darlin', what kind of a cop do you think I am? Better yet, what kind of a cowboy do you think I am?"

"Sorry, Ty. That was really silly of me to say. I apologize. I know that you waited to arrest Antoinette Chloe after the cemetery and after everyone left the breakfast. That was very nice of you."

He smiled, but I could tell that his heart wasn't in it. "This is your stop," he said, pulling into a space in the parking lot near my house.

I climbed down from the giant SUV. "Thanks for the ride. See you later."

"Later."

I looked around my property. It looked like a tent town. The Rubbers had finished setting up camp, and there were twelve royal blue potty stations and showers lining the woods by the parking lot.

Chad Dodson's zillion-dollar motor home was gleaming, though his front bumper was perilously close to touching one of the potties.

He was sitting outside on a director's chair, and it looked like he had a bottle of champagne chilling on a table at his side. He was sipping out of a flute.

He raised his flute in a salute to me. "Care to join me, Trixie?"

I didn't really want to, but I needed to talk to him if I had any hope of exonerating my friend. He opened another director's chair, poured me a glass of champagne, and handed it to me.

"Thanks."

I took a sip and knew that this was the expensive stuff. It was smooth, so smooth—except for the bubbles that tickled the back of my throat.

"Nice stuff," I said, sitting down.

He smiled his dazzling smile, and pointed his thumb at his chest. "Nothing but the best for this guy."

Ugh. What a show-off.

I took a deep breath and let it out. "Chad, about Nick's insurance policy . . . how did you know that Antoinette Chloe was the beneficiary?"

He shifted on his chair. "I guessed."

"Really? You didn't have inside information?"

His smile faded. "Why are you questioning me about this, Trixie? Did that cop send you?"

I wanted to kick the legs of his chair and send him sprawling on the parking lot. Instead I put on a smile as phony as his.

"No. Ty didn't send me. Matter of fact, my friend Antoinette Chloe was just arrested, and I want to get to the bottom of this mess."

He leaned forward and chuckled. "She was arrested?"

Jerk!

"Why are you laughing? I don't think it's funny. The real criminal should be behind bars, not her," I said, ready to send him to the nearest Walmart, a good hundred miles away, to park his rig.

"Maybe they *do* have the real criminal. And if she killed him, she won't get a dime of the insurance policy," Chad sneered.

Chad Dodson was way too pompous for Sandy Harbor. Actually, he was way too pompous for anywhere.

"I don't know why you're so concerned about insurance. You won't get a dime either," I said. "Unless you're listed as the secondary beneficiary after Antoinette Chloe is bumped out of the running, like if she was found guilty of the policyholder's death!"

I was mostly thinking out loud, but I caught a slight smile from Chad that he hid it by taking a sip of his drink.

He is the secondary beneficiary of Nick's insurance policy!

That's why the leading questions at breakfast. Maybe Ty put ACB into protective custody because he thought there'd be an attempt to kill her!

Maybe I shouldn't be so quick to bail her out. Though I think ACB would rather die than miss her chance at being the emcee of the Miss Salmon pageant, with its dancing-salmon routine.

I might as well keep talking to Chad in the meantime to see if I could get him to spill any more information. I held out my flute for a refill of champagne, not realizing that I'd sipped the whole glass dry.

"Chad, why would a rich guy like you worry about a mere million dollars' worth of insurance?"

"A million bucks is nothing to sneeze at, especially during these times."

"You didn't need Nick's money for the past several months. What happened?"

"The market." He took another sip. "And Nick wasn't worth anything until he was dead."

"How nice of you to say."

He shrugged. "Nick and I didn't part as friends. I'm sure Deputy Brisco knows that already."

"What happened between you two?" Liquor loosens the lips, and his were flapping.

He drained his glass. "We met at a restaurant I used to frequent in Boston. Nick was working there, and he made the most delicious meals. Just delicious. His pasta primavera and veal Parmesan were to die for. I hired him to cater a Christmas party one year at the family mansion, and everyone raved. Eventually, we talked about a partnering up to build our own restaurant. I'd be the face person, and he'd be the talent."

"And then what?" I prompted, pouring another hit of champagne into his empty flute and mine.

"And the restaurant was doing great. There

was a line out the door every night. We had the classiest people clamoring for reservations. The place was a hit, and we were swimming in money. Then he wanted to close the place for three days to feed *those people*." He swept his palm in the direction of Tent Town and the blue-plastic lineup of potties and showers.

"The Rubbers?"

"What a name. Can you imagine them in my— our restaurant? For three whole days. I would have had to cancel hundreds of reservations, and, on top of that, Nick didn't even want to charge the . . . Rubbers! He said that we could afford to pick up the tab for his friends."

"I see."

"Can you imagine such nonsense? Well, I put my foot down and told him that it wasn't going to happen. Then he hopped onto his bike, revved it up, and rode it through the restaurant. Almost everything was ruined. He knocked over tables and chairs, broke glass, destroyed the bar when he rammed it. And then he rode away and I never saw him again until last night at Manning's funeral parlor."

He drained his flute, and I poured him more. I'd have to make sure he didn't drive.

"Is that right?" I asked, my eyebrow raised.

"Oh, wait," he said. "I did see him at a fund-raiser I organized about six months ago. We fought. He broke my nose. And I slashed his arm with my switchblade."

"Your *illegal* switchblade?"

"One and the same."

"And, in the meantime, you had your lawyers and private investigators keeping an eye on him?"

"Yes. That's how I found out he broke our contract and changed his policy without my knowledge and put Antoinette Chloe first. I was next. His brother, Sal, is third. The two of us would have to die before Sal got anything."

"And Antoinette Chloe would either have to die before you got anything or be found guilty of killing Nick."

He held up his glass in a toast, and my desire to kick the chair legs out from under him returned.

"No one had better try to hurt Antoinette Chloe," I said as forcefully as I could. "They'd have to go through me first."

He grinned. "I'm not looking for a life behind bars. I'm having too good of a time."

"How long will your good time last? If you're chasing down an insurance policy, I'll bet you're almost broke."

"I'd say that's none of your business!" His nostrils flared like mine did whenever I smelled pizza. He quickly got himself under control.

"Like I said, Antoinette Chloe is my friend, pal. And you're not. I'm looking out for her."

"I think it's time for my overpaid lawyers to earn their retainer and file an order of protection for you to stay away from me, Miz Matkowski. Can't have you meddling in my affairs, now, can I?"

"Weenie." I am so brilliant when threatened with lawyers, I resort to name-calling.

He said nothing and glanced at his watch. "This conversation is over, Miz Matkowski. I have to shower and get ready for my interview with your detective friend."

Taking the hint, I left and went back to my Big House to see what was going on with the Miss Salmon contestants. They'd be gone in four days, so I could get my life and my house back.

The first person I ran into was Aileen Shubert. She was loading the dishwasher. Now, that was a woman after my heart!

"Thanks so much, Aileen."

"No problem at all." She was chirpy and friendly, and I still envied her hair. She had perfect makeup and tasteful jewelry and reeked of class.

If she didn't win Miss Salmon, she should be named Miss Salmon Congeniality.

We sat down at the kitchen table to have a cup of tea.

"Where are you from, Aileen?"

She tossed her hair. "A small town in Vermont, but I've traveled all over."

"Doing what?"

"Modeling, mostly. My credits are in my application that I submitted when I entered Miss Salmon."

"Have you entered other pageants?"

She tucked her hair behind her ears. "Several. Though this is the smallest one I've done."

"Why did you pick Miss Salmon? It's such small potatoes, Aileen."

She giggled. "I don't want to sound like a snob, but small pageants are easy for me to win."

She's right. That did sound snobby.

Betsy, Lisa, and Cher came into the kitchen and

sat down. They started complaining about being fish in the main number.

"Ladies, it'll be fine!" I said. "How are you finding the Roving Rubbers Motorcycle Club of New England?"

"The committee members won't let us near them," said Aileen.

"Good! Speaking of the committee members, where are they?" I checked my mental list of those who were on duty—it should be sisters May and June, and also Connie DiMarco.

"Talking to fisherman at the cleaning station," said a tall redhead.

Lord, I wish I could remember names.

"Trixie, Antoinette Chloe said that she'd lend me some earrings to match my evening gown. Do you know when she'll be back?" said a short girl with long black hair and white streaks.

"I don't know yet. She's had some difficulty and will be away for a while," I said.

For as long as possible, I wanted to put off telling the contestants that ACB was in jail.

Finishing off my tea, I picked up my purse. "Sorry, ladies. I'd love to stay and talk longer, but I have a couple of things to do downtown. What are your plans for the rest of the day?"

"We're going to practice our routine on the lawn," Aileen said.

I winked. "Be careful of the fishermen. They just might catch you."

That prompted a bunch of groans, so I exited stage left.

I went upstairs to change out of my funeral clothes. I slid on a pair of tan capris, a nice aqua striped T-shirt, and a pair of comfortable sandals.

I felt I looked presentable to see Janice Malloy, the lawyer. I called her on my cell phone as I was leaving to make sure she was available.

"Come right over, Trixie."

"Give me fifteen minutes, Janice."

"No problem. Just come into the hardware store, and I'll meet you there."

"Okay."

Fifteen minutes later, I walked into Malloy's Hardware and Gift Emporium. I scanned the gift area and saw wood carvings of salmon jumping out of the water, snow globes that said SANDY HARBOR, NY on them, salt and pepper shakers with the same logo, postcards, and various other knickknacks.

A very pretty woman with curly black hair up in a haphazard ponytail approached me. She was tall and thin and had deep-set brown eyes.

"Trixie?"

"Janice?"

"Yup. Let's go up to my office."

We walked up a worn staircase and entered a beautiful home. The walls were covered in knotty pine, and there was a huge stone fireplace taking up one wall. The kitchen had mossy green granite counters and tall birch cabinets. Beautiful.

Janice's office was off the main room. It was cozy and loaded with cute objects—an eclectic array of things that Janice said she'd collected over the years.

I sat down in the chair opposite hers. Her big desk had an overhang where I could pull up my chair.

"What can I do for you, Trixie?"

"I need you to represent Antoinette Chloe Brown," I blurted out. "She's currently in the Sandy Harbor Jail, and I'm afraid that her life could be in danger, too, so maybe it's better if she stays there. Oh, I don't know!"

"Wow!" She settled back in her chair. "First, I adore Antoinette Chloe. Second, what's she in jail for?"

"Murdering Nick Brownelli."

"Impossible. There's no way that she'd harm a flea."

"I know."

I filled her in on the events so far, and ended with her being arrested. She took copious notes on her computer and on a yellow legal pad.

"When's her arraignment?"

"Nine o'clock tomorrow morning."

"I'll be there. I'll ask for bail. After all, she's a longtime resident of the Sandy Harbor community and she has a business here. She's not a flight risk," Janice said.

"No, she's not. And she's been staying with me to help chaperone the Miss Salmon contestants."

"Excellent. Oh, Trixie, are you prepared to bail her out?"

"Absolutely."

"Let me explain what that would entail. You might have to put up your house, the Silver Bullet, and maybe even the housekeeping cottages to guarantee that she'll appear for all her court appearances."

"I'll put up the whole point to get her out of jail," I said. "But I'm worried that her life might be in danger if she gets out."

I told Janice everything I knew, guessed, or assumed.

When I had finished relaying everything to her, Janice slid her chair back and stood. "I'll drive over to the jail and interview Antoinette Chloe tonight. But thanks to you, I have a terrific start."

"I'm heading over to the jail now. I'll tell her that you're on board."

We shook hands and walked out together. Janice went back to her hardware business, and I drove over to the sheriff's department. It was really a beautiful building.

Knocking, I turned the brass knob of the thick oak door with frosted glass. It had thick black letters that said SANDY HARBOR SHERIFF'S DEPARTMENT.

Ty's feet were on his desk, and he was on the phone.

When he saw me, he cut his phone call short.

I sat down, and he removed his feet from the desk so I didn't have to look on the soles of his department-issued shoes.

"Ty, did you know that the secondary beneficiary on Nick's life-insurance policy is the not so charming Chad Dodson? Sal is third."

"Yes."

"Do you know that Chad Dodson is broke?"

"I know. He recently had a falling-out with his parents and extended family over his extravagant lifestyle and bad investments."

"How did you know that?"

He raised a perfect black eyebrow.

"Okay. Never mind," I said. "Do you think that ACB might be in danger from Chad Dodson?"

"Yes."

"Did you put her in jail to protect her?"

He hesitated. "Not exactly, but that's an extra benefit of her arrest."

"What else? Certainly not ACB's phony fingernail and earring and fascinator—oh, and yellow bunny—that were scattered like bread crumbs."

He ignored that. "There's also the fact that three upstanding ladies of the community, along with the rest of your diner patrons, heard her threaten to kill Nick and saw her ruthlessly stab an Italian sausage."

"I am convinced that she's being set up, Ty."

"What—someone put a gun to her head and made her stab the sausage and yell about how she wanted to kill Nick?" Ty asked. "Seriously, Trixie, who do you think is setting her up?"

"I don't know yet, but I will find out. You can bet on that! But do you know? Do you have a suspicion as to who is framing her?"

The other perfect black eyebrow went up. "Trixie, let me handle this. I mean it. I don't want you or anyone else to get hurt."

"If you're trying to keep her safe, I don't know if I should bail out Antoinette Chloe. She's supposed to be the emcee for the Miss Salmon pageant. If she misses it, she'll be a crazy woman."

"When is it again?"

"Four more days."

"Maybe I'll have the perp by then, and she'll be free to go."

"Are you that close?" I couldn't contain my excitement.

He folded his arms across his chest.

"So, I shouldn't bail her out now?" I asked.

"No. If you're really her friend, let her stay here. Believe me, she's very comfortable."

"Will you let me in to see her?"

"Of course. Follow me."

He opened another thick oak door and held it open for me. There was one cell.

"Where is she?" I asked.

"This is the men's side."

Another door led us to the women's side. ACB was on her cell phone. She was ordering curtains with "a garden display" and getting overnight delivery.

Her jail cell looked almost as cluttered as her room at my house. She'd been here only a couple of hours, and her cell was stuffed with all the comforts of home.

She had a pretty bedspread with big red peonies on it, a nightstand with a doily, a pink-tasseled reading lamp, a stuffed cat on her bed, and an assortment of clothes hanging on hangers from the cell bars.

She was eating takeout from the Gas and Grab.

"Trixie!" She hung up her phone. "Come and share my meatball sub."

"I'm good."

"Ty, would you bring in a chair for Trixie?"

"Yes, ma'am." He gave a salute and left the room.

When he returned, Ty opened the door to ACB's cell and let me enter. He put the chair next to her bed.

"Aren't you going to search me, Deputy?" I asked. "I might have a hacksaw in my purse to break this dangerous criminal out of here."

"Go for it," he said. "And take all her stuff with you."

He left without locking the cell behind him, and ACB kept eating.

"It's not so bad here in jail, other than the orange jumpsuit. It doesn't suit my coloring at all."

"But you have several muumuus here."

"They're my court clothes, but I don't think that Ty would mind if I change into them instead of wearing this orange thing. Do you?"

"I'm surprised he was able to talk you into putting that thing on." I chuckled, thinking of what Ty must have said to Antoinette Chloe to get her to do it. "Who brought you the other items—your comforter, doily, lamp, and all the rest?"

"Ty did. I made him a list, and he brought this all back."

That alarmed me. "You gave him the key to your house?"

"It's unlocked."

"But you let him go in there? Heaven's sake, Antoinette Chloe, he could search it. Maybe he'd even find things that could incriminate you."

"I don't have anything to hide, Trixie. Besides,

look at all my things that were found where Nick was buried. Someone else beat him to it."

Maybe I was being paranoid. In spite of my earlier annoyance at him, I knew that Ty was a fair and honorable guy. But he had a job to do. It was hard to explain that to ACB when she thought he was the best thing since mayonnaise cake.

I changed the subject. "I talked to Janice. She's coming to see you soon. And we'll both be with you when you appear in court tomorrow morning."

"Thank you. You're a good friend, and I trust Janice."

"By the way, I have your payroll things in the car. Fingers sent it all. You could do your payroll in here and write out the checks. I could pass them out or give them to Fingers to pass out. I'll go and get everything. Be right back."

I stood, but she put her hand on my knee. "Ty will get everything. Just give him a yell."

I didn't want to be waited on by Ty. He had better things to do.

"That's okay. I'll get them later." I handed her a napkin to wipe the tomato sauce that was all over her hands. "So, are you doing okay in here?"

"It's nice and quiet, and I'm getting a lot of things done. I've made a lot of phone calls regarding the pageant. Tying up loose ends. I think it will turn out great. I can't wait!"

"Antoinette Chloe, you can't emcee the pageant from jail."

"I'll just have to bail myself out," she said.

"Trixie, I hate to ask you, but would you be my backup plan just in case my bail is too high?"

I felt like crying. "I'd bail you out in a New York minute, but I don't know if I can. All my property is still in Aunt Stella's name. She wanted to put it all in my name, but I wouldn't let her until I pay her off completely. I'm so sorry, Antoinette Chloe. So sorry."

"I understand." She took my hand and held it. "Please don't worry. I can put up Brown's and my drive-in land."

"Yes, you probably can. We'll just have to wait and see how much your bail is going to be."

"Maybe they'll set my bail really high. I'm charged with second-degree murder, Trixie. I think that's one of the things Sal was found guilty of. Doesn't that sound just awful?"

"Yes, it does, but we both know that you didn't kill Nick."

"Who hates me enough to frame me?"

"I don't know, Antoinette Chloe, but I'm going to find out. Now, do you have anyone in mind?"

She shrugged. "There may be some women who are jealous of my couture. I mean, I'm pretty much of a fashion leader here in Sandy Harbor."

Yikes.

"And my restaurant is successful, and since I hired Fingers, it's really rocking. The man is a gem. I think I'll give him a raise."

ACB was just so generous. If the people of Sandy Harbor knew how generous she actually was, they'd be astonished.

If a farmer needed money to hold him over until his crop came in, an anonymous money order came in the mail. Single mothers often found boxes of groceries by their front door. If someone couldn't pay their doctor's bill, ACB anonymously paid it. If a family was struggling through Christmas, ACB bought candy and gifts for the children, along with a turkey and all the trimmings, and had them delivered anonymously.

When Sal was arrested, Antoinette Chloe came to me and asked if I could teach her to cook. Subsequently, she trained with all of my cooks for a good two weeks, and never missed a day.

As far as I knew, only the clerk at the post office, Mrs. Carol Dodd, who processed ACB's numerous money orders, knew how bighearted Antoinette Chloe was.

"Trixie? You're a million miles away."

"Oh . . . uh . . . just thinking, I guess. Antoinette Chloe, do you know that Chad Dodson is a beneficiary of Nick's two-million-dollar life insurance policy, after you?"

"Ty shared that information with me."

"What are your thoughts on that little tidbit?"

She shrugged. "If I were out of the way, Chad would get the two million, wouldn't he?"

"Yep, he would. He'd also get it if you're found guilty of killing Nick."

"Trixie, I'm not worried. I don't think that Chad is the type who'd kill me. And I didn't kill Nick, so I won't be found guilty."

"Antoinette Chloe, you're too trusting. Chad is broke, and I think he's pretty desperate. Why else would he come to Nick's wake in little Sandy Harbor? He wanted to talk to you and ask for the money that Nick allegedly owed him."

"If Nick owed him a million dollars and he can prove that, then I should pay the debt. I'll have Janice look into his claim."

"Great idea, Antoinette Chloe, but I still think that you should be careful of Chad."

"I will. Anyway, Ty said that the money has been tied up by the insurance company, depending on the outcome of my case."

"Oh! Your trial could go on for a year or so. Chad seems to want the money now."

She waved me away. "Trixie, it doesn't matter. I just have to get out in time for the Miss Salmon pageant. I'll ask Janice to look at my assets, and then I'll put it all on the line for my bail."

I didn't know how to tell her that getting out of jail *might* kill her. But I knew that not being able to emcee the pageant would *definitely* kill her.

What was a friend to do?

Chapter 9

I pulled into my usual parking space by the Big House. Tent Town was looking a little sloppy, and I would be glad when they were all gone.

I looked around for Toxic Waste, and was disappointed that I didn't see him. The pageant girls were over at the Silver Bullet for dinner, which gave me some quiet time, so I could catch some sleep before my graveyard shift.

Blondie greeted me like a long-lost friend and started whining, which I knew meant that she had to go outside.

I let her out the kitchen door, and she hurried down the stairs and headed for her favorite spot: by my red, white, and blue garden of petunias. The petunias were gasping their last, and I thought that I really should euthanize them and sweeten my compost pile.

Suddenly Blondie headed for a copse of trees and started barking.

"Go away!" I heard someone say. The voice was familiar. "Go. Get away."

More barking. A couple of unladylike swearwords came from the trees, followed by a couple of phrases of ungentlemanly swearing. Then the two individuals hurried from their hiding place and ran farther away from the house.

Toxic Waste and Aileen Shubert?

No way!

Blondie followed them, barking like crazy. She thought they were playing with her. I let Blondie torment them for a while; then I whistled, and she came back to me.

But what the heck was Aileen Shubert doing with Toxic Waste, other than the obvious? And where were the committee chaperones?

Probably eating at the Silver Bullet.

Didn't any of them know that Aileen was missing and playing kissy-face with the leader of the Rubbers?

Even though none of the ladies staying with me were underage, I still felt that they should be chaperoned. The grounds were crawling with Rubbers, fishermen, and various unknown customers of the Silver Bullet.

A dozen beauty queens might be tempting.

I let Blondie inside, then headed for the place I had seen the two lovebirds.

I found them rolling around on the ground by the border between my land and Antoinette Chloe's drive-in land.

"Excuse me, please." Nothing like coitus interruptus. "Excuse me!"

Aileen recovered first and pushed Toxic off her. He looked at me and had the decency to turn red.

"You know the rules. Please go back into the house," I said.

"I'm sorry, Trixie. Are you going to boot me out of the contest?" Aileen asked. "Please don't."

"We'll talk. Make some tea, and I'll be right there. I want to talk to Mr. Waste."

I waited until Aileen was well on her way to the Big House; then I turned to the leader of the pack. "Toxic, have you met Miss Shubert before?"

He looked at me as if I had snakes coming out of my ears.

"Uh . . . no."

"Did you just meet here?" I asked, feeling like a grammar-school principal.

"Uh . . . yeah."

He sure looked guilty. It crossed my mind that he was lying like a rug. "You two surely got acquainted fast."

He shrugged. "So?"

"We have rules for the pageant contestants while they are under my roof."

"I don't know of any rules." He looked down at the grass. "Yeah, okay. I won't bother Aileen anymore."

"Thank you."

"Can I go now?"

I felt like Sister Mary Mary of St. Margaret's school, who had wielded a pointer like a medieval sword and liked to rap knuckles.

"No, Toxic. I have something else I want to talk to you about."

"What now?" he said through gritted teeth.

"Nick's death. Can you think of anyone who might have wanted to kill him?"

"I thought you were a chef, not a cop." He put

his hands on his hips, trying to intimidate me. But he'd have to do better than that.

"I'm just a friend of Antoinette Chloe Brown, who's in jail for allegedly killing him."

"Maybe she did it."

"No way."

"Says you." He spit in the grass. "Look, all I know is that Nick ran off with my girlfriend and then left her at the altar. What kind of a guy does that?"

"It's awful, I agree, but maybe your girlfriend wanted to go. Maybe Nick didn't steal her. Maybe she wanted to break it off with you."

"Any way you put it, Nick still stole her."

I wasn't getting anywhere with this topic.

"What's her name?" I asked. Then I remembered what Sal had said. "Leslie . . ."

"Yes. Leslie McDermott."

"I wonder why Nick left Leslie," I mumbled to myself.

"He was a coward. He should have cut her loose before it got that far. Maybe she would have come back to me."

"I hear you, but why did he leave her?"

"I don't know, and I don't care. You have to know how to handle a woman like Leslie, and Nick didn't."

"You had to be pretty ticked off," I pushed.

"I was."

"I mean, you had to be really, really ticked off."

"What are you getting at, Miz Matkowski?" If looks could kill, I'd be pushing up crabgrass.

"Aww, Toxic, you know what I'm going for. Did you hate Nick Brownelli enough to kill him?"

"At one time I could have, but I've mellowed. In fact, Leslie and I have been talking. We might get together again."

"That's really nice, Toxic. Good for you."

"Anything else you wanna know?"

"No. Just stay away from Aileen Shubert, okay? You both can do what you want when the pageant is over."

He closed his eyes and gave a slight nod.

Then something hit me. "Toxic, why would you want to be with Aileen when you just said that you might get back together with Leslie?"

"Uh, well, you know how the song goes: 'Love the one you're with.'"

"You know how the other song goes: 'Your cheating heart will tell on you.'"

He clamped his teeth together, but spoke very clearly through them. "I gotta go. I have to talk to the cop."

Walking back to the Big House, I thought about what I'd say to Aileen Shubert. I got a lot of information from Toxic, but he'd be wary of ever talking to me again. I already knew most of what he'd told me, so his information wasn't too helpful.

I probably should tell the Miss Salmon Committee that Aileen wasn't salmon material in that she was already swimming upstream.

Trixie Matkowski, you are such a prude!

Maybe I should just keep this incident to myself. Aileen deserved a second chance.

She had tea ready and she was sitting at my kitchen table, hands folded and red-eyed.

"Trixie, I know what you are going to say," she said, softly. "You're going to tell me that my behavior was not appropriate."

"Yes." I poured water into my cup. "But you weren't the only one ordering off the menu. Toxic was doing the tango with you. That man is a fast worker."

"He can sweep a girl off her feet!" She smiled, remembering, then snapped back to reality. "And you're going to tell me that I'm not fit to be Miss Salmon. And that fooling around with a Rubber is not a good idea."

"Absolutely."

"And you're wondering if I knew Toxic Waste before."

"Sure."

"No. I did not. And that makes my actions even more heinous."

I shrugged.

"Please don't ban me from the pageant," she pleaded. "I couldn't bear it. I want to win, Trixie."

"Mmm."

"Are you going to ban me?"

I shrugged again.

"Oh, please. I'm so sorry. I totally apologize. Can I stay in? Please, please, please?"

"Okay. As long as you promise not to break any more rules."

She jumped up and hugged me around the neck. "Oh, thank you. Thank you! You can count on me." Then she bounced upstairs.

Whew! I was glad that we had that talk.

* * *

I was back in the Silver Bullet kitchen at midnight. I wished Cindy had called me to come in earlier, because she was swamped.

Springing into action, I took the next order in line. All six of them wanted the daily special: meat loaf with mashed potatoes and gravy; peas and carrots with a side chef's salad; and another side of macaroni and cheese, coleslaw, or homemade applesauce—made by yours truly.

Of course, some people wanted their gravy on the side, some wanted all of the sides, and then there were the various dressings for the salads. And then one person didn't want peas and carrots at all—he or she wanted corn instead.

Okay, I could do that.

Cindy and I did the Silver Bullet Shuffle until all the orders were complete.

"I wonder why we had such a rush tonight," I said. "Not that I'm complaining, but it seems like something's going on, or that something just stopped, so they all came here."

Cindy pulled some onions from the counter and started peeling them. "The new *Star Wars* movie is playing at the Bijou. It must have just let out."

"And then there's the ten Miss Salmon contestants and two of their handlers, Connie and Irene."

She looked out the pass-through window. "There were four handlers before. May and June must have just left."

Four committee ladies, and no one noticed that Aileen Shubert was missing? *Sheesh.*

"Why don't you head out, Cindy? It's been a

long day for you. Remember to put on your time card that I owe you time and a half for staying and helping."

"You don't have to. You gave my family all that food."

"Don't argue with your employer," I said. "Now shoo! By the way, Cindy, how did your date go?"

"Really nice, Trixie. He's a real sweetheart."

"Good. I can't wait to meet him." Cindy deserved a great guy.

Speaking of good guys, I spotted Ty Brisco taking a seat at the counter. He wore his good-guy white cowboy hat.

He saw me peeking at him and waved. I waved back and wondered how ACB was doing.

I went into the dining area and poured myself a cup of coffee. "How's our pal doing, Ty?"

"She's ordering more things to decorate her cell with. The last I knew, she was ordering some kind of room divider to put around the toilet. It is in the open. And she doesn't like the standard-issue metal john. She's ordered toilet-seat covers in purple and orange. Oh, and even a purple shag rug."

"Seems like she's planning on staying."

"I don't think so. She said that she's decorating for the next person to come in. She said that there's no reason why the Sandy Harbor Jail shouldn't be more homey."

"That's our Antoinette Chloe. How did her visit with her lawyer go?"

"Okay, I guess."

"Did you tell her about keeping ACB in protective custody?"

"Yes. She said that she can't go for that, and that every person has the right to bail. I think I'll talk to the judge myself."

I leaned over the coffee counter and whispered to him. "Did Nick have a will?"

"He did. We found it in his papers."

"And?"

Ty smiled. "Along with his house, he left his car, his bike, and some property on Blue Mountain Lake in the Adirondacks to ACB. Oh, and property in the Catskills, too, with a nice big lake on it. The state's looking at the property for a casino. Chad is next to benefit, and then Sal is after Chad. Just like his insurance policy."

"Who would have thought?" I said. I couldn't believe that Nick had been that rich. "Is it all paid for?"

"You bet. But he was land rich, not money rich. And he bought it ages ago for a song, when they were giving it away. He was smart to hang on to it."

"Wow."

"Exactly. Vern McCoy estimates that his property holdings alone are worth about two to eight million big ones, depending on who's buying it and what they want to do with it."

"Wow. ACB is going to be rich."

"Just what I thought. You know, Trixie, I talked to Chad Dodson, and in spite of his debutant attitude and remarks, I think he's running scared. He knows that he's a prime suspect."

"Did you talk to Toxic Waste?"

"He's a chef at a German restaurant, his own restaurant, and he pretends to be a rough-and-tough biker. But he's a real pussycat. And he cried like a baby in my office. He was afraid that he was going to be arrested for murder, and he said that after talking to you earlier, he was scared stiff."

"We didn't talk about anything so horrible that he had to cry."

"What did you talk about?" Ty asked.

"A little about Nick. I asked him if he was mad enough to kill Nick over his girlfriend running off with him. He said that he once was, but that it's water under the bridge now, and that he and Leslie—that's her name—were getting back together. But that was only after I scolded him for being in the woods with Aileen Shubert."

"What were they doing there?"

"Well, they weren't picking strawberries. What do you think they were doing?"

"Lust in bloom, huh?" He grinned.

"Must be something in the air. Perhaps they're copying the salmon."

On and on we went, bantering back and forth. I could do this all day, but Nancy put a couple of orders in front of me.

"See you later, Ty. I have to get to work."

"Wait a second, Trixie. I want to remind you to leave this investigation to me. I'll do the interviewing."

"Then I won't tell you about my conversation with Chad Dodson."

"Oh, I heard all about it. Chad wanted to file a restraining order against you with the district attorney, but I talked him out of it. I told him that you can't help yourself. It's your personality."

I couldn't help but laugh. "Gee, thanks."

"He's going to do it if you come near him again."

"Then he'd better move his behemoth of a motor home and his red Thunderbird off my property."

"I need him around here," Ty said, "where I can keep an eye on him."

Aww . . . damn. But if he thought that a piece of legal paper was going to stop me from talking to him, he was wronger than wrong.

"But I have a right to be on my own property," I mumbled to myself as I made two tanned three-story, pig-and-plants. That's Dinerese for a triple-decker bacon, lettuce, and tomato on toast.

When those were done, I made three rib-eyes, still mooing, with my homemade poker chips—er, potato chips. Three tuna subs with a whole garden—lettuce, tomatoes, and onions. Then three Silver Bullet daily breakfast specials: two eggs, two pancakes, two pieces of bacon, and two sausages, with either two pieces of toast or two biscuits. I put bread on the Ferris wheel to toast, tossed several bacon strips in the deep fryer, and started fussing with the eggs—up, over light, over hard. Oh, and two weepy eyeballs—aka eggs Benedict, which were my all-time favorite.

Through the pass-through window, I saw Nancy taking Ty's order. I could almost predict what he'd order at this time of the night: a slice of cherry pie and a slice of chocolate pie. He'd wash them down with another cup of coffee, which Nancy was pouring right now. Then he'd walk across the lawn to the bait shop next door and climb the stairs to his apartment.

On nice evenings, he'd sit out on the deck for a while. On rainy, cold, or snowy nights, he'd watch TV for about an hour. Then the lights would go out.

Not that I'd noticed.

There was a lull, so I decided to clean the kitchen a bit. I emptied the Ferris wheel of crumbs, straightened up the fridge by the stove, wiped down the stove with grease cutter, and took the trash out to the Dumpster.

While I was there, something caught my eye. Two guys talking . . . and drinking together. By the lights surrounding my parking lot, I could see that one had a black jacket on with the RR logo and chains draped from waist to knee. Toxic Waste. And the guy he was talking to looked dressed to command a yacht. He wore glaring white pants, shoes, jacket, and hat. It was none other than Chad Dodson, megaweenie.

I tuned in.

"So, we have an agreement?" Chad asked.

"Yeah." They shook hands.

"Don't screw me, Toxic. If you do, you're going to end up like Nick Brownelli," Chad said.

"The same goes for you," Toxic said. "Seriously, though, do you know who offed Nick?"

Chad shrugged. "I plead the Fifth on that."

They both laughed, like Nick's death was some kind of joke. I wanted to barf.

I wondered if they had known each other before, or if they were bonding over their shared dislike of Nick Brownelli and a mutually beneficial business experience.

Partnership with Chad wasn't beneficial to Nick in the least.

Either way, they made a strange pair of friends.

They walked toward Chad's motor home and shook hands again. Toxic walked to one of the potties and disappeared inside.

"Just don't make Chad a beneficiary of your life-insurance policy, Mr. Waste," I mumbled to myself.

I looked up at Ty's apartment. I could see him standing on his side deck. He also must have noticed Chad and Toxic together, laughing and joking.

Ty saw me and waved. I waved back.

I should have known that nothing much got past Ty Brisco.

Tossing the trash bag into the Dumpster, I went back into the kitchen. Washing my hands, I saw that there weren't any orders pinned to the wheel, so I kept on cleaning.

Then I decided to bake several mayonnaise cakes. I love how gooey and chocolaty mayonnaise cakes are, and how divine they are with cream-cheese frosting. Yum!

I thought I'd take one of them to ACB in jail. Then I could bring a couple back home for the pageant girls. They all could stand a little fattening up.

As I was measuring and mixing the ingredients, I couldn't help thinking of ACB sleeping in a jail cell. Sure, it was more like home than jail, but it was still jail, no matter how you decorated it.

Who wants to frame her?

Smarmy Chad Dodson had the most to gain if ACB was in jail—or dead.

Oh, and I couldn't forget about Sal, who had a love-hate thing going with ACB and his brother, Nick. Sure, he fell apart at Nick's wake, but it seemed that his "I forgive you, Antoinette Chloe, for taking up with my brother" speech was more than a little wacky.

Sal was still a suspect, but second under Chad Dodson on my list.

And what about Toxic Waste? He was ticked at Nick for stealing Leslie away from him. That kind of thing could last forever and turn into a mushroom cloud. He was even more ticked that Nick left Leslie at the altar. Go figure.

But Mr. Waste was being soothed by Aileen Shubert, so Leslie had to be far from his mind, right?

Oh! I just thought of something! I called Ty. I figured that he couldn't have been sleeping very long.

"Ty, it's Trixie. Tell me, was Nick knifed on the site where you found him or somewhere else?"

"Right next to the site. Remember, the perp had to bury him."

"I figured that. His house was really clean when ACB and I looked for him, so he couldn't have been killed there."

"What?" I could hear him without the phone to my ear. "When?"

"We were at his house before you found the body."

"Did you take something out of it, Trixie?"

Crap!

"Well, no. Actually, I didn't."

"Don't play word games with me. Did ACB take anything?"

"Two things. But, Ty, believe me when I say you don't want to know and it has nothing, absolutely nothing, to do with Nick's death. Nothing. And don't ask her about it. Please?" There was a long silence. Finally, I cracked. "Ty, are you there?"

"I won't say anything to her."

"Thanks."

"Do you want to know anything else?" he asked.

"Could someone lure Nick into his car, drive Nick out to the country, skillfully stab him in the jugular, dig a shallow grave, toss him in, and somewhat fix the vegetation that was messed up?"

"Sure, but it would have to be a hell of a lure. Nick was a pretty big guy."

"Could a woman do it?"

"Like ACB? She's no lightweight herself, but she's up there in years." He shrugged. "Depending on her adrenaline and anger and whatnot, maybe. But she didn't dig much—there was rain the day before. The dirt would have been heavy, and it was a shallow grave."

"So, you still think ACB did it?"

"When did I say that?" He was getting snippy.

"You said she didn't dig much."

"I was speaking about women in general, during that part of my answer. Now, is that all? I have to meet with Judge Butler in the morning before court. I need some sleep."

"Just one more thing."

He yawned. "What?"

"I know that you saw Toxic and Chad together."

"Yeah. I did."

"What do you think?" I asked.

"That it was interesting, but they're living right next to each other here, so why shouldn't they talk?"

Now, that was disappointing. I thought he was going to say something better than that.

"Do you think that they knew each other before . . . now?"

"They knew *of* each other, according to them. Anything else, Trixie?"

"I heard them talking that they are going to go into business together. Another restaurant. And Chad said something about pleading the Fifth when Toxic asked him if he knew who killed Nick."

"Interesting," Ty said. "But probably just guy talk. You know, just joking around."

I sighed. It seemed like Ty just didn't take things as seriously as I did. But what bothered me more was that he moved too slowly for me. "Are they suspects?"

"Everyone's a suspect until I catch the real killer."

"Are you close?"

"Good night, Trixie." *Click.*

Humpf.

I checked on my cakes. *Fabulous.* I let them cool, and made the frosting.

Then I continued with my shift. I made up more orders, and I rang the bell for Chelsea or Nancy. I drank more coffee and thought about who killed Nick Brownelli. Rinse and repeat.

Finally, as I was frosting the cakes, Juanita arrived to take over.

"*Hola*, Trixie. I came in early because I couldn't sleep."

"Why? What's wrong?"

"I was thinking of poor Antoinette Chloe in jail."

"She's doing okay, Juanita. She really is. Cheer up." I looked at the clock: seven thirty. "You know, since you're here early, do you mind punching in early? I want to jump in the shower before I go to court this morning. Antoinette Chloe is going to be arraigned."

"Go right ahead, and give her our best wishes. Tell her that we are thinking of her."

"I sure will." I hugged Juanita on the way out the back door to the Big House.

I was pacing out front of the bar/courthouse while I was waiting for Antoinette Chloe to arrive in one of the sheriff's cars.

Deputy Lou Rutledge brought her. She was in handcuffs, and it broke my heart. Thank goodness they didn't use the leg shackles on her. They probably figured that she couldn't run in flip-flops, so the shackles weren't necessary.

She wore a red muumuu with passion flowers

all over it, and what looked like every piece of jewelry she owned. Her sunflower hat glittered with sequins of all different colors, and on top of it sat a bluebird in a fancy white cage. Knowing ACB, it was a statement about her being in a cage herself.

Nice touch.

Lou took her by the arm and helped her up the broken sidewalk to the bar . . . er . . . courtroom.

She tried to hug me, but Lou held his arm out.

"Come on, Lou. I can't slip her my Uzi. I left it at the Silver Bullet."

He chuckled. "Standard protocol, Trixie."

"I know." Then I turned to ACB. "Antoinette Chloe, I'll be in court with you."

Her eyes watered. "Thanks, friend."

It was an effort for me to smile. I was so worried about her, and I didn't feel like I was getting anywhere proving that she didn't kill Nick.

All I'd done was to talk to the suspects I had in mind. I should be doing something more, but I just didn't know what yet.

Chad did tell me about the other beneficiaries in Nick's will. And Toxic Waste admitted that he had seethed about Nick stealing his girlfriend and then leaving her at the altar. Now I knew her name, Leslie McDermott, and I added her to my list of people who disliked Nick.

I followed Deputy Rutledge and ACB into the bar. She was seated at a table next to Janice Malloy, her lawyer.

"Please remove the handcuffs from my client," Janice said.

Lou looked at Ty, who was sitting on the DA's

side of the room. Ty nodded, so Lou unlocked her cuffs.

ACB rubbed her wrists. "Thanks, Lou, and thank you, Janice, for representing me."

Janice gave her a hug.

Then ACB waved at the court stenographer. "Oh, Sadie! We have to talk about the Miss Salmon pageant before I leave."

The court stenographer waved and nodded and got her black transcription machine set up.

"And it's good to see you, too, Marty." ACB waved to the judge, who sat at his own table in front of the room.

"Hi, Antoinette Chloe. How are you holding up?"

"I guess my answer depends on what happens here this morning."

Chapter 10

*T*he new assistant district attorney for the county introduced himself. "Your Honor, for the record, my name is Ronald Davies. I'll be representing the People in this matter."

"Welcome to Sandy Harbor, Mr. Davies," Justice Butler said. "As you can see, we're rather informal here. It's a bar. Just call me Judge or Judge Butler, but don't call me in the afternoon to go fishing. They bite the best in the morning."

That got everyone laughing and lightened the mood a little.

"Fine with me, Judge. I just came from an arraignment in a cow barn, so a bar is a nice change of pace."

Janice stood. "For the record, my name is Janice Malloy, and I'll be representing the defendant, Antoinette Chloe Brown."

Even though there'd been a ban on smoking in New York bars for years, smoke still clung to the walls and tables of the Happy Harbor Bar and Grill. The wood was yellowed with the damage, and it looked like the village justice of Sandy Harbor hadn't cleaned the place in years.

My folding chair was off balance and driving me crazy, so I sat in another one. Same problem. I stayed put.

Joan Paris, editor of the *Lure*, sat down in the wobbly chair I had just vacated. She pulled out a notebook from her tote and started writing.

Judge Butler shuffled his papers and seemed loath to read the charge against Antoinette Chloe. There was just one, but it was a biggie: murder in the second degree.

I already knew that, but when Judge Butler read out loud the New York State penal law pertaining to her murder-in-the-second-degree charge, it was ugly.

ACB looked back at me, and I sent her the best smile I could muster.

"Mr. Davies, do you have anything to say regarding bail for the defendant?"

Davies jumped to his feet. "The people request no bail due to the severity of the charge against the defendant."

"Miz Malloy, do you have anything to say?" the judge asked.

"Indeed I do. My client has the right to have bail set according to Section 180.80 of the New York State Penal Law, proceedings relative to a felony complaint."

"Mr. Davies, this court has decided that the defendant has the right to bail. Let's figure out an amount, huh? Or I'll set it myself."

Obviously, Ty hadn't succeeded in convincing the judge to keep ACB in protective custody without bail.

"Judge, the people request bail be set in the amount of three million dollars, cash or bond."

Janice jumped to her feet. "Judge Butler, the assistant district attorney's suggested bail amount is way out of line. My client definitely doesn't have that kind of money. I request bail in the amount of five thousand dollars, cash or bond."

"Mr. Davies?"

"Judge, the defendant definitely has the resources to abscond. She owns a successful restaurant and valuable lakefront property on Lake Ontario. She's a member of a motorcycle gang, so she has access to assistance. She has a van for transportation out of town. Additionally, we know that her husband, Sal Brown, as part of his plea deal, made full restitution to the defendant, and she was able to buy her property back. That amount is listed on the letter that I gave you earlier regarding her assets."

"Janice, what do you have to say?"

"Your Honor, the defendant is a lifelong resident of Sandy Harbor. And she would never abscond. He roots are here, as well as her restaurant and her land. She wants to develop the land and turn it into a drive-in, and—"

"A drive-in?" the judge interrupted. "Are you serious about that, Antoinette Chloe?"

"I sure am, Marty."

"But drive-ins are closing all over the States."

"Then everyone will come from all over to go to mine."

"Okay." Judge Butler shrugged. "Now, where were we?"

Mr. Davies shook his head and clutched the edge of the table. "We are talking about the same land where the victim was buried, Your Honor."

Antoinette Chloe tried to stand, but Janice put her hand on ACB's shoulder.

"I didn't know that I'd dig up Nick when Excavating Ed Berger started digging, Mr. Davies," Antoinette said.

"That's for damn sure," Joan Paris whispered to me.

Judge Butler used a glass as a gavel. "Antoinette Chloe, you can't talk during this thing."

"But it's true, Marty. I didn't know Nicky was there."

Judge Butler looked at Janice for help. "Do you have anything else to say about the bail issue, Janice?"

"Please consider that Antoinette Chloe has been a longtime resident of Sandy Harbor. We all know her character. She'd never run away."

Antoinette Chloe stood. "I sure as hell won't run. I'm not guilty of this and I hope that the Sandy Harbor Sheriff's Department will find the real killer soon. The jail is pretty comfortable, thanks to Sheriff Brisco, but I have things to do. I have to emcee the Miss Salmon pageant, and I can't wait to see the final routine that some of the contestants have worked hard to learn." She smiled. "Sadie, the costumes that your sewing committee made for the tableau are fabulous."

"Thanks, Antoinette Chloe," Sadie replied, still transcribing every word.

"Antoinette Chloe, please don't interrupt."

"For heaven's sake, Marty, this is my life you all are talking about. I'm not just going to sit back and say nothing to defend myself!"

The judge cleared his throat. "I've taken all the comments into consideration, and I'm setting bail at three million dollars cash or bond." He slammed down the glass. "Sorry, Antoinette Chloe, but I have to remand you back to the county jail until you post bail."

"Martin Butler, how could you? Don't expect me to vote for you on Election Day."

"Understood." He slammed the glass down on the table with such force, I expected it to break. "This court is adjourned."

I heard Janice tell ACB that she'd visit her later in the day and figure out her assets.

I saw Ty nod to the judge. He didn't get his wish for no bail, but the bail was set so high, it was just like no bail.

ACB flip-flopped out of the bar so quickly that Lou Rutledge had to run to keep up with her.

"Trixie!"

I hustled to get to her, yet was mindful not to get too close.

"Yes, Antoinette Chloe?"

"Trixie . . . please." There were tears pooling in her eyes. "I really, really want to be the emcee of the pageant. It means everything to me. I don't want to be in jail when the pageant is on. After all, this whole thing was my brainchild. I wanted it to be a nice fund-raiser for the town and . . ." She gulped, then hiccuped.

I felt awful. My heart was breaking along with

hers. "I'll visit you in jail later today. And we'll come up with a plan."

"Will you come right now?" She was so anxious that all the color had drained from her face and she was shaking like a leaf; I was worried about her health. All over a beauty contest. But that was ACB for you.

"I'll follow your car. I mean, the cop car."

"Thanks so much, Trixie."

In the back of the cop car, I saw her dab her eyes with the sleeves of her muumuu.

Then I noticed Toxic Waste by the Bubbly Clean Laundromat observing ACB leave. I wondered if he had been in the back of the bar during the arraignment. If he had been, I hadn't noticed him, but, then again, I'd been intent on watching the proceedings.

In the back of my mind, I filed his presence under *interesting*.

I stalled long enough to watch Toxic. Maybe he was doing laundry at the Bubbly Clean, and I was jumping to conclusions.

But I wasn't. He hopped on his motorcycle and headed in the direction of the point.

What a snoop!

I followed ACB to jail.

Ty was sitting at his desk with his feet on the top and was on the phone as usual. When he saw me standing there, he motioned for me to come over and take a seat.

I stared out the window until he got off the phone.

"That was painful to watch," I said. "I feel so sorry for her."

"She's fine. I got her a cell-phone charger, and she's burning up the cell tower now. That woman sure can talk."

"Ty, dress rehearsal for the pageant is in a couple of days. She has to practice being an emcee. Believe me, she has to practice."

"Trixie, a man is dead and you're worried about Miss Salmon?"

"I'm worried about Antoinette Chloe. I'm sure you saw the letter that the ADA gave to Judge Butler—the one listing the value of her assets. Did it add up to three million bucks?"

"No. Not even close."

"What about me?" I asked.

"What about you?"

"Do you think that the point is worth three million? The whole thing: the Silver Bullet, the Victorian, the eleven cottages, the thousand feet of prime lakefront?"

"Probably."

"Then I'm going to bail her out. Or, rather, Aunt Stella is going to bail her out—everything is still in her name. I know you want to keep ACB under protective custody, but has anyone tried to kill her?"

"Not yet. That's why protective custody is working. Although I did see Toxic Waste hanging around the Bubbly Clean. He was also in the back of the courtroom. I wonder why he's so interested in the case. I had Lou ask him if he'd voluntarily submit to a pat down, and he did. He was clean."

"I saw him, too, Ty. Oh my! Do you think he might've taken a shot at ACB, or something else?"

"Just trying to be careful."

"Ty, can't you just be her bodyguard while she's doing the pageant?"

"You know, all three of us have other duties. We just don't have enough time to be guard dogs for ACB."

"Then I'll do it," I said.

"You?"

"Why not me? You do it when you can, and if you're called away somewhere, I can dial nine-one-one if I run into trouble."

"It might be too late for nine-one-one."

"C'mon, Ty. Help me out here. I'll give you free meals for a week."

He chuckled. "I know I'm going to regret this, but all right. We'll both keep an eye on ACB."

I jumped up and impulsively gave him a hug around the neck. He smelled so good, like pine and cedar. Not that I noticed. "Oh, Ty! You're such a doll! I'm going to call Aunt Stella right now. I hope I can get hold of her. She was going to take one of those paddleboat tours out of Missouri or New Orleans or someplace watery like that about now."

"And here I went to the trouble of keeping ACB in here. Now I'm helping you bail her out. What the hell is wrong with me?"

"You secretly want to make the first annual Miss Salmon pageant a success."

"Oh yeah. That's it," he said sarcastically.

I stepped away from his desk and called Aunt Stella. No answer, so I left a message. Then I went to see ACB.

Her cell was looking pretty good. I'd venture to say that the Sandy Harbor Jail had the best women's accommodations of any jail in the United States.

"Trixie, what am I going to do? That damned Marty Butler! I remember him with a face full of acne, chasing Olga Baumgartner. She wouldn't give him the time of day."

"I'll get you out of here, Antoinette Chloe. I already put in a call to Aunt Stella. She's the one that actually has to bail you out, since everything is in her name."

She burst into tears. "Thank you."

"Hopefully everything will fall into place soon."

"Bless you." She sniffed.

"I'm going to go now. I have a feeling that I should get home and keep an eye on my squatters."

I rolled into my usual parking space and saw Chad Dodson entertaining in front of his motor home. About a dozen of the Roving Rubbers were there, and they all seemed to be drinking. Chad was pouring champagne into the flutes of a gaggle of female Rubbers, while others were pulling longnecks from a cooler.

Music was blaring so loud, it felt like it was going to shatter all the glass within a three-mile radius. I might be a party pooper, but I didn't like the looks of that party in the making. It wasn't even noon yet.

Tent Town seemed like it was jumping, too. There were Rubbers in groups, also drinking. And more loud rock music was playing.

This wasn't good. Not for the fishermen, not for

my customers at the diner, and certainly not for the Miss Salmon contestants, who needed their beauty sleep.

First, I marched over to Chad Dodson. "Mr. Dodson, end this . . . ah . . . party, please. It's too noisy, and I have guests and customers."

He gave me his usual mocking smile. "I can turn the music down. How's that?" He lifted his hand into the air and I saw that he was holding a remote. He lowered the music all of two decibels.

"That's not enough," I said.

He pushed a button. It barely made a difference.

"Shut it off completely, please."

There was a collective groan and at least two called me a party pooper.

Such tough talk from a group of chefs.

I waited, hands on hips, until Chad turned off the music.

"Better?" he said.

"Yes." I walked toward Tent Town, then changed my mind and turned back. "If you don't like it, you can find another place to park your rig."

"I'll have to go to Canada to find a spot."

"Well, what's stopping you?" I shrugged. "Oh, that's right. You have to stay in our little village for further questioning."

I smiled, and this time *my* smile was smarmy. His disappeared completely.

"And I heard that your pal had her bail set at three million dollars."

"Oh? How did you hear that?"

"A little bird told me."

Toxic Waste. He had been there. But why did he find it necessary to tell Chad Dodson?

Were they in cahoots together? My suspicions from the other night when I was taking out the trash were definitely confirmed now.

I turned and stomped over to Tent Town, heading straight for Toxic Waste's abode. I ran into Mad Dog first. "Where's the leader of the pack?"

"I don't know. Something you want me to tell him?"

"Tell him to turn down the music. If I can hear it, it's too loud. And tell him clean the place up and take the trash to the Dumpsters. My staff isn't waiting on you." The wind shifted. "And call to have the toilets emptied, for heaven's sake. And if Mr. Waste or anyone else doesn't like it, tell them to hop on their bikes and head out. I hear that there are a couple of spots in Canada."

"I'll take care of it."

"Thank you, Mr. Dog."

By the time I got to the door of my house, the music was off and a couple of Rubbers were emptying trash cans of their liners and walking toward the Dumpster.

I'd never been blessed with children, but it's good to know that my fictional children might have listened to me. After all, millionaires and biker-chefs did what I told them.

The house was blessedly silent.

In the kitchen was a note from Ty saying that he'd taken Blondie for a jog. *He sure got here quickly!*

That reminded me to give Aunt Stella another call.

"Trixie, how good to hear your voice! I was going to call you back after my classes, but I have a little time now. Now, what is it you want me to do? Bail out Antoinette Chloe?"

"Would you please, Aunt Stella? She's so pathetic sitting in jail. I'd do it, but everything I almost . . . sort of . . . kind of . . . own is in your name."

She sighed. "Antoinette Chloe is an eccentric dresser, but she's not a murderer."

"I know."

"I can't bail her out, dear. No. I can't," Aunt Stella said.

I had felt for sure that Aunt Stella would come through. A feeling of hopelessness hit me like a blast of cold. "I understand."

"It's not that I don't want to, but I did sign everything over to you," she said.

"But—"

"Trixie, all the papers transferring everything to you have been signed by me and are sitting in the gray file cabinet in the office marked MISCELLA-NEOUS. Just sign them and file them with the county clerk. You might have to pay some fees, but it shouldn't be all that much."

"Really?"

"Really! Remember how you didn't want me to transfer ownership to you until you paid everything in full?"

"I remember."

"Well, I still did the paperwork, because I knew

you'd pay me eventually, and no sense sending everything to Florida, so I did the next best thing. They're all legal and ready. Just sign 'em and file 'em, sweetie."

"You're a gem, Aunt Stella."

"So are you, Trixie, but are you sure you want to risk the point on Antoinette Chloe? She's awfully flighty."

"I'd put my money on her."

"Then sign the papers," she said. "Gray file cabinet. Call me if you need anything else, Trixie. I have to go to my Zumba class. Then tai chi and qigong."

"What's qigong?"

"I don't have a clue, but when I find out, I'll let you know."

"One more thing: Did you take your cruise?"

"My friend Vivian, who booked the trip, got it all wrong. It was a paddle-wheel boat, and it never left the dock, but I won two hundred bucks on the slots."

I laughed. "Talk to you later. Have fun with your classes and qigong-ing!"

"I will. Bye, now."

Hurrying to my office, I found the gray file cabinet and found a file marked EVERYTHING INCLUDING THE KITCHEN SINK.

In the folder was a thick packet of papers, survey maps, and whatnot. I saw by the light-blue paper attached that said Janice Malloy was Aunt Stella's attorney and Anthony Ricelli was the surveyor from Syracuse.

I signed under Aunt Stella's name and left the

papers on the kitchen table, ready to go to the county clerk's office.

But before I left for again, I needed to see if Aunt Stella had a nice purse upstairs in the attic that would go with the dress.

Going upstairs, I passed ACB's bedroom. I really should clean it, maybe change the bed, for her release.

In the attic, I placed a call to Janice Malloy. I got her voice mail, but I left a message telling her how I was going to file the papers that would make me the owner of the point.

"So, I'm going to bail Antoinette Chloe out. Tell me how."

I looked out the window as I was talking. There was a turret with windows on four sides where I remembered playing Cinderella with Susie. This was our castle.

Seeing two people way off in the distance, almost to ACB's land, I wondered who they were, and guessed that it was Toxic Waste with none other than Aileen Shubert.

At least they weren't rolling in the grass together again, or maybe I had missed that part, thank goodness.

Even though I'd had a little talk with Aileen and she'd vowed to adhere to the rules, she hadn't. Why wasn't she up at the Silver Bullet with the other ladies having lunch?

I found a pretty black, glittery purse that would go perfect with Aunt Stella's dress. Great. Now I didn't have to stop at the Spend A Buck, but I did need panty hose.

But what should I do with Aileen?

Nothing. The pageant would be over soon.

Thinking of Aileen got me thinking of Toxic Waste. *What a two-timer! Here he said that he was getting back with his girlfriend, Leslie McDermott, but he can't seem to stay away from Aileen.*

And Aileen must be attracted to bad-boy biker-chefs who owned Bavarian restaurants.

I could see that Aileen and Toxic were walking away from each other. She jogged to the Big House, and Toxic meandered to Tent Town.

I rushed out of the attic and walked down the hall to my room. I decided it was time to try on the dress. It was okay in the boobs, and it fell nicely to midcalf. I loved how it looked, especially the copper-colored sequins on the bodice. Antoinette Chloe's sequin obsession must be rubbing off on me.

The purse worked with the dress. My black flats matched, too. Hooray!

I heard footsteps down the hall. *Must be Aileen.* I opened my door and stuck my head out.

Her hand flew to her heart. "Oh, Trixie! I didn't know you were here." She oozed guilt like my corned beef sandwiches oozed corned beef.

"Obviously. What have you been doing?"

"Nothing. Just taking a walk. It's such a beautiful day."

"Yes. It's a beautiful day for fall."

We were making small talk, and I could tell that Aileen was ready to bolt. She wouldn't look me in the eye and she was squirming like a worm.

"Where are the rest of the ladies?" I asked.

"One of the committee members arranged a

pontoon boat tour of the coast. That's where they are. On a boat tour."

"Why on earth didn't you go?"

She shifted on her feet. "I get seasick."

"Gee, that's too bad," I said, not wanting to tell her that the Miss Salmon winner should embrace water sports.

"How did Antoinette Chloe's court appearance go?" Aileen changed the subject.

"She's going to make bail."

"Really?"

"Really," I said.

Her eyes sparkled. She seemed to really be happy that ACB would be out of jail. Well, any friend of ACB was a friend of mine.

"I gotta go, Trixie. I have studying to do."

"You're in school?"

"Graduate school. I'm in the business-management program at Syracuse University."

"Fabulous," I said, wishing that I'd gone to grad school for my business degree, or maybe culinary school. I still want to do that someday. "Well, I don't want to keep you, Aileen. Go and study!"

But I didn't believe her for a New York minute. Not at all. Especially since I didn't remember any of the Miss Salmon applicants saying that they'd gone to my alma mater. So, once I arrived at the courthouse, I pulled into a nice parking space and called Syracuse University. Eventually I got ahold of my friend from first grade, Lorraine Fletcher, who, as luck would have it, worked there.

Lorraine said that the graduate school of business management never heard of Aileen.

Surprise, surprise!

I wondered why she lied. *To make herself shine so she'd make a better Miss Salmon contestant? She knows I'm a judge, and maybe she thought that being in a graduate program at SU would impress me because I had a football banner in my living room. Go, Orange!*

But I wasn't impressed.

After going from office to office at the courthouse like a steel ball in a pinball machine, I finally got the papers filed.

Then I met the bail bondsman in front of the courthouse by the war memorial. As I waited, I read the names of all the residents of Sandy Harbor who had served in various wars—starting with the Revolutionary War and ending with the Gulf War. They'd soon have to add Afghanistan. I said a few prayers, and noticed a man approaching. It was Shaun Williamson, who ran the florist shop, Buds and Blooms, on the corner of Tulip Terrace and First Street.

"Shaun, you're a bondsman, too?"

"I am."

It must be some kind of Sandy Harbor code that everyone must have two different occupations.

"Well, okay." I took a deep breath. "I want to put up the point. Hopefully you'll think everything is worth three million bucks so I can get Antoinette Chloe out."

"You really want to put up the point?"

"Not particularly, but it's the only way to get her out, so write the bond, please."

He knew what Aunt Stella had owned. He'd been over at the Silver Bullet enough times. Besides, he had grown up here.

Shaun Williamson, bail bondsman and florist, opened his briefcase and pulled out a packet of legal-looking papers in the smallest font known to humanity. I pulled out my glasses from my purse.

We walked over to a picnic table and sat down. I waited for him to start.

"When Janice Malloy called me, I looked at the survey maps of everything on the point, priced similar properties, should I have to sell it all, and I can absolutely bond you for three million."

I broke out in a sweat in spite of the cool weather. "Sell it all?"

"If Antoinette Chloe doesn't appear for her court dates or absconds, I can sell your property to reclaim the money that I spent insuring her release, or I can keep it."

"Wow."

"Usually, people put up their own homes and property, but Antoinette's holdings aren't worth three million bucks. Although I'd love to get my hands on her waterfront land."

"Shaun, don't you think Antoinette Chloe will appear in court?"

He shrugged. "I don't know if I'd stick around with a murder charge hanging over my head like a guillotine."

"Well, she would. She'd want to prove that she didn't kill her boyfriend. Besides, she's lived here forever, and her business is here."

"It's your call." He leafed through the papers. "Sign here, here, and here. Initial that this is your signature. Sign that those are your initials."

Sign my name where I initialed? This was more legal than my divorce!

"I'll walk it over to the sheriff's department." He checked his watch. "Ty will be there. I think he's on office duty. He'll process her out."

"I'm going over to the Spend A Buck. Then I'll be over to the jail to pick up Antoinette Chloe and drive her to my house."

Shaun laughed. "While it's still your house!"

"Knock it off, Shaun. You are about as funny as being laid off at Christmas."

He gave me a salute; then he just about skipped in the direction of the jail. I walked in the other direction to buy a pair of panty hose and visit Antoinette Chloe.

Chapter 11

*T*y leaned back in his chair. "Sorry, Trixie, but apparently the county clerk has to do a bunch of things to your paperwork before he can put the point in your name. Shaun went over to the courthouse to yell at everyone, but they'll probably let it go in one ear and out the other. He's known for his hissy fits."

"And inconsiderate jokes."

Ty grinned and looked way too smug.

"C'mon. You said you'd be her bodyguard. Can't you make a couple of calls, turn on your Texas cowboy charm, and speed things up?"

He raised his blue eyes to the ceiling and mumbled—something he did all the time. Ty's a very religious man. *Ha!*

He picked up the phone and started punching in numbers.

"Ty, can I see Antoinette Chloe? I'd like to tell her that she might not get out today."

He picked up a metal mess of keys from the top drawer of his desk and separated two of them.

"The small one is for the entry door. The bigger one is for the cell."

"You're trusting me?"

"Sure, but I'll be calling in some favors from you. Like your fried chicken."

I laughed. I loved to cook for someone who enjoyed it.

As I entered the cellblock, I saw Antoinette Chloe sitting on a rocking chair, crying.

"Oh, sweetie. Are you okay?"

She sniffed. "I'm just feeling sorry for myself."

"Don't. I got Aunt Stella to sign over the point to me in my name. A couple of county departments have to do a couple of things to the paperwork first; then you'll be bailed out. Oh, and Ty's helping to speed things up."

"You put the point up for me?"

"Yes. I told you I was going to. Too bad I had to deal with Shaun Williamson."

"He's a punk."

"Yes, I know, but he's the punk who's going to help get you out of here."

"*Bueno!* Let's go." Whenever ACB was stressed, she always spoke in another language.

"Not so fast," I said.

"Shall I pack up my things?" she asked.

"Yes. Absolutely, but I thought that you were going to leave some of these things for the next inmate."

"Not all of it."

I did not want to haul all of her stuff out of here, not now anyway. I'd just moved her to the Big House not too long ago.

"Can you just pack up what you absolutely need for now?"

"Of course."

She removed some muumuus that were hanging on the bars. "I'll need these."

She went to a big plastic cart on wheels and tapped it with a finger. "My fascinators and hats are in here. Oh, and I'll need more underwear and flip-flops—just the sequined ones. And I have another cabinet with all my makeup, too."

A five-drawer cart filled with makeup?

"You really need all this stuff?"

"I might. I don't know until I'm putting an outfit together."

We rolled two plastic carts as far as the hallway, when Ty entered.

"What's going on?" Ty asked.

"We're moving ACB out of Heartbreak Hotel."

"You can't touch a thing until she's bailed out," Ty instructed.

We moved the cabinets back into her cell.

His phone rang, and he answered it. "Deputy Brisco."

There were a lot of *okay*s and *right*s and *thank you, darlin'*s but eventually, he stopped talking and turned to us. "Okay, now you can officially leave."

As ACB was settling back in, I looked out the windows for Ty, who was supposed to be protecting ACB.

Then I saw Vern McCoy in his unmarked silver-green Prius. As my cheating ex, Deputy Doug, used to say, he should really patrol the perimeter. There were four entrances into the Big House.

But I got distracted when I saw today's issue of the *Lure*. It seemed that while I was in court, Aileen had entered the salmon derby and had come really close to winning. She caught the third-largest salmon of the day.

Mr. Farnsworth, the owner of the bait shop next door, had taken her out on his guide boat.

Joan Paris even printed her picture in the *Lure*. It showed Aileen with her white blond hair, shorter-than-short shorts, halter top, and magnificent tan, holding up her third-place salmon as several hulky fishermen gathered around her.

Where were her shoes? More importantly, where were her ugly green rubber waders? Even better, what happened to her story that she got seasick on the water?

Another lie, Aileen? Looks like you don't get any more seasick than I do.

As I was sitting on the porch, Aileen came around the corner, saw what I was reading, and giggled about the picture to the other girls.

"My father taught me how to fish," she said.

"And you bait the hook?" asked Betsy Dyson.

"Of course I do." She tossed her hair.

"What about cleaning them?" I asked.

"Oh, sure. I clean them, too."

"You're going to have to prove that one, Aileen. Right, girls?" I was egging her on just to prove that she was a liar in front of all the girls.

I hurried to the basement to find one of Uncle Porky's fillet knives.

Oh! There was an empty hook on the Peg-Board where another knife should have been. I remembered four fillet knives hanging from those hooks. Only three were left.

Maybe Ty had borrowed it. I did give him blanket permission to help himself to any of Uncle Porky's fishing things. I reminded myself to ask him when he stopped by later.

I grabbed one of the other fillet knives and went back upstairs. Then I walked across the lawn to one of the fish-cleaning stations and asked one of the men if I could borrow a couple of salmon, and when he said yes, I motioned for Aileen to come over.

The other pageant girls came with her.

"Okay, Aileen. I'd love to see how you fillet."

Joan Paris happened to be nearby, taking photos of everyone's catches. I motioned for her to join us.

"This could be another photo op for you, Joan."

"I'm always looking for those."

When I handed Aileen one of Uncle Porky's knives, she hesitated for a second, then took it and stared at it for another moment.

Then she got right to work, gutting and filleting the fish like an old pro. She handled the knife like an expert, posing for pictures and tossing her hair.

The fishermen who were watching cheered her on, and she filleted three salmon in no time.

When Joan stopped taking pictures, Aileen stopped smiling. Bored with the whole thing, she announced that she was going to go jogging. Some of the other girls decided to join her.

And I decided to do a little jogging of my own, over to the diner to get something to eat. I was so busy trying to find a way to bail out Antoinette Chloe that I didn't remember to eat anything. Which just went to show how stressed-out I'd been—I never, ever, never miss a meal.

Well, I didn't really jog. I walked a little faster than usual because I was hungry. On the way, I called ACB and asked her if she wanted me to bring her anything.

"A bacon club," she said.

"You mean a bacon, lettuce, and tomato club?"

"No. Just bacon."

"Got it," I said, thinking how I might add a B-B-B club to my menu.

"And a chocolate milk shake."

"Okay."

"And maybe one of Sarah Stolfus's cherry hand pies. No, make that two hand pies."

"You got it. See you soon."

Ty was just walking into the diner as I was. "Let's get a booth, Ty. I want to share information with you."

"Okay."

There was one last booth, way in the back. I slid onto the red vinyl bench seat.

Chelsea hurried over to us.

"Chels, I'll have a bowl of split pea soup and a grilled cheese and ham sandwich on white," I said.

"I'll have the same, but I'd like tomato soup instead of pea, and a Reuben on dark rye with coleslaw instead of the ham and cheese."

He was just so funny—not!

Chelsea doubled over with laughter. She was

overdoing it a little, but like every other woman within a thousand-mile radius of Sandy Harbor, she had the hots for Ty.

I didn't. I had a wall surrounding me that I'd built brick by brick. And it was completely cop-proof.

Well, maybe I could blast a section off for Ty.

No, I couldn't.

Yes, I could.

"So, what do you want to tell me?" he asked, snapping me out of my reverie.

"I wanted to get your advice on one of the Miss Salmon contestants, Aileen Shubert."

"Do I know her?" Ty asked.

"She's the one with the picture-perfect blond hair with white streaks. She's tall, beautiful, has a toothy white smile, and is Miss Personality and Miss Congeniality combined."

"Real short white shorts with a fringe on the bottom and pockets that hang lower than her hems? Did she have an aqua tube top on today, along with gold hoop earrings? And she never wears shoes and has bright pink nail polish on her toes with a sparkly ankle bracelet?"

I rolled my eyes. "Oh, so you haven't noticed her?"

"No. I haven't noticed her at all."

"I can tell." I grinned. "But anyway, I think she lied on her Miss Salmon application."

"That's a crime punishable by life in prison!"

"Ty, what I'm trying to say is that I think Aileen Shubert is intentionally trying to fool the pageant committee."

"Now you're talking. That's the electric chair."

I took a deep breath. He wasn't taking me seriously.

"She said she was going to the graduate school of business management at SU. And, well, they don't know her. I didn't remember anything on her application about her taking graduate courses at Syracuse, so, for the heck of it, I called a friend of mine who works there."

"Trixie, it's probably nothing more than some beauty queen trying to look good and win the pageant."

"Yeah, but she'll win a whopping five hundred dollars and a ride in Hal Manning's relic of a car at the front of the Salmon Parade. And I won't stand for that."

"All right, all right. I'll run a record check on Aileen Shubert. Give me her date of birth from her questionnaire."

"It's February 21, 1986. I remember that distinctly. It's the same date as a friend's birthday."

He pulled out a little notebook from his shirt pocket and wrote it down with the stub of a pencil.

"Will you let me know what you find out?"

"I doubt it," he said.

"You know, I give you everything I find out, but you don't give me any information at all."

"Trixie, you know I can't give you information from a current investigation."

I knew that. I did. However, when the good Lord passed out patience, I got out of line because the line was moving too slowly.

"Okay, Ty. In the spirit of me telling you *everything* and you telling me *nothing*, here's some major information: One of Uncle Porky's four fillet knives is missing from the basement. Did the murder weapon look like this?"

I plopped the knife on the table.

He hesitated, but I shot him a look that would wither a dozen roses. "Uh, yes, it did."

"Uncle Porky's have unique handles—ivory. They're probably illegal now."

"They are, but a lot of the old ones have ivory handles. Nick's fillet knives, for instance, have ivory handles. And so do Sal's."

"Do you know whose collection the murder weapon came from?" I asked.

"I can't tell you that."

"Oh yes, you absolutely can."

"No. I can't. I'll have to have this one compared to the one we found wrapped in Antoinette Chloe's Easter fascinator. Do you know if all of your uncle Porky's knives looked alike?"

"I—I don't know. I can give you the other ones, too."

"Good."

Ty didn't have to tell me whose collection the murder weapon came from. It was Uncle Porky's. Somehow the murderer snuck into the basement and stole a knife.

Our meals arrived, and we stopped talking about the case for a while—just a little while. Then I made a U-turn back to the investigation.

"Ty, when are you planning you let the Rubbers go? And how about Chad Dodson?"

"I'm getting there. Give me a couple of days."

"I don't want you to let them go! You need to find one of them guilty, so ACB will be off the hook."

"Trix, you stick to cooking, and I'll stick to my job."

"But tomorrow's dress-rehearsal day."

"I know. And I'm on ACB watch. I can't think of anything more fun than the Miss Salmon dress rehearsal." He made a painful face, then grinned. "But Aileen and all the other gorgeous girls will be there."

"Along with the five Wheelchair Grannies from the Sandy Harbor Golden Age Apartments."

He smiled. "I don't age discriminate."

It was my turn to roll my eyes. Was I doomed to banter with Ty Brisco until the end of my days? But I had to admit that I enjoyed his company immensely.

Ty insisted on paying for his meal, but I pried the check out of his fingers and tore it up.

"Leave Chelsea a nice, big tip, and we'll call it even," I said.

We parted ways, and I went into the kitchen to thank Juanita for the fabulous meal.

"Juanita, the pea soup and grilled cheese and ham sandwich were delicious, and Ty loved the tomato soup and Reuben. And the little garnishes you do are adorable."

"Thanks, *amiga*."

Other restaurants put a tomato slice on a lettuce leaf and call it a garnish. We try to make the garnish edible and unique.

Juanita is all about carrot curls, radish roses, and zigzagged cucumber chunks. In season, she'd add rosemary sprigs or edible flowers that looked like orchids. She was very creative and had taught Chelsea how to dress up plates with garnish.

Juanita has taught me, too. I'd found a book at the library's book sale about making garnishes, but I haven't had a chance to read it. She would probably like it.

"The kitchen looks absolutely fabulous," I told Juanita.

"You did most of it the other day. I just kept on going, and so did Cindy."

"Then we all did a good job. Anything you need Juanita? Anything I can do to help?"

"*Nada.* I'm good." She paused for a second, then whispered to me. "I see you sitting with Deputy Ty. He's a good man, Trixie. And very handsome."

My mouth went dry. "*Chica*, are you trying to match-make?"

"*Sí.*" She peeked at me through her long black eyelashes. "You two make a nice couple."

I shook my head. "He's not my type."

And I'm not his type. I thought of what he said about Aileen Shubert and her short shorts. *Not my thing at all.* However, I was planning on stunning him with my sequined dress—well, Aunt Stella's sequined dress.

No! I was wearing the elegant dress for myself, not for any transplanted cowboy from Houston.

What was I thinking?

I was thinking that I should get my hair colored

or low-lighted. My blond hair looked a little washed-out. And maybe some white streaks in it would jazz it up. Wait. Aileen had white streaks, and I didn't want to look like her—not that I could. So I'd skip the streaks, and go with the low lights and one of those new cuts with lots of layers.

"See you later, Juanita."

"Adios."

I called Harbor Hair before I forgot. They had a cancellation and could take me in fifteen minutes. Other than that appointment, they were all booked with Miss Salmon contestants and couldn't fit me in until after the pageant.

"I'll be there. Fifteen minutes."

I delivered to Antoinette Chloe her B-B-B, chocolate milk shake, and two cherry hand pies. When I arrived, she said that she was cleaning her room.

I didn't see any difference.

Antoinette Chloe shook her head. "I can't believe that my glittery pink fingernail is gone from the set. So is my motorcycle earring that I wore on my last ride with Nick. My favorite fascinator and the little yellow bunny are gone. That was the cutest bunny. I remember putting the hat and bunny on the windowsill. I was going to glue the bunny back on." She reached for the take-out container. "Ty said that I'd get everything back when the case is over."

She sat down on the edge of the bed, and the old springs groaned in protest. Popping open the white foam container, she took a bite of her B-B-B club.

"This is good," she said. "Lots of mayonnaise."

Yikes.

"And the milk shake is nice and thick," she said.

"Uh, Antoinette Chloe, I'm going to get my hair cut and dyed at Harbor Hair. Are you going to be okay here alone?"

"Of course. I'm going to bed early."

"Do you mind if I take your van? I'm about of gas and I don't have time to stop along the way." I checked my watch. I had to get moving.

"Of course." She reached across her bed and handed me a fistful of key chains with one or two keys attached somewhere.

As I left, I knocked on Vern McCoy's car. Oops, I forgot to bring him a sandwich. That was thoughtless of me.

"Vern, call the Silver Bullet and have Clyde or Max bring you a sandwich or something. It's on me. Oh, and Antoinette Chloe said that she's going to bed early, but don't believe her. She always changes her mind when she thinks of something better to do. I'm going to get my hair done."

"Okay, thanks, but I don't want to blow my cover."

"When Ty relieves you, go to the diner, then."

"I will. Thanks."

It was dark before I drove downtown. I was driving fifty-five on the highway as posted, but high beams glared at me from the car behind me, blinding me.

What the hell? I was going the speed limit.

I felt a bump from behind, and instead of slow-ing down like I should have, I sped up. The car behind me gunned it and hit me from behind again.

What a psycho!

My heart was thumping in my chest, and I was barely breathing. I couldn't take my eyes off the rearview mirror. The car bumped into me again.

I screamed, "Stop it!"

I turned onto Route 13. The speed limit on Route 13 was thirty. As I slowed down to thirty, the car bumped me again. I pulled into Mrs. Green's driveway and waited. If the car pulled in behind me, I was going to spray him or her with my Save A Buck Evening Melody body mist.

The car kept on going, and by the glow of the streetlights, I could see that it looked like a red T-Bird. Chad Dodson's red T-Bird.

He could have killed me!

Shaking, I drove to Harbor Hair, even though I'd rather just drive home and have an iced-tea glass full of lime green Kool-Aid and a glazed donut and relax.

However, I had to press on, or I'd never get another appointment.

But when I saw Chad Dodson again, he was going to get a piece of my mind. Then I was going to kick him off my property. I didn't particularly care where he went either, or if Ty would have to track him like Davy Crockett.

Almost two hours later, and after way too much Harbor Hair chatter, I looked gorgeous. Though my head was about to explode from my near-death experience on the highway, the chemicals, and all the gossip. I was ready to go home.

Rachael Diamond, the owner of Harbor Hair, walked me out, still talking. "I'm so glad that Antoinette Chloe is out of jail. We were all going to pitch in and bail her out, but there was no way this place is worth three million. I'm glad you got her out, Trixie."

"How did you know it was me? Shaun Williamson?"

"Oh yeah. He's the biggest gossip this side of the Mississippi." She held up a large coffee can. "We also have a pool as to who killed Nick. Do you want to place a bet? The choices are: Sal, Toxic Waste, Chad Dodson, Antoinette Chloe, or a Sandy Harbor resident other than Antoinette Chloe or Sal."

"Who's the Vegas favorite?" I asked, just wondering how public feeling was leaning.

"Chad Dodson. Everyone feels that he has the most to gain with the insurance thing. With Nick dead, Sal in jail, and Antoinette Chloe heading there if she's convicted, he's the logical choice."

"Even though Chad's rolling in dough?" I knew that his family disowned him, so that was a trick question.

"His family is rolling in dough, not Chad. Rumor has it that his family disowned him," Rachael said. "But Antoinette Chloe is running a close second. You know, that sausage-stabbing incident at the Silver Bullet propelled her up the chart."

Wow! The gossip at Harbor Hair was almost better than my entire investigation so far. I should hang around here more often.

"Who's your source?" I asked.

"You know I can't give away sources. Then we wouldn't get any information."

"Do you cut Vern McCoy's hair?"

"Why . . . yes."

How about Lou Rutledge's hair?"

"Uh . . . sure. Lou comes here."

"Ty Brisco's?"

"No. He goes to Joe the barber."

"I see."

I stuffed a tip in her right hand and a five in her left hand. "Put me down for five on Chad Dodson."

"Will do, Trixie. See you at the pageant."

When I got home, I marched right up to Chad Dodson's mega motor home and knocked. His T-Bird was still in place, like it had never left.

He opened the door. "What?"

"What do you mean bumping my car from behind? I could have been killed!"

"You're going to have to translate that sentence for me."

"Chad, don't mess with me. I'm not in the mood."

"Nor am I." He yawned—it was a phony yawn, like I was boring him. I wanted to grab him by his golf shirt and pull him down the stairs.

"You bumped my car—well, it was actually Antoinette Chloe's van—with your red T-Bird at least four times on Route 3 and Route 13, and don't deny it."

"My car never left here tonight—ask anyone— and without a doubt I wouldn't ruin a vintage car. Now, is there anything else?"

I mumbled a few blue words as I walked to his car to examine his front bumper. I didn't see any scratches, but it was shadowy in spite of the lights around the parking lot.

"Well?" he said.

"I'll be back, and while I'm gone, you'd better make plans to clear off my land."

"I would, my dear Trixie, but I can't. Your cowboy friend, the deputy sheriff, stopped by tonight and reminded me not to leave again. He said he wanted to talk to me again and wanted me where he could find me. What do you make of that?"

"I don't know, Mr. Dodson, but I'll tell you what I'm hoping."

"And what's that?"

"I'm hoping that he arrests you. After all, I have a five-dollar bet riding on you."

Chapter 12

I found Ty sitting on my porch, the one facing the lake. He was surrounded by the pageant contestants living in my house and the notorious Antoinette Chloe, murder suspect.

"Trixie, your hair looks fabulous!" ACB said. "All you need is one of my fascinators to jazz it up."

"Thanks, Antoinette Chloe, but I never wear hats. I look hideous in them."

Ty's eyes twinkled. "Your hair does look nice."

My mouth suddenly went dry.

"Where did you get it done?" ACB asked. "Harbor Hair?"

"Yes. It's the only place in town other than Joe the barber's. Two-thirds of the Sandy Harbor Sheriff's Department goes to Harbor Hair." I shot a "your deputies blab too much" look at Ty, but he was too busy flirting with Aileen to pick it up on it.

Jane O'Clemmons got up and sat cross-legged on the floor of the porch, at Ty's feet. "Take my chair, Trixie."

"Thanks, Jane."

ACB put a hand on the arm of my Adirondack chair. She wore at least four pounds of bracelets on that wrist and the same poundage on the other side—for balance.

"Trixie, we all were thinking. When the other contestants arrive for the dress rehearsal, how about if we have a little reception for them so everyone can meet?" Antoinette Chloe said.

"What a nice idea."

"We were thinking that we could have it at the auditorium in front of the stage. I'll arrange everything with Fingers."

"I'm working tonight," I said. "I'll make cookies."

"That's very generous of you, sweetie. You've done so much already for everyone." She started to cry.

I patted her hand. "Antoinette Chloe, dry your eyes. Be happy. Our first pageant will be a success, with all the hard work you did."

"That the committee did."

"Let's hear it for Antoinette Chloe, Trixie, and the committee!" Aileen said in her best cheerleader voice.

There was a round of applause and cheers. Even Ty joined in.

He sure was enjoying his role as a cop surrounded by beautiful young women. Oh, wait, he *was* a cop surrounded by beautiful young women.

ACB and I included!

At least we were young compared to the Wheelchair Grannies of the Sandy Harbor Golden Age Apartments.

And that got me thinking. "Antoinette Chloe, how are the Wheelchair Grannies going to get to and from the auditorium?"

"Bonnie Hoff has a wheelchair lift on her van. She's going to transport them."

"Great. Anything I should do?" I asked, holding my breath. I didn't know if I could add one more thing to my already very full plate.

"No. Just show up to judge. I'll have the score sheets there."

"Who are the other judges?" I asked ACB.

"My ex-friend Marty Butler, Kathy Prellman from the car repair, Lois Valton from the candle shop, and Rachael Diamond from Harbor Hair."

"Five of us?"

"Well, we don't want ties."

The girls were getting excited. I could tell by the high-pitched conversations and giggles.

"What about you, Miss Shubert? You seem pretty calm," Ty said. "Are you excited?"

"Of course."

"But you must be used to competing in pageants."

"Each one is new and different."

"How?" I asked.

"This one is very small-town. The last one I did, in Vegas, had more hype and glamor," she said, looking at her nails. "I won that one," Aileen said.

"What was it called?" one of the girls asked, just as I was about to.

"Uh . . . Miss Casino," Aileen said.

"Which one?" Ty asked.

She winked one of her deep-blue eyes. "Why, all of them."

ACB grunted as she rose to her feet. "Ladies, I think we should all head up to bed and get our beauty sleep. Tomorrow is going to be a jam-packed day."

There were nods, and just about all the contestants voiced agreement. All except Aileen. "I could stay here forever and listen to Ty's stories."

He sat up taller in his chair. "I probably should get going, too. It's been a nice evening, ladies. Happy trails and happy dreams."

He tweaked his hat brim. And I saw all the ladies start to swoon. *Oh, brother.*

I waved to everyone as they left, but I stayed to talk to Ty. "A car followed me to Harbor Hair. He bumped the van a couple times."

"Are you okay?" he asked, scanning my body for boo-boos. How sweet.

I flushed. "I'm fine, but it scared me."

"Were you driving your car?"

"No, Antoinette Chloe's white van."

He pushed his hat back with a thumb and shook his head.

"Oh my! He must've thought I was Antoinette Chloe! That slimeball!"

"That's my guess. Did you get a good look at the driver?"

"It was Chad Dodson in his red T-Bird."

"You saw him?"

"No, but nobody else has a car like that around here but him."

"But I've been here most of the night. And I think I can safely say that he never took his car out."

"It had to be him, Ty."

He shook his head. "You didn't see his face, so

you have no proof. It could have been some kids fooling around. Or someone in town for the pageant, or a drunken fisherman looking to have a little fun."

"It wasn't funny."

"I know. I'll check some of the area car-rental places for a red T-Bird. You never know. And some of the used-car lots. If the perp is around, I'll know soon."

"Thanks. And by the way, what's Toxic Waste been doing?"

"Lying low. He and his second, Mad Dog, haven't made a peep since you snuffed out their loud music. The most I've caught is a whiff of marijuana, purely medicinal, I'm sure."

"And what about Aileen Shubert?"

"Her record was as pure as the driven snow. No hit. It looks like she's clean."

"Could that be?"

"Of course. But it's hard to be one hundred percent certain. I'd need to run her fingerprints to see if they are tied to any arrests," he said.

"I'm going to check out her Miss Casino story on the Internet," I said.

"Wait. I'll use my phone."

He did some typing and some scrolling. "Nope. Aileen wasn't Miss Casino. Matter of fact, there really isn't a Miss Casino pageant that she could even enter."

"Another lie." Then I had a scathingly brilliant idea. "If I can get you her fingerprints on a glass or something, can you run them through the system? I just don't want her to swindle the fund-raiser out of money if she's lying."

"It'll take a while. I'd have to send it to the State Police headquarters in Albany. They have the equipment for that kind of thing and the database of prints to go along with it."

"I'll get it to you tomorrow," I said.

"No need." He held up a can of soda pop. "Got them already."

"You're good, Ty!"

"That's what all the women say."

It was about ten o'clock, and I decided to take a walk through Tent Town.

Grabbing a sweater from the hook on the back of the door, I did a lap around the Big House first. ACB's window was open a bit, but her light was off.

Aileen's light was off, too. The other rooms were still brightly lit, and I was sure there was nail polishing going on, along with some shaving and exfoliating.

I walked down the main path through the tents. Most of the grass was gone and mud was left. I walked on, trying not to slip and fall on the mud. Then I heard an unmistakable laugh.

"Antoinette Chloe?"

"Trixie! Come here and pull up a lawn chair. Join us. Toxic was telling us some fun motorcycle stories."

"Aileen? Is that you?"

She hurriedly pulled her hand out of Toxic's.

"Oops, caught again." She giggled, covering a hiccup.

"And you're drinking?" I asked her.

"No. Just ginger ale," ACB said. "What kind of a chaperone do you think I am?"

"I don't know."

I felt like blasting her. She was sitting with a suspect and a contestant who was breaking the rules, although ACB didn't know the extent to which Aileen had broken them.

Since when were ACB and Aileen so chummy? Not to mention being chummy with Toxic Waste.

"I'm talking Toxic into taking me with him to Sturgis, the big motorcycle rally, only he doesn't want to put a sidecar on his bike."

"Maybe Toxic will think of someone else in the Rubbers who'll take you," Aileen offered.

"That'd be nice," ACB said.

"Toxic, don't you have to get back to work someday?"

"I lost my enthusiasm for cooking since I lost a star with Michelin, thanks to Nick. I also lost my reputation with the Rubbers and the respect of my nephew when I didn't produce the Panhead. And I lost my girlfriend. That was the most heartbreaking." He was unabashedly drunk.

"Isn't that romantic?" ACB sang, but apparently didn't know the rest of the song.

Aileen sat with her hands on her lap, head down.

Toxic stared at Aileen with puppy-dog eyes.

What was going on?

Toxic shook his head. "Yeah, I've been mad at Nick—hated him, even—but, hey, I never wanted him dead. He was a good guy when he wasn't being a jerk."

"He definitely sounds like a jerk," Aileen mumbled.

I looked at her. Did I hear that right? How did she know Nick enough to label him a jerk?

"I never thought he was a jerk," ACB said quietly. "I thought he was terrific. He was a sweet man—very attentive and romantic. Boy, was he romantic!" She giggled, probably remembering her personalized thong.

I glanced at Aileen. She was glaring at ACB. When she saw me looking at her, though, she quickly looked away.

"What's your background, Toxic?" I asked.

"I don't have much of a story. I'm a cook at my Bavarian restaurant."

Then I turned to Aileen. "And what was your last job?"

"Not a cook or a chef—that's for sure. I was an administrative assistant for a . . . corporate lawyer."

Aha! Seems like she'd forgotten what she wrote on her questionnaire. But I remembered, since I'd re-read her application right after I found out she was lying about attending SU. She said that she was an administrative assistant for a pharmaceutical company.

"How long have you known Toxic, Aileen?"

"Why, we met here. We were both taking walks, and we started talking, and we just clicked."

You did more than just click, pumpkin.

"Isn't that a nice story?" ACB asked.

"Very nice." I smiled at Aileen. "Well, I'd better go back to the house. Lots of things to do yet before I start work, like take a power nap. Don't be late, ladies."

They all said good-bye to me, and I waved. I walked back through the muddy path and made the turn to the Big House. As soon as I did, something or someone jumped out of the shadows.

I was just about to scream until my lungs popped, but Ty put his hand over my mouth. I shoved his hand aside.

"Are you trying to give me a heart attack, Deputy?"

My knees were ready to give out. I needed to sit down.

"Trixie, why aren't ACB and Aileen in the house? What are they doing sitting with Toxic?"

"I . . . don't . . . know! Ask ACB—she's supposed to be the chaperone. Instead she's hanging out and chitchatting. By the way, I caught Aileen in another lie. I'm going to search her room, Ty. Maybe I can find out who she really is."

"Not a good time. Here she comes."

Ty disappeared as quickly as he had appeared. ACB and Aileen turned the corner.

"Oh, Trixie, you're still here?" ACB asked.

"Yeah, I was just looking at the stars. Bright, aren't they?"

"They're so close, I could just reach out and touch them," Aileen said. Then she yawned. "I'd better get my beauty rest now. Good night, Trixie. Good night, Antoinette Chloe."

"G'night," I said.

ACB hugged her. "Good night, sweetie."

I held ACB back from walking inside. "Antoinette Chloe, Aileen may not be the sweet girl you think she is."

"I know. She's lied a couple of times on her questionnaire. I don't think she was a classical dancer. She really has no rhythm. And her age? If she's twenty-eight, then so am I! That's why I wanted to get close to her—maybe there're more lies."

If I had false teeth, they would have fallen out of my mouth. ACB and I were on the same track. "How? What?"

ACB shrugged and shook her head. "We can't have a fibber as our first Miss Salmon, and we can't let her dishonestly win the prize money. But we don't want to cast a shadow over the whole pageant by disqualifying her, so I think the judges have to make sure that Aileen Shubert doesn't win first, second, or third place."

While my friend was worried about Aileen disgracing the pageant, I was wondering if that's all Aileen Shubert was really up to.

I heard a scream. One of the ear-piercing screams that meant someone's life was in danger.

Ty appeared from somewhere. "Upstairs! Stay here, Trixie!"

I followed him anyway. All the girls were milling in the hall, looking scared, pointing to ACB's room.

Ty drew his gun and kicked the door. The door didn't move. He kicked it again. Again, the sturdy oak door didn't budge.

I reached around him and twisted the handle. The door opened like I knew it would.

"None of the doors lock. I don't know why," I babbled.

"Get back!" he ordered me.

I followed him. ACB was standing in the middle of a mess, even more of a mess than usual. Her muumuus were slashed, the drawers in her plastic carts were out of the frame, and the contents were thrown on the floor.

Jewelry was everywhere. Her fascinators were slashed; so were her tote bags and purses. Even her flip-flops were pulled apart.

"Who hates me enough to do this?" she asked. "And where are my pageant notes?"

Ty shut the door and whispered, "It had to be an inside job. I've been watching this place. Trixie, check your room."

Mine was a mess, too. Stuff everywhere, swept off the top of the dressers, drawers tossed on the floor. Even the bedding was pulled off the bed.

With my heart in my throat, I looked at Aunt Stella's gown, praying that it wasn't in tatters. It was still hanging on the back of the door to the bathroom, where I'd left it. Thank goodness nothing had happened to it. Nothing in the bathroom was disturbed.

There goes my power nap. I had to clean up this mess and help ACB.

Then I noticed that my spiral notebook was missing. It contained my Miss Salmon notes, but there was nothing exciting in it. Just committee plans. There was nothing about any of the contestants in it.

I went back to ACB's room. Ty was taking photos of her room. He stopped, waiting for my report.

"My room was just tossed. It's a mess, but nothing was cut. Nothing important is missing that I can tell, except my Miss Salmon notebook. But there was nothing exciting in it."

"My folder had the timetable for the ceremony. I need it for the dress rehearsal and the pageant. Oh, what am I going to do?" ACB said.

Ty had his hands on his hips. I knew from my past experiences with him that he was beyond angry.

"I want to know who did this and how they got past me."

"It could have happened earlier, Ty. On Vern McCoy's watch. Who knows? My house is always open."

"But your rooms were specifically targeted," he said. "I asked when everyone was in the hall, and none of their things were bothered."

"But our rooms are the first ones that someone would come upon when they came upstairs." I paused, letting that sink in. "They seem to have unleashed their fury on Antoinette Chloe's room. Mine seems more like it was an afterthought, unless they were interrupted and didn't get to the slashing."

ACB plopped down on a Queen Anne chair by the window. "Who hates me enough to do this? I don't have any enemies. I'm kind to everyone."

She really was kind to everyone. I went over to

her and gave her a big hug and let her cry for a while.

"Whoever did this wanted the pageant stuff," I said. "Why else would they do it?"

Ty pulled out his notebook and stubby pencil. "You ladies figure that out. I'm going to talk to the contestants and see if they saw or heard anything."

"Thank goodness my dress muumuus are still at the jail."

"That's good news," I said. Always a silver lining with ACB.

Ty noticed a piece of paper on the floor. I could see the black print bleeding though. He read it and swore under his breath.

"What is it?" ACB asked.

Ty hesitated.

ACB had a white-knuckle grip on the arms of the chair. "I want to know."

Ty handed her the paper, and I read over her shoulder:

YOU ARE NEXT!

I double-checked my measurements for peanut butter cookies, because I couldn't get my brain to focus. All I could think of was how ACB's room had been trashed and her muumuus slashed.

ACB had been with Aileen most of the evening. Toxic and Dog had been there. The only one missing from the scenario was the less-than-delightful Chad Dodson.

I spooned out the peanut butter from an industrial-size jar and got my big mixer turning. Slow at first, so the flour didn't slop all over the floor, then faster.

I prepared my pans, cutting parchment paper to size. I swear by parchment paper and use it for cookies all the time.

With a soup spoon, I scooped out the mixture, rolled it into a ball, and put it on the parchment, spacing the balls evenly. Dipping the bottom of a glass in sugar, I squished each ball. Then I took a fork and made a crisscross pattern on the top, for no reason other than that my mother used to do it and they look cute that way.

I gathered what I needed for my chocolate chip cookies. But first I had to eat some chips for quality control.

Just as I finished mixing the chocolate chip cookie batter and started taking the peanut butter cookies out of the oven, Chelsea came bouncing in.

"The Roving Rubbers are here. It looks like all of them."

I checked my watch. It was two in the morning. Didn't those motorcycling chefs ever sleep?

"What's up with them?"

"They're leaving at sunup. Something about eating and roving where the rubber meets the road," Chelsea said.

I wondered if Ty knew that two of his suspects were going to rove.

"Well, bring on the orders. I'm ready."

"Trixie, here's a good one. Toxic Waste said to tell you that he'd like to cook with you."

I thought about that for a bit. "I guess it's okay."

Actually, it was more than okay. I'd be able to question him more.

I almost fainted when Toxic walked into the kitchen through the swinging doors. He wore a white chef's coat and white hat, black jeans, and black sneakers. He was freshly shaved and looked so unlike the Toxic Waste that I knew.

"Can I call you by your real name in my kitchen, Chef?"

"Billy. Last name is Gerard."

"Billy it is," I said. "Before the orders come in, I need to get my chocolate chip cookies out of the oven and onto the cooling rack."

"I'm on it," Billy said.

"Then I'll start the batter for snickerdoodle cookies."

Billy loaded the last pan of cookies, then yelled over to me. "I'll chop up more lettuce for salads. I see that the special is spaghetti and meatballs. Got enough?"

"How about boiling more spaghetti? I'll throw a pan of meatballs into the oven to heat them up." Luckily, I had a pan already cooked and sitting in the cooler.

"How about sauce?"

"In the cooler. A huge pot of it. Needs to be heated."

"I'll get it," Billy said.

I was impressed. Billy was a self-starter.

He got everything bubbling on the stove, and I got the snickerdoodle dough covered with plastic wrap and in the cooler. It needed to chill for four hours.

By then, the Rubbers should be on the road. Which reminded me . . .

"Billy, are you going to be leaving town with the rest of the Rubbers?"

"I asked Deputy Brisco if I could go, and he said no. I still have to stick around," he said. "I'm going stir-crazy, so I figured I'd help you out."

"I can put you to work. Graveyard shift." I couldn't believe that had just come out of my mouth, especially when I was just criticizing ACB for fraternizing with the questionable.

But I did need a break. At least to get my house back in order and find a spa and pamper myself.

"I'll take you up on that," he said.

Billy and I worked side by side as the orders came in. Most everyone ordered the special with a side of today's soup—chicken noodle—and a chef's salad. Several ordered breakfast.

Then the poker club came in, about twenty-two of them. They had just played a high-stakes game—a dollar—and the winner of the game got to have dinner on the treasury.

Margie Grace was the winner. She wanted fried chicken with mashed potatoes, gravy, and peas.

Billy and I did the Silver Bullet Shuffle, crossing back and forth in front of and behind each another. Billy sure could dance. I enjoyed my time with him, and we laughed and joked. I felt that we bonded.

Finally, I blurted, "Billy, who do you think killed Nick?"

He didn't speak for several seconds. "I think Cowboy Ty arrested the right person: Nick's nutso girlfriend. It's a money thing. It always is."

"You think Antoinette Chloe did it? She doesn't have it in her."

"Each one of us can kill if the conditions are right," he said. "Maybe they had a fight and she saw her opportunity to off him and collect some money to boot."

"The insurance won't pay if she's convicted of killing him. Chad Dodson would get it," I said.

"No kidding?"

Oops. Chocolate chip cookies loosen the lips.

"Maybe I shouldn't have told you that." I plucked another order off the clip and started putting it together. Corned beef and cabbage on rye with Thousand Island dressing.

"You know, I don't care. I just want to get back to my restaurant," Billy said, chopping lettuce with a knife like the pro he was.

He sure was skilled with a knife.

"Maybe you're right. I remember you telling me that you could have killed Nick because of the things he did to you. I think that stealing your girlfriend was the worst. But, Billy, didn't you think she wanted to go?" I sliced the corned beef on the big slicer.

"He charmed the pants off Leslie and then left her broken and mortified. She came back to me for a while and I helped her pick up the pieces, though things were never the same between us. But I still love her."

"But you're dating Aileen Shubert. Maybe things will work out all right this time."

I put the rye bread on a plate, heaped on the corned beef and the cabbage, and squirted the dressing on it all. I put long, fancy toothpicks in it and cut it in half.

"Maybe you're right."

"And Antoinette Chloe is *not* nutso."

He laughed as he spooned tomato sauce on a plate of spaghetti.

"Billy, speaking of Antoinette Chloe, what were you doing at her arraignment? I saw you hanging out by the Laundromat, and then you came into the bar—I mean, courtroom."

"I was wondering if a friend would be there."

"Was she?"

"What makes you think I was waiting for a female?"

He had a twinkle in his eye. Yeah, I'd bet one of my cottages that he was waiting for a woman. But he wasn't going to spill the details.

Curious.

Billy was such a skilled chef, and I was kind of . . . sort of . . . mostly liking him.

But I couldn't rule him out as a suspect. After all, he was really skilled with a knife.

Chapter 13

I finished my snickerdoodles, packed all the cookies in separate trays, and covered them with plastic wrap. I shook hands with Billy, welcomed Juanita, and zombie-walked to my magnificent brass bed.

As I reached the Big House, I saw Ty sitting on the front porch, facing Tent Town. He must have been watching the exodus.

There was not much left except overflowing trash cans, litter that didn't make the cans, and lots and lots of mud.

Oh, and one tent: Billy's.

The potty and shower vendor was loading the blue plastic facilities on a truck. One potty and one shower remained behind: Billy's private facilities.

I took a seat next to Ty. "What's going on with the contestants?"

He smacked his lips. "Two committee members brought breakfast over. I smell bacon and coffee, and I'm drooling."

"I'll bring you something."

I went into the Big House and found everyone gathered around the oak table. The food was set up on my counter, like a buffet. Picking up a plate, I fixed breakfast for Ty, and poured him a cup of coffee. Black.

"Anything new on the room mess?" Aileen said. "I see that Ty's watching the house."

"Yeah, he is. This plate of food and the coffee are for him. Did any of you ladies hear anything yesterday?"

"Nothing," said Jane. "But I did tell Ty that I smelled something."

"Like what?" I perked up.

"Cologne. Strong stuff," she said. "Like the stuff Antoinette Chloe wears."

ACB heard her name and turned. "I make my own perfume from essential oils, and I wouldn't destroy my own things, Jane, dear."

"Oh! I didn't mean that you did. I meant that I smelled perfume like yours. It's unique—and overpowering."

"Maybe a bottle was spilled by the criminal," I suggested, noting that ACB's feelings were hurt. "But I was in the room right after, and didn't notice a strong smell of perfume."

I turned to the committee members, Pam Grassley and Jean Harrington, who were on duty today.

"When are you leaving for the auditorium? I want to go to the reception and meet the rest of the contestants," I said.

"We're rolling out in exactly a half hour," Pam said. "It's finally pageant dress-rehearsal time!"

The screams that came from the contestants— and ACB—had to be disturbing the salmon on their swim upstream. I could envision them all making a U-turn and doing the breaststroke back to wherever it was that they came from.

Ty ran into the room, ready for action. At the sight of his drawn gun, the contestants launched into more screams. He holstered it as the ladies ran upstairs.

"What the devil?" Ty looked baffled. He probably expected a hale and hearty criminal, not a bunch of screaming Miss Salmon hopefuls.

"They're just excited. It's dress-rehearsal day," I said, putting his plate and coffee on the kitchen table. "Have a seat, Ty."

He moved his plate and coffee where he could see the stairs and the side of the Big House through the bay window and sat down.

Pam and Jean smiled at Ty, leaned closer to him, and hurried to pass him the cream and sugar, in spite of the fact that he'd told them four times that he liked his coffee black. He seemed amused as they went back and forth to the buffet to refill his plate and microwave it back to hotness.

In the meantime, I was putting everything away. If we were rolling in a half hour, I'd better get the Big House cleaned up.

And thank goodness they'd all be leaving with their parents or whomever after the pageant tomorrow night.

I'd have my house back, and peace and quiet would reign once again.

Blondie whined loudly. It was her "I really have to go" whine. I must have missed the pre-whine before with all of the commotion.

I let her out the front door, and sat down on the

stoop to call Clyde and get him working on the cleanup of Tent Town. Right now, with only Billy's tent left, it looked like Little Tent on the Prairie.

Surprisingly, Chad and Billy were talking together. I don't know why that surprised me again. I'd seen them talking before.

Maybe they were chatting about the break-in. Maybe they were the ones who broke in. I could believe anything about Chad Dodson, but since I had gotten to know Billy, I liked him. But I couldn't rule him out as Nick's killer yet.

I got ahold of Clyde, and he was already on the scene with his four-wheeler, dragging the utility wagon behind. He was picking up all the trash cans and probably taking them back to the fishing stations after he dumped everything into the Dumpster.

Then my mind wandered. I wondered if I could squeeze any more information out of Sal. He'd just hate the fact that ACB was arrested.

I needed a trip with Ty to Auburn Correctional Facility to see Sal again. Or maybe I could just call him.

I hurried back inside with Blondie. Ty was still eating, but everyone was out of the kitchen.

"Ty, does Sal know that ACB was arrested for killing Nick?"

"Not that I know of."

"But her arrest is important to him. If he still loves her like I think he does, he'll be crazy with worry. Do you think he'd be persuaded to help with ACB's future on his mind? Maybe he was holding something back."

He thought for a moment. "I don't know if he could tell us anything more than he has already, but it's worth a try."

"Road trip?" I asked, wondering how I could possibly fit in a trip to the real Big House.

"I'll call him, Trixie. Stay out of it."

I poured him another cup of coffee. "Do you have any information about the goof who kept banging into ACB's van?"

"It was a rental car that was stolen from Harbor Rentals. They were washing the car and cleaning the inside. The keys were in the car, and someone wearing a black hoodie, black sweats, and sunglasses drove it away. They think it was some kid who just wanted to drive a hot car and get into a little trouble."

"And this car looked just like Chad Dodson's? What are the odds?" I asked.

"Nah, the colors were the same, but he has a T-Bird. What was stolen was a Camry."

"Camry? I was that far off?"

"You were in panic mode. It's totally understandable, Trixie."

"So, you think it's a kid out for a joyride? Must be that I was in the way, so he had to keep bumping me."

"Vern McCoy found the Camry in a ditch on Cow Path Road. It was out of gas. Vern dusted for prints. We'll find the person."

Cow Path Road wasn't far from the point, and it ran parallel to Route 3. It was all hills and valleys, and the kids loved to race on it.

"Ty, are you sure that the driver of the Camry

wasn't trying to run ACB off the road? I mean, it was me driving, but it was her van."

"It's possible."

We said good-bye because I had to get ready for pageant practice.

Then I wondered if I could call Sal before Ty did. I wanted to appeal to him as a friend of ACB's, which I was. If he had any more information, I'd try to get it out of him.

But when I went upstairs to my room and dialed the number that I had been given by jail personnel, I found out that I wasn't on Sal Brown's call list, so Auburn wouldn't put me through to him, no matter how I pleaded and whined to Correctional Officer Stone.

Darn! Antoinette Chloe would have to call Sal.

Or maybe I could pretend to be ACB to get by Correctional Officer Stone.

"Hello, Correctional Officer Stone. I'd like to speak with my ex-husband, Sal Brown. My name is Antoinette Chloe Brown."

"Miz Brown, don't you know that you must speak with the inmate's counselor first? Depending on how many personal calls he's received already, he might not be eligible to talk with you. If he's eligible, his counselor will then have to go to his cellblock to get him and call you back. Then, finally, the counselor will put the inmate on the phone."

Officer Stone recited his spiel like a robot. He must be bored to death. I wondered whom he offended or what rule he broke to be assigned to phone duty.

I cleared my throat and tried to imitate the fluttery way that ACB spoke. "Would you kindly put Sal's counselor on the line, Lieutenant Stone?"

"Uh, it's Correctional Officer Stone . . . but stay on the line for Correctional Officer Cuddy, please."

"Thank you so much!"

Officer Cuddy had such a high voice I thought that I was speaking with a member of the Vienna Boys' Choir, but he stated that Sal was eligible for one personal call and I was to stand by. I also had to answer several personal questions that only ACB would know the answer to, but, being a close friend of hers, I could answer correctly—with the exception of her Social Security number.

I fluttered and stammered and finally flirted enough with Officer Cuddy that he gave me another question. Success!

I was on edge. I couldn't control the jumping of my foot or the drumming of my fingers on the phone stand. Then I thought about how Ty would kill me if he ever found out that I beat him to Sal.

He'd be one ticked-off cop—that's for sure.

But he just didn't move fast enough for me.

The phone rang, and I jumped twenty feet in the air. As I returned to my chair, I greeted the incarcerated-for-life Sal Brown.

"Don't say anything, Mr. Brown, but this isn't Antoinette Chloe. This is Trixie Matkowski."

"Oh, joy. Wassup?"

"I just wanted to tell you that Antoinette Chloe was arrested for killing Nick. I need you to help me out, for Antoinette Chloe's sake. She asked me to help her, so I'd like to ask you a couple of questions."

"I heard she was arrested. I'm in jail, not on Mars. How is my dearest darling? Is she doing okay?"

"You know her. She always lands on her flip-flops."

"Yeah. What a broad! I wish she'd never divorced me."

"I don't know what she was thinking," I said with frost hanging from each word. "And *broad*? Did you really say *broad*?"

"Oh, excuse me, Miz Matkowski. I'll immediately enroll in a politically correct terminology class in the cellblock."

He was being sarcastic, and I tried not to laugh, but it was nearly impossible when he was trying to be the star of a 1950s gangster B movie. Maybe it was simply a case of jail survival, but I think that Sal should update his slang for the times.

"Sal, didn't you say that you were jealous of Nick dating Antoinette Chloe?"

"Yeah. It tore my heart out when I heard about them. When I told Nicky to take care of her, I didn't mean sleep with her." I could hear the sadness in his voice. "But she could never kill anyone. Has Ty's cheese slipped off his cracker?"

Sal Brown was absolutely right about ACB, but I felt a need to defend Ty.

"I think someone is trying to frame her, Sal. I don't know who yet, but it's obvious. Her stuff was littered around the crime scene. It was obviously planted there. Ty had no choice but to arrest her. Besides, it was for her own protection, but she begged me to get her out so she could emcee the Miss Salmon Contest."

"Who would want to frame my beloved Antoinette Chloe?"

"I was hoping you could tell me."

"Damned if I know. She's a saint." Suddenly Sal shouted, "I did it. I killed Nicky. Tell Ty that I'll give a statement that I did it. I killed Nicky. I killed my brother. I didn't like the fact that he was sleeping with my wife."

"But, Sal, you were in jail at the time Nick was killed."

"You can get anything done in here, if you know the right people, and I do," he said. "I'll take the rap for killing Nicky, not my Antoinette Chloe."

"Sal, that's really so sweet of you, but I don't believe you, so I doubt Ty will. So, listen. Can you think of anything—anything at all that could help Antoinette Chloe?"

There was silence for a while. "Okay. I didn't want to tell Ty this because I was afraid that they'd audit our restaurant, but I was involved with Chad Dodson and helping him launder money. It was gambling money from hot games in the basement of Nicky's restaurant."

"Go ahead."

"One day, Nicky stumbled into our private gambling club that was meeting in his basement. His restaurant was closed on Monday, so why the hell didn't he stay away?"

"So, you were all gambling, Sal?" I asked.

"I love Texas Hold 'Em, and I would disappear every Sunday night. I told Antoinette Chloe that I was seeing our friend, Alan Lohman, at a nursing home in Boston, but Al died years ago. Instead I was going to play cards. We would start early on Monday morning and play until eight o'clock. Chad had a great business going with the private club. He charged a couple of grand for players to belong, and the house took a cut on each game. The money would go through the restaurant and come out squeaky-clean."

"And then Nick found out?" I asked.

"And he had a fit—said that no one was going to use his restaurant and smear his good name to launder money from illegal gambling or illegal anything. He hopped on his motorcycle and drove through the dining room and kitchen and wrecked the place, and took off down the highway. Crazy fool. It was a gold mine for me and Chad. We would have cut Nicky in, but he was too straight. Everyone was scared that Nicky would go to the cops, so we all took to the wind."

"Did you launder money through Brown's Four Corners, too?" I asked.

"Yes, ma'am."

"And Nick broke his partnership agreement with Chad and left him high and dry. Now Chad is broke. You should also know that Chad is sniffing around Nick's life-insurance policy that names Antoinette Chloe, then Chad and you as beneficiaries. Do you think that someone's trying to get Antoinette Chloe into jail and out of the way?"

Sal let loose a few nice swearwords. "Sorry,

Trixie." Then he took a deep breath. "Well, I'm not the one trying to get my darling in jail. My sweet lady would fade like a cut rose in jail. I'd place a bet on Chad, though. He's a slippery one, and he needs fast money. If I find out that Chad is doing anything against my Antoinette Chloe, I'll take care of him. I got nothing to lose."

"Sal, this was very helpful, but I have to go. Antoinette Chloe and I have to get going to the Miss Salmon reception and the dress rehearsal."

"My Antoinette Chloe should be entered in the pageant. She'd win. She's just beautiful," Sal said just before a tape recording told us his time was up.

"She's the emcee. She can't enter." I thanked Sal for the information and promised to watch out for ACB.

I was thrilled. I got a lot of information from Sal. I knew I'd have to tell Ty and incur his wrath, but I'd postpone that for later. I was a pro at procrastination.

Climbing the stairs, I found the pageant contestants and ACB in a state of panic. How hard was it to pack up all their stuff for a dress rehearsal? They just had to hang their evening dresses in garment bags and pack the rest of their things—shoes, a bathing suit, and a salmon costume—into a tote bag.

I hadn't seen the salmon costumes yet. The other members of the committee had sewed the costumes from yards and yards of shiny gray material donated by Notions and Potions, a sewing and New Age store downtown.

I wasn't a part of the sewing. Knowing my lack of skills, the committee decided that I was doing enough just by being a judge, opening my house, and feeding the contestants at the Silver Bullet.

ACB was supposed to be in charge of breakfast and lunch, but because of her unfortunate stint in her comfy cell at the Sandy Harbor Hilton, the committee had to help out more.

I knocked on her open door and walked in. "Antoinette Chloe, you can drive with me. I'm not going to be at the entire dress rehearsal, just the reception. You'll have to get a ride back."

"I can do that."

I sat down on the Queen Anne chair, since her bed was once again loaded with clothes. Sighing, I remembered how that bed was once cleared off after the slasher incident. ACB and I worked like rented mules putting everything back together and throwing wounded muumuus and fascinators away. But ACB had a system, and she knew just where everything was.

Pam, one of the Miss Salmon committee members, stomped into the room.

"Are you two coming to the high school with us? The reception is starting soon and the van is leaving!" Pam said impatiently.

"Pam, thanks anyway, but Antoinette Chloe and I are driving to the reception together. Go ahead without us. But would you stop at the Silver Bullet first and pick up my trays of cookies, please?" I said, shutting the door before she had a chance to answer.

Then I filled in ACB on my conversation with

Sal and why I had pretended to be her when I called Auburn.

She listened as she stuffed a couple of pairs of flip-flops into a tote bag. "I never knew about the money laundering, and I guess it's good that Sal didn't tell Ty, so I wouldn't be audited. And I never knew the truth about the big argument that drove a wedge between Chad and Nick. Nick would never tell me."

I shook my head. "I think that Ty needs to move Chad Dodson up the suspect list to the number one position. Chad couldn't start another poker club until Nick was out of the way, or Nick might squeal. Sal was already out of the way. With you in jail for murdering Nick, Chad would hit the beneficiary bonanza. Plus he's broke and has to act fast. Right?"

I felt that I'd gone over this information before, but the laundering of gambling money was a new twist.

As I left ACB's room, I gave her ten more minutes to stuff everything she could into her tote bags and into her cleavage.

Then I decided to check the contestants' rooms. Like Ty, I thought that the trashing and slashing was an inside job. It was probably illegal for me to paw around their rooms, and Ty was in the process of getting warrants, but this was my house, I reasoned, so I could do whatever I wanted.

And I was going to start with Aileen Shubert's room. It was right next door to ACB's, and Aileen could probably hear everything that ACB was doing and saying.

Antoinette Chloe wasn't exactly demure and talked in a booming voice, mostly to herself.

So I twisted the knob and let myself in. Talk about perfume! The place smelled like the cosmetics corner at Spend A Buck.

Aileen's bed was made, her room was spotless, and nothing was on the dresser except makeup, perfume, and a huge jewelry box.

I was a bit of a jewelry snoop. I never really wore it, but I had a couple of nice pieces for weddings, funerals, and the like. Nothing expensive, just semiprecious stones and some colored glass.

Opening Aileen's jewelry box, I was dazzled. It looked like the real thing, but I didn't know a real diamond from cubic zirconia.

I pulled open every drawer of the box, being careful not to touch anything. In the bottom drawer I found an envelope. Of course I looked inside and found a newspaper clipping from the bridal section of the *Boston Globe*. I read:

SOCIALITE LESLIE McDERMOTT TO WED RESTAURATEUR DOMENICK BROWNELLI

Leslie McDermott of Greenwich, Connecticut, will marry Domenick Brownelli of Sandy Harbor, New York, at a moonlight ceremony Saturday evening at the home of the bride's family.

The bride is the daughter of Irene (O'Connor) McDermott and Bart Francis McDermott. The bride's mother is a corporate efficiency consultant.

The bride's father owns sixteen car dealerships across New England.

The bride works for her father's company. The groom formerly owned Chef Nick's Restaurant on Beacon Hill and enjoys designing and making custom motorcycles.

After a honeymoon cruise to Hawaii, the couple will reside in Sandy Harbor, New York.

Poor Leslie. She was ready to get married, but it never happened. I stared numbly at the picture of Leslie McDermott, with her perfectly straight blond hair and her beautiful gown and flowers. . . .

And that's when it hit me. The woman in the picture was Aileen Shubert!

Chapter 14

So, Leslie McDermott was really Aileen Shubert. No. It was the other way around. Aileen Shubert was really Leslie McDermott.

No wonder Toxic Waste and Aileen were hotter than dinner rolls from my oven. They were picking up where they had left off before Nick drove a wedge between them.

But why would she enter the Miss Salmon pageant under another name?

When we finally walked down the stairs, I was carrying several tote bags for ACB. She had even more.

Ty jumped to his feet. "Need help?"

"We got it. We just need to keep walking to keep our momentum going," I said, trying to avoid him. I still felt guilty about going behind his back and calling Sal, and prayed that Sal wouldn't tell him. "I'm driving us to the high school in my car."

"I'll follow you both," he said.

I felt my face heat, and I knew I was getting the red Crawling Crud of Guilt. It starts on my neck and stops at my cheeks. I also had to spill that I had searched Aileen/Leslie's room.

Why would Leslie want to enter the Miss Salmon pageant? To hang around Sandy Harbor so she could be near Nick and maybe get back with him? Or simply to kill him?

Finding out that Aileen was Leslie was big news! I wanted to tell ACB, but my gut told me to tell Ty first, because I knew ACB would go off the deep end.

I'd have to wait to get Ty alone.

Hiding my face with tote bags because Ty knew my guilt tell, I put everything in the trunk of my car. ACB's items, too. Everything barely fit.

As ACB went back into the house to get more of her things with Ty, I called Juanita. "Did Connie pick up the cookie trays?"

"*Sí*. Not too long ago."

"Good. Is everything okay?"

"Lots of business. I've been busy," she said.

"Do you need me to help you?" I could skip the reception, if I had to, although now I wanted to keep an eye on both Antoinette Chloe and Leslie.

"Everything is good. Mr. Billy came in to eat and he helped me for a while. He said that he cooked with you on the graveyard shift, so I said okay. He said that he's bored waiting around. I like Mr. Billy."

"He definitely knows his way around a kitchen."

"*Sí*. And he likes Raymond. The two of them were throwing a football back and forth on Ray's break."

Ray was the best dishwasher and all-around kid that I've ever hired, and when he quit hacking into his school's computer to raise everyone's grades, I paid him extra to be my computer geek.

"Okay, I'm going up to the reception with Antoinette Chloe, who's basically a wreck because the slasher took all of her notes. I think she's more worried about being a terrible emcee than the murder charge. Talk to you later."

"Have a good time."

Followed by Ty, Antoinette Chloe finally emerged. They were both carrying garment bags, probably more muumuus that weren't maimed. They laid them across the backseat.

Finally, we were off and headed to the auditorium. ACB looked particularly festive today. She wore a muumuu with palm trees and colorful surfboards all over it, sparkly purple flip-flops, and a straw hat with a toucan and a palm tree on top.

What—no surfboard?

Her jewelry consisted of various shells—shells hanging from her ears, wrists, neck, and ankles, and several places in between.

A South Pacific ensemble for a Great Lake in New York State? Knowing ACB's luggage and tote bags, she had a variety of wardrobe changes in store for us.

Maybe I'd stay for a while and see the contestants' swimsuits or stay longer and see their evening gowns. I wasn't sure how ethical it was for a judge to get a sneak peek, but it wasn't like this was the Miss America pageant.

I turned right onto School Road and noticed that another vehicle was following Ty, a motorcycle. It was Billy, Mr. Toxic Waste. Must be that Juanita didn't need him to help her cook after all, and he decided to go to the pageant.

Was the pageant really his thing?

Probably not, but Aileen—or, rather, Leslie—certainly was. Obviously they had renewed their relationship with the romantic backdrop of spawning salmon.

We found parking spaces right near the door. Good. ACB had a lot to unload. Even Billy helped. It took all four of us to get ACB's stuff inside the high school and in the back where makeshift dressing rooms were set up through a creative use of curtains. School desks were set up with mirrors of all different sizes.

Evening gowns hung on racks made of pipes.

ACB was walking around in a state of horror. "No wire hangers!" she kept saying, and directing the contestants to find wooden hangers for their gowns.

Calm down, Joan Crawford!

Finally, ACB and I went to where the food was set up in front of the stage. The contestants were too focused to eat the baked ziti, the salads, the rotisserie chicken, the mixed veggies, the meat platter, and the steak fries.

More for me.

The contestants munched on my cookies instead and walked around with bottles of water.

"Antoinette Chloe, Chef Fingers did a fabulous job," I said, bypassing the salads for the pan of steak fries.

"I know. I think I'll give him another raise."

Was that two raises in two weeks? I think I'll go work for her.

ACB and I mingled with the other contestants. Luckily, one of the committee members thought to make stick-on name tags, so that broke the ice.

Finally one of the committee members grabbed ACB's attention, and I walked around, trying to find Ty.

I found him and was ready to catch him up with the investigation when Aileen came over to talk to us.

"This is a wonderful event. I'm just so excited!" She turned to Ty. "What do you think my chances are of winning Miss Salmon?"

I could see Ty taking in her shiny hair, her perfect makeup and jewelry, and her short, short sundress with brown leather sandals. Her blue eyes were twinkling with excitement.

Oh, brother!

"I'd say you have a great shot," he said, and flashed a big grin. He had a little dimple on his left cheek that liked to appear on occasion, and it chose to do so now.

Not that I noticed.

I took Ty's arm. I needed a private place for us to talk, so I led him to the girl's locker room. No one was in there, but just in case, I tugged him into the shower and pulled the white vinyl curtain shut.

"This is interesting, Trixie. You must have something important to tell me."

"What I want to tell you will rocket your cowboy hat off your head."

"You have the red crud creeping up your neck. You're feeling guilty about something. You'd better spill it."

I sat down on the bench in the shower. "You'd better sit down for this, too." I moved over, but it still didn't give Ty much room for his butt.

The two of us sat glued together on a seat in a shower stall in the girl's locker room at the Sandy Harbor High School, in the middle of a reception for Miss Salmon. If Ty thought it was strange, he didn't say anything.

"C'mon, Trixie. Spit it out. I have a feeling I'm not going to like it."

I decided to get the Impersonating an Ex-Wife Confessions over with first. "I called Sal."

"You have to be kidding! I should lock you up for interfering in my investigation."

He tried to stand, but my hips had a lock on his. "Just listen to me."

"Go on," he said between gritted teeth.

"Sal wanted to talk to you and confess to Nick's murder."

"I know he didn't do it," Ty said firmly. "He couldn't have killed Nick."

"How do you know that?" I asked.

He looked at me with an arched eyebrow and didn't say a word, so I continued.

"Anyway, I asked him if there was anything—*anything* at all—that he might have forgotten to tell us that would help Antoinette Chloe, the love of his life."

"And?"

"And get this: He said that he and Chad Dodson

had been running an illegal gambling club in the basement of Nick's old restaurant on Monday nights. Chad and Sal were laundering money through the restaurant and through Brown's Four Corners. Nick found out and was so livid that he skipped out on Chad."

"I know," Ty said. "I went back up to Auburn to see Sal early this morning."

"Ty, why didn't you tell me?"

"Because I'm the investigator here, not you. Seems like I keep reminding you of that fact."

"But ACB is my friend."

"But you're not a cop."

I wiggled on the bench seat, just to make him uncomfortable. *Take that! And forget your discount for meals at the Silver Bullet.*

"Anything else, Trixie?"

"Shouldn't that make Chad your lead suspect? Chad was probably worried that Nick would spill the beans about the gambling and the fact that they were making tons of money. Sal told Chad that Nick would never tell and never bring down the cops on their restaurants, but Chad didn't believe him. Then Sal went to jail for murder and couldn't keep track of Nick to keep him in line. So Chad killed Nick and set up Antoinette Chloe with those dumb clues. And jackpot!"

"Makes sense."

"Aren't I right? Chad did it, didn't he?"

"I didn't say that."

"What are you saying?" I asked.

"That Chad is a prime contender for Suspect of the Year."

"But you had ACB arrested anyway."

"You know that I arrested her partially to protect her. I could have safely held her for five days before that Section 180.80 would kick in, but, no, you had to swoop in and get her out!"

"All right, all right. What's done is done. I probably shouldn't have bailed her out. But she's fine, so it doesn't matter. But I do have more news to tell you about."

"Tell me."

"Aileen Shubert is really Leslie McDermott, Toxic Waste's former lover and the woman that Nick Brownelli left at the altar."

"How on earth do you know that?"

"I searched her room. I found her wedding announcement in the paper, along with a picture. The picture was of Leslie McDermott—we know her as Aileen Shubert. What do you think of that?"

"Trixie, you searched the room of a tenant?"

"Not really. I just searched her jewelry box and found the clipping. And anyway, she's not really my tenant; she's a guest in my house."

He sighed. "I'm concerned that Aileen is really Leslie McDermott. Go figure. I wonder if this is an identical-twin type of thing." He seemed to be talking to himself, then turned to me and said loud and clear, "I'll handle the investigation from now on, and I mean it, Trixie. If I have to, I'll arrest you, and you can enjoy ACB's decorating."

"Oh, you're so infuriating! You should be thanking me for all the information I gave you. You don't tell me anything at all." I sighed. "Let's get unstuck and get out of here."

That was easier said than done. After unsuccessful wiggling on both our parts, Ty swiveled to the marble wall and pulled himself up on the grab bar. Then he offered me his hand. I shunned it and got up myself using both grab bars.

"You're mad at me?" he asked. "Just because I won't feed you information about an official investigation? Why don't you ask Vern or Lou? They blab a lot."

"Maybe I will." I wasn't going to throw Vern or Lou under the bus, but obviously Ty knew that they had loose lips.

He mumbled something under his breath, and we both went back to the reception.

The parade of contestants in bathing suits was going on. ACB must have already given her speech, because she wasn't at the podium.

June Burke went up to Connie, who was in charge of this portion of the program, and asked for her to have the contestants march again, but much slower this time. June changed the music to a waltz instead of Beyoncé, which ACB had picked.

They all looked wonderful, but the five Wheelchair Grannies were definitely going to steal the show. They wore beach cover-ups with colorful beach hats and sandals instead of bathing suits. Everyone loved them, and the Grannies were content with rolling over the feet of the other contestants or wheeling into their legs.

Aileen was the picture of poise and confidence. She wore a one-piece cherry-red suit with gold looping designs that shimmered under the lights. She had on shiny red five-inch heels that had intricate gold piping designs along the sides. Everything was perfectly matched.

I had to admit that it was the perfect choice for her coloring.

Aileen, the woman scorned.

Aileen, left at the altar by charming, sexy, bad-boy Nick.

Aileen the liar. She doesn't get seasick. She isn't a grad student at SU.

And then I remembered that Aileen was the one who had been nagging ACB about a place to stay. What if she had been in Sandy Harbor the whole time? Since no one in Sandy Harbor ever locked their doors, Aileen could have helped herself to things from ACB's house and from the Big House.

But so could have Chad. And Chad had lots and lots of money to gain from it all.

Chad could have easily buried Nick on ACB's land. Aileen was a skinny beauty queen with perfect hair and nails, who'd probably squeal at the sight of dirt, but revenge was a powerful motivator.

We sat through the whole rehearsal again, and—merciful heavens—the Wheelchair Grannies sang and played the bells. They chose a song that they all had written together called "I'm a Sexual Camel Because I Haven't Had Sex in Fifty Years."

That sent Ty and me under the seats with laughter. They had to do it several times because they kept forgetting the lines or forgetting to ring their bells.

"I called Vern McCoy to check out Leslie. Now

that we know her real name, maybe something will turn up," Ty whispered to me.

Then it was time for Margie Grace and ACB's unique choreography of salmon swimming upstream. According to the program, it was called *Salmon Swimming Upstream*.

When the New Age-ish music started, they fluttered onto the stage wearing their grayish-silver fish outfits. I thought they looked more like the stars of Shark Week instead of salmon. The salmon did a tango with the fishermen holding rods, and another dance that looked like an exercise routine or an exorcism—it was unclear. Finally the salmon were caught and the salmon cried as the fishermen marched around them in hip waders, twirling their fishing poles like batons.

Unable to keep a straight face, I said to Ty, "I'm going to see if ACB is okay. She has been angsting over her emcee duties since her script was stolen."

"ACB just slipped offstage to change into her next muumuu. Do you want me to go stand outside the door? Or should I barge right in as everyone is changing?" he asked.

"I'll take over now and check on her."

"Bless you."

I stopped at the buffet table and grabbed a snickerdoodle cookie. It was fabulous, if I do say so myself.

Backstage, I looked for ACB. She wasn't in her dressing room. She wasn't in the ladies' room.

I moved a curtain to see if I had missed her, and saw the salmon swimming upstage as fishing rods tempted them. I counted. There were eleven. One girl was missing.

Where was Aileen? And where was Antoinette Chloe?

Oh, crap!

I didn't want to jump to conclusions, but both Chad and Toxic Waste were sitting in the audience. Then again, Aileen was supposedly in rehearsal. Perhaps she was somewhere backstage where I couldn't see her.

Just as everyone was changing into their evening gowns, Janice, ACB's lawyer, came around the corner along with Shaun Williamson, the bail bondsman and florist. He was carrying buckets of flowers.

He nodded at me. "Where should I put these?"

"I don't know. You'll have to ask Antoinette Chloe."

"Where do I find her?" Shaun asked.

"I'm not sure. I'm looking for her, too," I said.

Janice, ACB's lawyer, put her arm around my shoulder. "I'm here to do my volunteering, but I need to talk to Antoinette Chloe first. It's about her next court date."

"Uh, when I find her, I'll send her to you both."

"You mean you can't find her?" Shaun asked with a greedy gleam in his eyes. "I can picture myself owning the point now. I'll use one of the cottages for my floral shop. No. I'll put up another building right on Route 3. How much road frontage do you have?"

"Knock it off, Shaun," Janice said.

"Yeah, knock it off," I echoed.

I cupped my hands over my mouth. "Anyone see Antoinette Chloe?" I yelled to everyone backstage.

"I saw her go outside with Aileen. They were huddled together about something," said Pam, one of the pageant committee members.

"Thanks, Pam."

I ran outside looking for ACB and called her cell phone. No answer. She always answered. She'd answer today's calls for sure. They'd be all about the pageant. Then I noticed a seashell on the ground beside some car tracks. She had to have gotten into Aileen's car. But why?

I hurried to my car. I started it and called her again. Nothing. Where would they have gone?

I drove to ACB's multicolored Victorian near downtown Sandy Harbor, thinking maybe she'd forgotten something there that she needed for her outfit change. I rang and knocked, but everything was dark. She wasn't there.

I raced back to my car. Now what?

I was near Nick's, so I turned my car toward his house. It was the only other place I thought they would go.

My heart was pounding in my ears, and I took a couple of deep breaths as I parked my car a couple of doors down.

A dim light peeked out from under the garage door. As quietly as I could, I snuck over to the side door and opened it a crack.

Aileen was holding a fish filleting knife on Antoinette Chloe!

ACB's hands and ankles were tied with black

electrical tape, and she was attached to Nick's motorcycle by a boat rope. She looked uncomfortable sitting on the cement floor with her legs out in front of her. Her sequined flip-flops were barely hanging on to her toes. She did have on her faux-leopard cape, so at least that kept some of the cold off her.

I had to admit that Aileen looked lovely in her evening gown. It was white and fluffy and the Swarovski crystals shimmered in the light. She could have won the competition hands down, but I digress. . . .

I reached for my cell phone to call Ty, but I was too little, too late. Aileen knew I was there.

She hurled herself at me, and I fell to the cement floor. As much as I squirmed to get away from her, she clung to me like plastic wrap.

Aileen and I struggled for the knife.

She won.

"Aileen, you're going to ruin your beautiful evening gown for the competition. There's grease all over the floor," I said from my spot on the cement.

She stood over me. "Get up, Trixie."

It took me a while, but I got up and faced the point of Aileen's fillet knife.

Aileen shook her head and got a strange look on her face. She rubbed her right temple.

"Look at how beautiful I am! How could Nick fall for a frump like her? I left Billy for Nick. And then Nick left me. I'm a McDermott. No one does that to a McDermott!"

ACB grunted. "So . . . you're really Leslie Mc-

Dermott? I knew you lied on your Miss Salmon application. And I'm not a frump. I'm colorful."

I saw the hurt look on my friend's face and couldn't resist throwing a zinger at Leslie.

"Um . . . Leslie, why do you think that Nick skipped out on your wedding?" I asked.

I felt the prick of her knife on my neck. Okay. Bad timing. When would I ever learn to shut up?

"Leslie, put the knife down and go practice for the pageant. That gown looks like Donna Karan. Am I right?" I asked.

"It's vintage Dior," ACB said from the floor. "And white is a great color on you—very angelic."

"Thank you. Why . . . how . . . how do you know that it's Dior?" Leslie asked.

"I studied design in Paris and in New York City," ACB said.

"Impossible! Look how you dress . . . and your makeup is a disaster!"

"I like being vibrant," ACB said.

"You mean that you like being gaudy," Leslie said.

"Colorful," I said, still sticking up for my friend.

"Leslie, you set me up!" ACB suddenly shouted. "You scattered enough of my things all over my land to make it look like a yard sale. And how dare you enter my house and do something like that, especially after how nicely I've treated you!"

"Your house looks like a Victorian garbage heap. So did your room at Trixie's house. What a dump."

"I thought you couldn't find a place to stay," Antoinette Chloe pointed out. "You whined enough to me about the lack of accommodations. So, where were you staying when you killed my Nick?"

"The Wishing Well Campgrounds. They had an immediate vacancy in a cottage after someone got sick at their nighttime campfire and had to move to the hospital." She tossed her hair and crossed her arms, looking smug. "Something about rat poison in his beer."

My stomach turned. "How can you hurt some-one like that?"

"It's for the greater good. *My* greater good. I wanted to get back with Nick, but he only had eyes for . . . her!" She held the fillet knife at waist level, ready to lash out . . . at ACB.

"Nick loved me," ACB said. "And I loved him. He was good to me at one of the worst times in my life, and I will always love him for it."

I held my breath. Not a good thing to say when Leslie was ready to make a shish kebab out of her.

"I loved Nick, too. He was a great kisser and he was fabulous in bed," Leslie said.

"Absolutely!" ACB laughed. "Nick sure was out-standing. Sal was good, but Nick . . . wow!"

Leslie chuckled. "You know what? I like you, Antoinette. I wish that I didn't have to kill you. But that's what I'm going to do. I entered Miss Salmon and came here to get back with Nick. After he cast me aside like yesterday's newspaper once again, I couldn't handle it, so he had to go. If I couldn't have him, then no one would. But it was actually Antoinette that I came here to kill."

"You don't have to kill her," I said. "Just put down the knife."

"Leslie, how did you get Nick out on my land?" ACB shifted on the cement.

I wished she'd shut up. Anything could trigger Leslie into filleting the both of us like a fish.

She waved the knife in the air. "Nick was surprised to see me, and at first he wouldn't even give me the time of day. But I convinced him that I just wanted to drive and talk for a while, and he said okay. Then I told him that I wanted to go for a walk. I knew that Antoinette owned that land. I figured that killing Nick on her land would put another nail in her coffin."

"Then you planted everything at the scene?" I asked.

"It was a piece of cake. Antoinette's house is always unlocked—just like yours, Trixie—so it was easy to steal a knife from your basement. My intention was to trick the cops into thinking you were in cahoots with her, but it made an excellent weapon." She laughed. "You small-townies really should lock your doors, huh?"

I was still waiting for a chance to catch Leslie off guard.

Sheesh! It might help if I could take out my phone and call Ty. . . .

Oh, but I could! I didn't need to see the screen to call him from my phone! I reached into my pocket and pressed the number one on my phone's keypad to speed-dial Ty without Leslie seeing me. Why on earth didn't I think of that before?

I heard Ty answer.

"What's that noise?" Leslie asked, thrusting the knife under my nose.

"That's my stomach growling, Leslie. I'm hungry," I said loudly. Maybe Ty could hear me. "Uh, Leslie, can we get out of Nick's garage, and can you put that knife down before you kill us like you killed Nick?"

I looked at Leslie and now she had crazy eyes. She was walking in circles around ACB and mumbling to herself. "Look at how beautiful I am!" She twirled in her evening gown. "How could Nick leave me at the altar for someone like you, Antoinette?"

"Leslie, my name is Antoinette *Chloe*."

Sheesh. ACB was correcting a murderer about her name?

"I still can't understand how could Nick dump me for you, Antoinette *Chloe*. You can't dress. You look like a luau in a hurricane." She sniffed. "How could Nick embarrass me like he did? My picture was in the paper. Everyone saw."

Suddenly Leslie lunged at ACB, with the knife held high. I yanked at her gown as hard as I could and then she turned her attention to me.

Luckily, Antoinette Chloe was on the ball and tripped Leslie. She fell like the skinny contest junkie she might—or might not—be.

I jumped on top of her and smacked her hand against the cement floor until she let go of the knife. Then I tied her hands with the electrical tape that ACB kicked over to me.

Ty Brisco, Vern McCoy, and Lou Rutledge—the entire Sandy Harbor Sheriff's Department—ran into the garage. Lou rushed over to ACB, cut her free, and helped her up.

ACB and I closed the distance between us and hugged.

"Nice job, Trixie," she said.

"Nice job, Antoinette Chloe."

I looked at Leslie lying on the floor and sadness washed over me. She definitely needed help, and I hoped that she'd get it wherever she was sent.

I took Ty, Vern, and Lou aside along with ACB and we huddled. "Be careful, guys. She's not as helpless as you might think."

Leslie tossed her hair. "I can't go to jail right now. I have to get back to the high school to rehearse that lame salmon tableau. I have a pageant to win."

I shook my head. I couldn't believe that Leslie the Lunatic still wanted to win the pageant. "I think you're going to miss the competition, Leslie."

ACB turned to Ty. "But I can't miss my opportunity to emcee. This event is my life. Can I hitch a ride with you to back to the high school, please?"

"Sure. I'll even turn on the siren for you two. You both deserve to finish the event."

That was nice of him, but all I really wanted was a carton of nut chocolate-fudge brownie ice cream and a spoon.

Epilogue

E-MAIL TO AUNT STELLA
Hi, Aunt Stella!

I have so many things to tell you and you seem to be traveling somewhere, so I always rely on e-mail to reach you.

First, Antoinette Chloe Brown wound up being *not* guilty. We found Nick Brownelli's real killer with help from Ty Brisco. He's really a great cop, but you know how impatient I get. I know I should leave him to his job, but ACB's my friend, and I wanted to help her.

I actually feel bad for the murderer, Aunt Stella. Of course, I feel sorrier for Nick Brownelli. He lost his life way too early.

Sal Brownelli, currently residing in Auburn Correctional Facility in Auburn, New York, was actually a big help in providing motives for whoever might have wanted to kill Nick. Sal is still desperately in love with ACB, and I think a part of her still loves him, too, in spite of everything he's done to hurt her. She has such a big heart.

One of the major suspects was Chad Dodson of *the* Dodsons of Beacon Hill in Boston, Massachusetts. They are the big cheeses of banking and insurance, and they had dumped Chad, since he was using up too much of their money. Chad was sniffing around Nick's life-insurance policy, but his story about Nick owing him money was a lie. He figured that Antoinette Chloe was a soft touch and would buy his story and try to make good on Nick's debts. Shame on him.

Antoinette Chloe is the beneficiary of Nick's policy, free and clear. And she decided that she's going to continue building her drive-in, and plans on remodeling her restaurant with the check from Nick's insurance company. The rest will go for her secret charity work.

She wants to name the drive-in after Nick. Specifically, she wanted to name it Nick at Nite, but I pointed out that the name was already taken by a TV channel, so she's still thinking about the name.

Chad went home with his tail between his legs, but before he did, he arranged some kind of partnership with Billy Gerard, also known as Toxic Waste. Chad and Toxic want to open an American-type of restaurant somewhere around Alexandria Bay in the Thousand Islands area.

Billy Gerard is a fabulous chef who owns a restaurant called Billy's Bavarian. He's quite devastated by the events, but I think the winner of the Miss Salmon pageant, Cher LaMontagne, has the hots for him, and vice versa.

Billy hasn't had much luck in the girlfriend department, but Cher seems to be nice and a real change from Leslie.

Oh, and Billy knew that Leslie was masquerading as Aileen Shubert. But he's been totally in love with Leslie for years, even after she dumped him and was going to marry Nick. Anyway, he kept his mouth shut and tried to figure out what Leslie was up to, but that didn't stop him from frolicking in the grass with her, if you catch my drift. It's a long story, Aunt Stella, but you get the idea.

Oh, one day someone was bumping me from behind as I drove to Harbor Hair. Leslie McDermott confessed to Ty that she thought that ACB was driving, not me. Please don't tell my mom about this. She hates my frequent brushes with death!

But I don't want my e-mail to be all gloom and doom. The Silver Bullet and the cottages are filled to the brim with fishermen and tourists. I'll be able to make a balloon payment to you at the end of the quarter. As Ty would say, yee-haw!

The first annual Miss Salmon pageant was a success. The auditorium was packed, and Margie Grace and ACB prepared a dance that memorialized the salmon running upstream, complete with dancing fishing poles and the fishermen doing the tango with the salmon. It probably would have been better if Margie Grace had left a little to the imagination when the contestants depicted the salmon laying eggs. LOL!

ACB was a success as emcee. I think that the audience was more interested in her costume changes than watching the pageant; she had some real doozies.

God bless her! She enjoys putting together colorful outfits.

In closing, I just have to say that I looked fabulous in one of your gowns. Well, because of my height, it was a tea-length dress on me, not a gown. It was the one with the copper sequins on the bodice and a cream-colored skirt.

Ty waited for me to change for the pageant, and when I walked down the stairs, he whistled—a long, low wolf whistle. And he smiled that great smile he has. His little dimple on the left made an appearance.

Not that I noticed. No way.

Love you,

Trixie

Family (and Friends'!) Recipes from the Silver Bullet Diner, Sandy Harbor, New York

Cousin Virgie's Holiday Broccoli-Corn Casserole

Virgie used to make this easy, quick casserole for holiday gatherings, and we all looked forward to it. Yum!

1 (16 oz.) can creamed corn
1 (10 oz.) package frozen chopped broccoli, cooked and drained
1 egg, beaten
1 Tbsp. minced onion
2 Tbsps. melted butter
16 crushed saltine crackers
Salt and pepper to taste

Preheat the oven to 350°F.

Combine all ingredients in casserole dish. Bake for 35 to 40 minutes or so until golden brown and bubbly on top.

Makes 5 to 6 servings.

Giant Snickerdoodle Cookies

A friend I previously worked with gave me this recipe. His mother used to make them for his school lunches, and all the kids wanted to trade him. He said to mention that these are big and need room to expand. Don't try to get more than 5 or 6 on a large cookie sheet.

Prep: 20 mins.
Chill: 4 hours
Bake: 12 mins. per batch

4½ cups all-purpose flour
2 tsp. baking powder
1 tsp. baking soda
¾ tsp. salt
1¼ cups shortening
2 cups sugar
2 eggs
1½ tsp. vanilla
½ tsp. lemon extract or 1 tsp. finely shredded lemon peel
1 cup buttermilk
½ cup sugar
2 Tbsp. ground cinnamon

Preheat oven to 375 degrees. Lightly grease cookie sheets. Set aside.

In a medium bowl, stir together the flour, baking powder, baking soda, and salt. In a large mixing bowl, beat the shortening with an electric mixer for 30 seconds. Add the 2 cups of sugar. Beat until combined, scraping the sides of the bowl. Beat in the eggs, one at a time, beating well after each addition. Stir in vanilla and lemon extract or peel.

Alternate adding the dry ingredients and the buttermilk to the creamed mixture, scraping down the sides of the bowl as necessary. Cover and chill for at least 4 hours. Meanwhile, combine the ½ cup sugar and cinnamon. Set aside.

For each cookie, use a ¼ cup measure. Roll each scoop of dough in the sugar-cinnamon mixture to coat. Place three inches apart on the cookie sheet. With the palm of your hand, gently press down the cookie to ½-inch thickness.

Bake for 12 to 14 minutes, or until the bottoms are a light gold. Transfer to a rack to cool. The cookies bake more evenly if you bake just one batch at a time.

Makes about 24.

Dick Green's Famous Caramel Corn

Dick and Judy are old friends of my family. Judy said that she always made this caramel corn when they took their kids to the drive-in, and they loved it! Dick adds that it's absolutely delicious, and I wholeheartedly agree!

6 qt. popped corn
2 sticks butter
2 cups brown sugar
½ cup light corn syrup (such as Karo)
Dash salt
½ tsp. baking soda

Preheat the oven to 250°F.

Spread the popcorn in a shallow pan. Keep warm in the oven.

Combine butter, sugar, corn syrup, and salt in a heavy saucepan. Bring the mixture to 248°F, checking frequently with a candy thermometer.

Stir in the baking soda; it will foam.

Drizzle over the popcorn; stir and toss to coat. Return the popcorn to oven for 45 minutes, stirring every 15 minutes.

Store in an airtight container.

Dog Biscuits

Blondie loves these!

1⅛ cup whole wheat flour
1⅛ cup unbleached white flour
½ cup peanut butter or other nut butter
1 cup water
2 tablespoons vegetable oil

Preheat the oven to 350°F.

In a bowl, blend the wheat flour and white flour. Set aside.

In a large mixing bowl, combine the vegetable oil, peanut butter, and water. Add the flour, one cup at a time, and mix to form a dough. You will need to blend the final bit of flour by hand, kneading until a nice, firm ball of dough is formed.

Let the ball of dough stand for about 10 minutes to allow the gluten to relax; this makes rolling easier.

Roll the dough to about ¼-inch thickness on a sheet of waxed paper. Cut with the desired cutter. I like to use a cutter in the shape of a dog bone! Score the tops of the cookies with a fork so the steam that builds up inside the cookies will be released.

Bake on an ungreased cookie sheet for 25 minutes, rotating the pan a couple of times during baking. The cookies should be hard to the touch before being removed from the oven. Continue to bake in five-minute increments until they reach the proper hardness, usually around 30 to 35 minutes.

Allow the cookies to cool completely, then store them in plastic bags or airtight containers.

Big Jim Kocik's Potato-Cheese Soup

Big Jim was Uncle Porky's golfing partner and had to make this soup each time he lost to Uncle Porky—which was a lot of times!

7–8 strips thick-cut slab bacon, diced (½-inch dice)
2 cups sweet onion, diced (½-inch dice)
3 cups Swanson chicken stock (not broth)
3 Tbsp. butter
2–3 tsp. jalapeño slices, finely chopped
½ tsp. black pepper
½ tsp. of your favorite mixed seasoning
6–7 cups red potatoes, peeled and diced into ½-inch cubes
12 oz. Velveeta cheese, cut into ½-inch cubes
1½ cup half-and-half
1 Tbsp. dried chives

Notes:

Use *red* potatoes; they hold up best in soups. After dicing, rinse 2 or 3 times to remove excess starch. Soak in cold water until needed.

Easy way to dice bacon: Cut a stack of strips lengthwise, then cut ½-inch slices.

After frying the bacon, do not drain away all the grease. Easy method: Push the fried bacon to one side of the Dutch oven or pot and absorb about half the grease with 5 or 6 paper towels.

Two teaspoons of chopped jalapeños just barely register in this recipe but add to the flavor, so don't leave them out. If you want a little more heat, add an additional 1 tsp. at a time. Just remember that you can always add more, but you can't take them out.

Swanson chicken stock comes in a 26-oz. container; use the whole thing. Homemade stock (from leftover strained chicken soup) is best, if you have any.

Don't be tempted to substitute cheddar or any other hard cheese for Velveeta, because Velveeta does not curdle and provides a very creamy texture to the broth. If you want more cheese favor, garnish the soup with shredded Asiago or some other favorite cheese.

In a Dutch oven or stockpot over medium-high heat, fry the bacon until crisp. Remove about half of the grease.

Add the diced onions and continue cooking until the onions are translucent, about 5 minutes.

Add the chicken stock, butter, jalapeños, black pepper, Accent, and drained potatoes, and simmer on medium-low heat until the potatoes are just tender, about 20 minutes.

Add the Velveeta cheese, half-and-half and dried chives and turn up the heat to bring the soup to a simmer. Stir until the cheese is well melted and blended into the soup. Adjust the heat to low and simmer for an additional 10 minutes, stirring frequently.

Trixie's Raisin-Cider Sauce

This sauce is absolutely perfect with ham or pork!
I serve it all the time.

> 3 Tbsp. brown sugar
> 1 Tbsp. cornstarch
> ¼ tsp. salt
> ¼ tsp. cloves
> ⅛ tsp. cinnamon
> A few grains nutmeg
> 1 cup apple cider
> ½ cup seedless raisins
> 1 tsp. lemon juice

In a saucepan, mix the brown sugar, cornstarch,
salt, cloves, cinnamon, and nutmeg. Stir in the ap-
ple cider and raisins. Bring to a rapid boil over
high heat, stirring slowly and constantly. Cook
until the mixture is thick and clear, about three
minutes.

Remove from the heat and stir in the lemon
juice.

Makes about 1½ cups sauce.

Cowboy Beef Stew

I cut this recipe out of a magazine ages ago. The recipe was dog-eared and yellowed, so I rewrote it when I was making it (times fifty!) for the Silver Bullet's Tuesday Special last week.

Total recipe time: 2¼ to 3 hours

1 package (12 to 14 oz.) dried bean soup mix with
   seasoning packet (not quick cooking)
2½ pounds beef for stew, cut into 1-inch pieces
2 Tbsp. vegetable oil
2 cans (14.5 oz. each) diced tomatoes with green
   peppers and onion
1 can (14 to 14.5 oz.) beef broth
3 cups frozen diced or hash brown potatoes
Salt and pepper to taste

Soak the beans in water overnight in the refrigerator, according to the package directions. Reserve the seasoning packet.

Coat the beef with the seasoning packet. In a large stockpot over medium heat, heat 1 tablespoon of the oil until hot. Brown ⅓ of the beef in the hot oil. Remove from the stockpot. Repeat two more times. Add additional oil as needed. Pour off the drippings, and return the beef to the stockpot.

Drain the beans and discard the water. Add the beans, tomatoes, and beef broth to the stockpot. Bring to a boil. Reduce the heat and simmer 1¾ to 2 hours, until the beef is fork tender.

Stir in the potatoes. Bring to a boil. Reduce the heat, and continue simmering, uncovered, for 5 to 7 minutes, or until the potatoes are tender. Season with salt and pepper to taste.

Makes 6 servings.

I just loved wintry Sunday mornings in my Silver
Bullet Diner.

It was organized chaos as families filed in after
church, workers came in for breakfast after their
shifts, and snowplow drivers came in to get warm,
refill their coffee, and get something to eat.

Speaking of coffee, as I was refilling my mug
behind the counter, I paused to listen to the chatter
of my customers and the clatter of silverware on
plates—more of my favorite things.

The smell of bacon frying and bread toasting
permeated the air along with the strong aroma of
coffee brewing. Mmm . . .

Arriving customers shrugged out of their winter
regalia and helped their children out of theirs. They
stuffed mittens, hats, and whatnot into the pockets
of their coats and hung them on the pegs near the
front door. If they were lucky enough to find a red

vinyl booth right off, they shuffled over to claim it as their own by hanging everything from the brass treble hooks screwed into the frame.

Heads were hunched over my big plastic menus, and fingers were pointing to the colorful pictures as my morning-shift waitresses walked around with pots of coffee—regular and decaf—and exchanged friendly banter.

Because Sandy Harbor was such a small town, most everyone knew one another. Joking, shouting, and table hopping were common, much to the confusion of my waitresses. There were plans being made for ice fishing, shopping trips to Syracuse or Watertown, and discussions about dairy cows and buying hay if there was a shortage.

Weather was always a big topic. I tuned in to a conversation between Guy Eastman, who owned a zillion cows and grew the best butter and sugar corn during the season, and Dave Cross, who was our area plumber and fishing guide.

Dave stirred his coffee absentmindedly. "My bunions tell me that we are going to have one hell of a blizzard. This is going to be bad for so early in November."

"My right elbow was aching this morning, so I think you're right, but my left knee was calm, so you might be wrong," replied Guy. "My hammer toe was throbbing and so was this blister I got from my new work boots. I wonder if that means anything."

Dave shrugged. "My right knee was creaking this morning. That's usually a sign of frost, but we're beyond frost. Maybe it's warning me about more sleet coming."

"Creaking? Both of my knees were creaking when I walked in here—it's my bursitis and arthritis. Oh, and I had pain shooting up and down my right leg. That tells me that we're in for a couple feet of snow soon."

"Oh, for heaven's sake, Guy! That's not a snow predictor—that's your sciatica."

A big laugh started in my stomach and was making its way to the surface. I was in trouble. I had just taken a big gulp of coffee and was just about to spray it all over my pretty diner if I couldn't swallow both the coffee and the laugh at the same time. Leaning over, I opened one of the cooler doors below the counter, and made like I was looking for something until I could tamp down the laugh and the liquid.

These were the sights, sounds, and smells of my diner this Sunday morning in mid-November and really most every morning.

But both Guy and Dave were right, according to our local weather person, Heather "Flip a Coin" Flipelli, the daughter of the station manager, who had no weather training and who was too young to have weather predictors like bunions and sciatica. Too bad she didn't have them—maybe she'd have done better predicting the weather.

Heather was currently closed-captioned on an ancient TV hanging from the rafters at the end of the counter. I shivered when I saw that she was wearing a sleeveless tank top and a denim miniskirt. Heather noted, with a toss of her shiny black ponytail, that it was sleeting outside—a combination of rain and heavy snow and whatever else Lake Ontario was throwing at little Sandy Harbor,

New York. Heather named it a "weather event" and identified it as a "lake-effect polar vortex," but I, Trixie Matkowski, called it another "Massive Weather Mess."

"It's supposed to turn into a blizzard," said Huey Mobley, new to the scene and who had missed out on the bunion conversation. Huey was delivering the Sunday edition of the *Sandy Harbor Lure*, our local newspaper, and stocking the paper box. "And this base of sleet will be slippery and icy. It says so right here in the *Lure*."

And the *Lure* was sacred in this area.

"Your friendly Department of Public Works has the icy conditions under control, Huey." Snowplow driver Karen Metonti set her fork down on her plate, which had supported a stack of blueberry pancakes and crispy bacon, and raised her coffee mug in salute. "My hopper is loaded with sand and salt, and I'm ready to go at it again just as soon as I refill my coffee."

"It's on me, Karen," I said, bobbing to the surface of the counter. "And help yourself to a couple of donuts for the road on your way out."

"Thanks, Trixie. It's going to be a long day or two," Karen said, zipping up her padded orange jumpsuit. She slipped on sheepskin mittens and a hat, which were so stuffed with fur that they looked like they lodged a whole sheep. Then she clomped out in snowmobile boots, stopping to have Nancy refill her coffee and slip a couple of donuts into a white bakery bag.

After spotting several fruit hand pies that my Amish friend Sarah Stolfus had made revolving in slow circles in the pastry carousel, I walked toward them as if in a trance.

"Beatrix Matkowski, don't you dare eat one of those hand pies, particularly not the cherry one. You just started another diet this morning," I mumbled to myself. Maybe myself would listen, since I hated to be called Beatrix.

With my coffee cup leading the way and before the hand pie could jump into my hand, I zoomed past the carousel and hustled back to my usual spot in the kitchen between the steam table and the huge black stove.

I'd been here since midnight. My shift would end at eight o'clock—in about ten minutes. I enjoyed working the graveyard stint because customers who came in to eat then were an interesting group. We had loners who relished the camaraderie in the diner, loners who just wanted to be left alone, and customers who were full of energy and thrived in the night. Most every shift, I had customers who simply ran out of steam, maybe after their work shift, and would snooze in a booth.

But they all had wanted something to eat—something warm and comforting—and that was my specialty.

Right now, I had four different kinds of soup on the stove in huger-than-huge pots: chicken noodle, broccoli and cheese, New England clam chowder, and bean soup. That was quite a variety, but there were a lot of people who worked out in the elements who needed thawing out, and that meant soup—lots and lots of comforting soup.

It also meant chili, mac and cheese, meat loaf . . .

I could go on and on, but first I want to get a batter started for chocolate chip cookies.

I looked at the clock on the wall. Juanita Holgado, my morning cook, should be arriving momentarily. She loved to bake, so she could finish them for me. I was dead on my feet and yawning.

Maybe it was the weather. But thank goodness I didn't have any bunions or other body parts that could predict the weather. I usually took my chance on "Flip a Coin" Flipelli.

All I needed to do was look outside and see the snow falling in big, wet flakes. I could barely make out the outlines of Max and Clyde, my jacks-of-all-trades when they weren't napping on the job, through the plummeting snow. They were trying to shovel and snow-blow the sidewalks around the Silver Bullet so my patrons wouldn't slip, twirl, and triple flip and get a low mark from the Olympic judges.

But thank goodness for Karen, the first female snowplow driver in Sandy Harbor, who let the blade down on the village's snowplow and made a couple of swoops in my parking lot.

Karen wasn't supposed to use village equipment to do personal things, but sometimes we close the rule book here in Sandy Harbor.

In gratitude, I was going to make sure that Karen was never without free coffee and donuts whenever she stopped into the Silver Bullet.

Deputy Sheriff Ty Brisco, a Texas transplant who lived above the bait shop next door, would accuse me of bribing a governmental official. I'd just call it being neighborly.

Ty was getting too stuffy anyway. He needed to loosen up, but maybe he had weather-predicting body parts that were giving him a hard time.

Just then, I saw Ty's big monster of an SUV do a half spin into the parking lot. He got it under control before he ended up in a ten-foot-high snowbank, and he safely parked in a spot cleared by Karen.

I peeked from the corner of the pass-through window, waiting for Ty to walk into the diner. It wasn't because I loved to watch the way he walked or listen to that sexy cowboy drawl of his, or because I just enjoyed bantering with him.

No way.

I wasn't interested because I was still cementing bricks around myself due to my divorce a couple of years ago from Philadelphia deputy sheriff Doug Burnham, slimy cheater. He had found a fertile twentysomething, who gave him twins, Brittany and Tiffany, and I became last week's birdcage liner. I wanted to get serious over another deputy like I wanted to clean the grease vent fan in the kitchen.

But I was slowly chipping away at the bricks since I bought everything on "the point," a hump of land that jutted out into Lake Ontario, from Aunt Stella after Uncle Porky died. She had wanted to retire, and I wanted to start fresh.

Trying to be casual, I continued looking through the pass-through window, waiting for Ty to appear.

The pass-through window didn't have any glass in it and wasn't used for passing anything through it, but it was my window to the happenings in the front of the diner whenever I was in the back.

And right now, I was hoping to enjoy some cop-cowboy eye candy.

The door opened and there was a collective groan when snow blew into the diner and landed onto the customers near the door.

Sheesh.

Ty should have waited until the outside door had closed before he opened the inside door, but the wind grabbed it. He mumbled, "Sorry," took his cowboy hat off, and brushed off the plastic bonnet that protected his hat.

How cute!

The plastic bonnet reminded me of my aunt Helen's living room with her plastic-covered sofa and chairs. I used to stick to the sofa whenever I wore shorts, and my father loved to joke about the covers as he drove us all home after our visit. But Aunt Helen was proud of how the plastic kept her furniture just like new.

"When is this stuff ever going to stop falling?" Ty snapped as he unzipped his bomber jacket, shook it out, and hung it on a peg.

"August," someone shouted.

"I believe it," Ty said.

"Amateur," I mumbled. It was only beginning.

I think that this was Ty's third winter in Sandy Harbor. It was my second as owner of the Silver Bullet and the eleven housekeeping cottages (which used to be twelve, but that's another story). I also own a big Victorian farmhouse with three floors, a bunch of rooms, and a bunch of bathrooms because my late uncle Porky loved company and loved porcelain.

I had left Philly and headed for my favorite place on earth, Sandy Harbor, New York. The planets aligned and Aunt Stella decided that the diner, cottages, and farmhouse weren't going to be the same without her beloved Porky, and she offered to sell everything to me with the "family discount and easy payment plan."

We worked out the details on a Silver Bullet place mat. After the dust settled, she handed me a wad of keys and I handed her the contents of my purse, my bank accounts, and all the change I had in the ashtray of my car. Aunt Stella then took off for Boca Raton and an Alaskan cruise with her gal pals, leaving me overwhelmed with balloon payments scheduled throughout our lifetime and a diner that was OPEN 24 HOURS A DAY, AIR-CONDITIONED, BREAKFAST SERVED ALL DAY.

I loved it here in Sandy Harbor. I loved my staff, the villagers, the closeness, and the camaraderie. If someone needed help, then help they'd get!

Nancy arrived with some orders. "Two cowboys on a raft, wheat. One dead-eye with sausage, sourdough. One pig between two sheets, sourdough. And two cows, done rare—and make them cry. And, Trixie, the two cows are taking a walk."

Nancy loves her "Dinerese." I've come to love it, too. It's like our own special language. I got the two Western omelets frying and the wheat bread onto the Ferris wheel—that's what I called the revolving toaster. I got the water boiling for the two dead-eyes—poached eggs—and put two orders of sourdough bread on the wheel. I cut slices of raw onions to make the cows/hamburgers "cry" and toasted their buns. When the meat was ready, I plated everything and boxed up the hamburgers for their walk.

Just then the back door opened and Juanita Holgado, my morning cook, arrived. "This weather sure is something. I need a vacation, Boss Trixie. Like, now!"

"Whenever you want a vacation, just let me know."

Juanita shook off her coat, pulled off a brightly colored hat, and stomped the snow off her boots. Unzipping her boots, she slipped into a pair of rubber clogs.

Today, Juanita wore her chef pants with red and green peppers on them. My pants were covered in red tomatoes, my signature. The other cook, Cindy, had pizza slices on hers.

As I loaded bread onto the Ferris wheel, I thought of my alleged other cook, Bob, whom I've never met.

Bob served in the army with Uncle Porky and it was Uncle Porky who hired him as a cook. When I took over, Bob kept calling in sick from Atlantic City, Vegas, Connecticut, and other casinos . . . er . . . I mean specialist physicians.

Bob had only ever called in sick to Juanita, but the next time he called, I told Juanita that I wanted to talk to him. Bob was probably in Vegas right now. At least he was warm, unlike us.

Juanita was ready to start her shift, and mine was over. I grabbed my mug of cold coffee and tossed it down the drain. I rinsed my cup off, ready to get a fresh cup in the diner.

As I was pushing open the doors, I paused. The diner patrons were completely silent, but there was relentless pounding on the roof, which sounded as if the place was going to shake apart.

"What on earth?" I said to no one in particular.

Ty answered. "It's hail. And it's as big as softballs."

"Terrific. What's next?"

Just as I said that, lightning flashed and thunder rumbled. There was a collective gasp from my customers.

I hoped the Silver Bullet would hold up.

After filling my mug with coffee, I refilled everyone's coffee at the counter. Just as I was about to do likewise for those in booths and at tables and chairs in the side room, Colleen, another waitress, took the pots (regular and decaf) away from me.

"You did your shift, Trixie. You must be tired. Go—sit down and talk to that delicious cowboy," she said, her blond ponytail dancing as she walked.

I could barely hear her. The hail seemed to be pounding on every side of my diner.

I hoped that Clyde and Mac had taken shelter. No sense in trying to keep up with the current Massive Weather Mess.

The hail stopped, and everyone took easier breaths. The cordial din of everyone talking returned.

Both Ty and I walked over to the side window at the same time.

"Back to snow," he said as we both looked out.

"And it's really coming down again. I'd better get going. I'm sure that some crazies are trying to drive in this."

I sighed. Why would anyone risk their life or anyone else's to drive in these conditions?

Ty's radio went off. So did most everyone's cell or radio. He listened to the static-filled device to what seemed to be Deputy Vern McCoy's disjointed voice.

I flashed back to my days with Deputy Doug and the "let's get together code" that he and his twentysomething-year-old chickie devised via his radio.

"What?" I asked Ty. "What's going on?"

Ty didn't have to answer. "The library's roof collapsed" was the response twittered around the diner, after dozens of phones and radios were shut off.

Just about all my customers stood up at the same time and shrugged into coats and gloves and plopped hats on their heads.

"Thank goodness the library was closed," Ty said, slipping into his jacket.

I sighed. "A couple of years ago, it was the court house. Last year it was the American Legion and now the library. What next?" I asked.

He adjusted the rain bonnet on his cowboy hat. "Maybe we need some roof inspectors before anyone gets seriously hurt. The weather here is just plain . . ."

"Hideous," I supplied.

"Yeah." He swung his hat and plopped it on his head, tapping it with a couple of fingers into a comfortable spot.

"Ty, it's awful out there to drive, and all these people are going to drive down the highway, where there is zero visibility, and into town, where there're narrow streets and nowhere to put the snow even if the plows got there. Can you at least call Karen and get her or someone else to plow your way?"

"Already done. You must have missed that on the radio."

"A police radio is like Dinerese. You have to develop an ear for it. I never did."

He put his gloves on and turned to the big line of villagers down the center aisle of my diner ready to respond.

Ty raised a hand for quiet. "Ladies and gentlemen, I want everyone to take their time driving in this weather. The village plows have cleared a path for us, but it's still treacherous out there. From what I understand, no one was in the library, so there is no rush. We'll try to tarp it to save some of the books and whatnot, but first, the town engineer, Emmett Woolsey, will decide if what's left of the roof is stable enough for us to go in there."

Ty's radio went off again. Same type of mumbling, same static.

"I stand corrected," Ty said. He hooked his radio onto his belt and was ready to rush out the door as if his jeans—which fit perfectly (not that I noticed)—were on fire. "I've got to go."

"Is anyone hurt?" I asked.

"Can't say."

He never can say.

"Please call me. I have a diner full of people who care," I instructed.

He didn't answer. He was sliding down the sidewalk to his big black monolith of an SUV. I kidded him about it, but a megatruck or an SUV was pretty much mandatory in these parts.

"Did I hear the words 'Tidy Trio' on the radio?" Leo Sousa, an EMT, asked.

"I heard that, too," Megan Hunter said, then turned to me. "The Tidy Trio is Donna Palmeri, Sue Lewandursky, and Mary Ann Malone. They've been cleaning the library for years." Megan Hunter owned an antiques shop and restoration business in downtown Sandy Harbor and was a bundle of energy like an elf at Christmas. "I sure hope they're okay."

Everyone's phone went off yet again. "Tidy Trio" was murmured throughout the diner. What customers were left dropped their forks and stood, then slipped into their coats.

I held open the exit door as most everyone hurried out.

"Be careful!" I said. My plea was echoed by those they'd left behind with unfinished meals and stuck with the bills.

The Silver Bullet was quiet now. Only a handful of customers dotted the inside of the diner, eating in relative silence, thinking and praying that the Tidy Trio was okay.

It seemed like an eternity before Ty called. I was buzzed on enough coffee to float a battleship.

"They're all okay," Ty said. "They were just scared out of their wits with the cracking of the wood and the noise. The big stained-glass dome is now in shards on the floor. Luckily, they were all away from the worst part when the roof collapsed."

As I looked up, every pair of eyes was trained on me. "They're all okay, Deputy Brisco said. Just scared."

There was a round of applause and a jovial atmosphere returned to the Silver Bullet.

"How did the rest of the library fare?" I asked Ty.

"Everything's wet with the exception of the archive room and a couple of offices. When this roof decided to cave-in, it did a bang-up job. It's too late to tarp the books. They are gone. Very gone."

"Oh, no! All those beautiful books," I said. "And all that marble."

"The marble is okay. It's now a marble swimming pool."

"Sheesh."

"I gotta go, Trixie," he said.

"Wait! Ty, tell everyone there that I'll deliver hot coffee and sandwiches."

"You're a good egg, Trixie Matkowski."

I smiled. "Good to know."

"Bye," Ty said.

I turned to the patrons again. "Deputy Brisco said that most all of the books are ruined."

My heart was breaking. I grew up in libraries and loved the sounds and smells of them. A voracious reader, I loved to touch, feel, and smell a book in my hand and get lost in the world of words.

"It's such a beautiful building. I sure hope that all that beautiful wood doesn't get ruined," Megan Hunter said. "And those beautiful desks and brass lamps! What a shame!"

Nursery school teacher Lorraine Matthews stood.

"We definitely have to have a fund-raiser to repair the library and get replacement books."

"Yeah!" Several fists pumped the air.

"We should have a chili cook-off during our Winter Carnival," Lorraine added.

"Please, no." I shook my head. "Everyone does chili cook-offs. We need to come up with something bigger—something different."

"Like what do you have in mind, Trixie?" Megan asked, listening intently.

I thought for a while, then snapped my fingers. "How about a macaroni and cheese cook-off? It's pretty easy, and we'll see who makes theirs stand out the most. They'll get first prize. We could have three prizes—gold, silver, and bronze."

"I nominate Trixie Matkowski to be the chairperson of the library fund-raiser," said Jean Vermer, whom I'd hunt down later.

"Wha—"

"Don't worry, Trixie," said Megan. "I'll help you out. So will most of the town, whoever's able."

"I second the nomination," said Tess Drennan.

"All those in favor, say aye," Megan yelled.

This was just way too crazy.

"I don't even have the time to tie my sneakers these days. Don't say aye. No ayes!" I pointed my finger down the aisle. "Don't you guys dare!"

"Aye!"

I sat down, trying to think of a way out of this. It's not like I didn't want to help—I just didn't have the energy or the time to chair it.

"The ayes have it," said Megan. "You're the chairperson of the library fund-raiser, and we are having a macaroni and cheese cook-off."

"I'll do my best."

"I'll be your cochair," Megan announced to a round of applause. "I'll contact an old sorority sister of mine. I hear she's breezing through town to go to Ottawa to tape her TV show there. I'm sure I could get her! Just wait until you all hear this name: Priscilla Finch-Smythe. 'Cilla' for short."

There was a general sense of awe. Add me to the list. I loved watching Cilla on TV. She was noted for making basic comfort food and for her published cookbooks, her latest being *Comforting Comfort Food*.

"So, what do you think about Mabel Clunk coming to town to judge the contest, Trixie?" Megan asked while actually patting herself on the back.

"Mabel Clunk? Who's that? I thought you said Priscilla Finch-Smythe would judge it."

"They are one and the same person."

I guess you can't be a TV personality with a name like Mabel Clunk.

"Oh, Trixie!" Megan shook my biceps until my teeth were ready to fall out. "The first prize could be a weekend in New York City with Cilla and an appearance on her TV show to cook the winning mac and cheese recipe. Wouldn't that be incredible? We could get real chefs and wannabe chefs from all over the world by relentlessly using her name. We could charge an enormous entry fee. Incredible idea, huh?"

"Just incredible," I repeated. "Mabel Clunk." I took a deep breath. "And everyone will help?"

My patrons nodded and clapped, excited to rebuild the library. I was overwhelmed. All I'd said was "macaroni and cheese" and now I was in charge of an international cook-off?

Mac and cheese was definitely a comfort food. With enough help, I could pull this off.

But why didn't I feel comforted?